NECROMUNDA

FLESHWORKS

IN THE FUTURISTIC hive city of Necromunda, from the top of the hive spire to the very depths of the underhive, there is only one rule: survival of the fittest. Brutal gangs prowl the darkness, hideous mutants and unspeakable monsters lurk in the forgotten and lonely places. For the enterprising mercenary, a respectable living can be made. But be warned: allies become enemies all too quickly when the ultimate prize is survival itself...

For the spies of the secretive House Delaque, survival is even more of a struggle. When Uriah Storm is told that his next target is his friend Soren, a spy working within rivals House Van Saar, he is surprised – Delaque spies are never supposed to know their targets personally. Realising that the real target is not Soren, but his biomechanical implants, Uriah begins to suspect the game is more complex than even he imagined and is forced into a race against time to find his friend before the Van Saar or his fellow assassins do.

WITHDRAWN

NECROMUNDA

FLESHWORKS

LUCIEN SOULBAN

A BLACK LIBRARY PUBLICATION

First published in Great Britain in 2006 by
BL Publishing,
Games Workshop Ltd.,
Willow Road, Nottingham,
NG7 2WS, UK.

10 9 8 7 6 5 4 3 2 1

Cover illustration by Clint Langley.

A CIP record for this book is available from the British Library.

ISBN 13: 978 1 84416 329 8
ISBN 10: 1 84416 329 6

Distributed in the US by Simon & Schuster
1230 Avenue of the Americas, New York, NY 10020, US.

Printed and bound in Great Britain by
Bookmarque, Surrey, UK.

See the Black Library on the Internet at
www.blacklibrary.com

Find out more about Games Workshop
www.games-workshop.com

In order to even begin to understand the blasted world of Necromunda you must first understand the hive cities. These man-made mountains of plasteel, ceramite and rockrete have accreted over centuries to protect their inhabitants from a hostile environment, so very much like the termite mounds they resemble. The Necromundan hive cities have populations in the billions and are intensely industrialised, each one commanding the manufacturing potential of an entire planet or colony system compacted into a few hundred square kilometres.

The internal stratification of the hive cities is also illuminating to observe. The entire hive structure replicates the social status of its inhabitants in a vertical plane. At the top are the nobility, below them are the workers, and below the workers are the dregs of society, the outcasts. Hive Primus, seat of the planetary governor Lord Helmawr of Necromunda, illustrates this in the starkest terms. The nobles – Houses Helmawr, Cattalus, Ty, Ulanti, Greim, Ran Lo and Ko'Iron – live in the 'Spire', and seldom set foot below the 'Wall' that exists between themselves and the great forges and hab zones of the hive city proper.

Below the hive city is the 'Underhive', foundation layers of habitation domes, industrial zones and tunnels which have been abandoned in prior generations, only to be re-occupied by those with nowhere else to go.

But... humans are not insects. They do not hive together well. Necessity may force it, but the hive cities of Necromunda remain internally divided to the point of brutalisation and outright violence being an everyday fact of life. The Underhive, meanwhile, is a thoroughly lawless place, beset by gangs and renegades, where only the strongest or the most cunning survive. The Goliaths, who believe firmly that might is right; the matri- archal, man-hating Escher; the industrial Orlocks; the technologically-minded Van Saar; the Delaque whose very existence depends on their espionage network; the fiery zealots of the Cawdor. All striving for the advantage that will elevate them, no matter how briefly, above the other houses and gangs of the Underhive.

Most fascinating of all is when individuals attempt to cross the monumental physical and social divides of the hive to start new lives. Given social conditions, ascension through the hive is nigh on impossible, but descent is an altogether easier, albeit altogether less appealing, possi- bility.

excerpted from Xonariarius the Younger's
Nobilite Pax Imperator – the Triumph
of Aristocracy over Democracy.

PROLOGUE

SOREN WAS A dead man, each step a countdown to his own execution, but that didn't stop him from running faster. He no longer cared that his calves were numb or that his ribs ached hard and stabbed him in the gut with every stride.

In the mad, wild panic to escape his pursuers, Soren had taken too many side corridors, too many unfamiliar passages. Left, right, left again before he lost his bearings. He was lost, running blind past endless walls of rivet-punched plates the colour of dull metal. Soren stumbled down flights of grated stairs, their ceilings pressed down by the crushing weight of ten miles worth of aging city.

Finally, fatigue robbed Soren of his footing; he slipped on a greasy patch of pooling machine oil that leaked from the braided intestines of ceiling pipes and tubes. His ears roared from the surge of pounding blood and the piston-hiss of the servos in his augmented arm. The sounds of gunfire that had hounded him through the warrens of the Underhive had stopped. It was silent, his heart beating as if from behind his eardrums.

Soren wiped the black oil from his face and stood with a steadying hand against the wall. His legs quivered with fatigue and his artificial eyes strained to detect thermal variants in his surroundings, but to no avail. He was near a smelting plant and the heat from all that molten metal bled through the walls' multiple skins. The casing protecting his implants grew warmer against the connective tissues of his flesh, and while not painful, it would be uncomfortable soon. The air felt thick with humidity; the walls perspired. It was several degrees hotter than the human body. That rendered his pursuers invisible to thermal optics, and Soren's normal sight couldn't see much better in the corridor.

Soren hadn't escaped. He felt it and it found voice in his panicked whimpers. Fate wouldn't let go that easily, if at all. Fate was patient; fate was hungry; and fate seemed blessed with an endless supply of ammunition. Shots rang out in the corridor; a round punched a dent in the wall above Soren's head. He turned and ran, catching a fleeting glimpse of someone in the dark, a thermal ghost washed out by the surrounding heat.

Soren continued running, until the last shot rang out; until he staggered to a drunken, sloppy halt; until he looked down at the wet, crimson flower blossoming on his shirt, the flesh petals of a blackened, scorched hole in his chest that sizzled; until he quietly wondered if his heart had burst or if getting shot normally hurt this much…

CHAPTER: ONE

A good falsehood is more comforting than the truth.

– Delaque Operational Commandments
from the *Book of Lies*.

THE EAR-POPPING crack of gunshots and the hiss of lasfire was almost deafening; it echoed off the walls, amplified to storm's pitch by the thick, pockmarked plascrete. Uriah Storm ignored the racket. He focused on his target, both hands wrapped around the bolt pistol's grip, and angled down to the floor. His blue eyes drifted, as though lost to some silent conundrum.

Suddenly, with an experienced snap, he brought the pistol up – one hand to aim, the other to steady – and squeezed off four shots, his finger barely tapping the hair trigger. The untamed weapon kicked in his hand with each shot; four of four rounds found their target. A fleeting smile escaped his lips and Uriah chuckled. He felt like a child with a new toy.

The firing range was crowded today, a line of twenty men and women unleashing a blistering array of punishment. Uriah didn't look at them. Instead, he watched the steel-alloy targets scattered at various intervals along the range, hidden behind collapsed walls and blasted archways. That the targets all bore some semblance to the thick-necked, low-browed members of House Orlock was mere coincidence, or so the Delaque agents claimed with a smile. Still, too many of their shots were errant. Too many House members believed that filling the air with a steady hail of death was equal to being a crack shot.

Uriah clucked and smiled at his own sudden mischievous inspiration. He pivoted and fired another four shots into the other targets along the range, hitting the ones others had missed. A few people stopped firing and craned their heads to look in his direction. Most of the shooters scowled at him, though a couple returned his easy grin. Those of poor humour, Uriah decided, were likely to be equally poor shots.

Pleased with himself, Uriah ejected the pistol's clip and cleared the round in the chamber. He mouthed a quick 'thank you' to the Machine Spirit empowering the weapon. It was only when he turned the gun over to the weapons master standing next to him that he noticed the man had been talking.

'She is loud, isn't she?' Uriah said, removing the earplugs. 'You were saying?'

'What were you mumbling?' weapons master Coryin replied.

'Nothing,' Uriah said with a grin before waving dismissively. 'A mantra, I suppose, actually. *Hail to me*, or something to that effect.'

Coryin grunted. 'Your shots are drifting,' he said. 'Kept hitting other targets.'

'Yes, surprising that,' Uriah said, admiring the engraved handle, 'but she has spirit. I like the gun. She's untamed.'

'Too much for the likes of you, I suspect,' Coryin said. 'And too loud for your line of work.'

'Perhaps,' Uriah replied, taking a moment to unfurl the braid in his hair before tying it up into a simple ponytail. He noticed the bald Delaque man studying his crop of brown hair – a rarity among the Delaque, but necessary to someone in his position. 'There are times when the only proper response is a loud one,' Uriah said. 'I want her.'

'Get the requisition forms signed and she's yours. Oh, and Uriah, no forgeries this time. I'm double-checking every signature with Percal. Understood?'

'Coryin,' Uriah said, slapping the other man's shoulder, 'I'd never use the same trick twice on you.'

Coryin scowled as Uriah walked away with a laugh.

THE CORRIDORS WERE dark, the lights dimmed by half. The Delaque preferred their illumination on the darker side of grey; less harsh on their normally sensitive eyes. And they whispered while they spoke – even in passing conversation. The Delaque stronghold of Shadowstrohm was typical of the House's other assets throughout Hive Primus, all plascrete walls and endurasteel floors, their sky low, dark and lined with pipes. The walls bled history in dulled stains, the collected moisture of centuries and the occasional spatter of blood from days when the Houses waged their wars more openly. It did not share the opulence of the main House compound several miles above their heads, but Shadowstrohm was among the more active listening posts. It was closer to the streets, and thus nearer to the action and bustle. It was also considered part of the trenches, the first line of defence against the other Houses.

To Uriah it was home in an unfriendly household. Several Delaque gangs made their residence in Shadowstrohm, at the insistence of the House's masters. It was a ploy against outsiders, making House Delaque seem larger and more organized than any of the other Houses, but behind the walls, Uriah belonged to one of several factions, and surviving meant knowing how to navigate the other groups.

Fortunately, Uriah was good at his game. Despite the youthful mien that cast his age some years short of thirty, in his line of work, that meant he was a veteran of 'the game', the same game that killed Delaque spies with facile routine. Still, if the game's mortality rate ever bothered Uriah, it didn't show. He walked through the hallways, annoying the serious-minded Information Cullers with his smile and mystifying the Seductresses as to the motivation behind his grin. Uriah flashed teeth to disarm the unwary and to unhinge those who knew better. Why serve one purpose when an action can serve two?

Uriah navigated the labyrinthine corridors without a second thought, ignoring engraved markers that pointed him in wrong directions, official-looking hallways that suddenly dead-ended and doors that opened to plascrete walls and gunports. The Delaque believed that a proper defence was a good deception, and that axiom reflected itself in the very architecture of their bases. That is what brought Uriah to the plain door hidden deep in the shadows of a thin, seemingly ignored corridor.

Uriah knocked five times in erratic fashion, mentally counting between each knock. On the final tap, something clicked on the other side. What that sound entailed, Uriah never knew, only that it was a bad idea walking through before hearing it. That said, Uriah entered carefully.

The room was small, but served the needs of the bald man sitting behind the desk, with some comfort to spare. It was surprisingly clean, with a metal desk, two chairs and a black pict screen to adorn the otherwise austere space.

Well actually, there was also that thin seam in the wall extending from floor to ceiling that Uriah suspected was a hidden door. He never asked about it or volunteered his suspicions that something was there. It was to his advantage to pretend he knew nothing.

The only personable touch to the otherwise basic room was a thick regicide board with bronze and silver tiles set upon a small stand in the corner. Upon the surface flickered low-rez holographic pieces caught in the middle of a match's static ballet. How the bald man managed to procure such a piece of archeotech was a mystery, but whenever Uriah visited, the pieces had been moved around. It was never the same game on the table.

Percal, the man sitting behind the desk, was bald and stout in all his proportions, thick of chest, arms, legs and neck. He might have been like any other venerable, but relatively indistinguishable agent in House Delaque, but a knife scar hooked his lip into a scowl and two slits rested where an Orlock knife had claimed his nose. He was proof that surviving the game had its costs, costs Uriah never intended to willingly pay.

Most men couldn't stare into Percal's beady black eyes, one partially clouded by white, but Uriah had no qualms maintaining eye contact with his superior, and he did so with a smile.

'Sit,' Percal instructed, reading a data-slate in his hands.

Uriah closed the door behind him, and heard the familiar whiz-click-whir. Apparently they weren't to be disturbed. He sat in one of the unyielding metal chairs, instantly uncomfortable. The trick, was not looking bothered. This is how the game between Percal and Uriah always began.

'Comfortable?' Percal asked, putting the data-slate down. He studied Uriah, his eyes that of a carrion eater seeking the prize morsels of meat on his subordinate.

'Indeed,' Uriah said, acting half-distracted. 'I requisitioned the very same chairs for my quarters.'

'Did you now?'

'Yes, I wanted my guests to experience the same comfort that you offer your visitors.'

Percal offered a thin smile. 'I can't abide company either.'

'Then to what do I owe the pleasure of your invitation?' Uriah asked.

'Work.'

'Same as always.'

'Not quite this time,' Percal said with a purr. 'You know the target.'

Uriah was instantly aware that Percal was studying him, waiting to gauge his reaction to *something*. He said nothing. Even asking questions surrendered too much information, at least in theory.

Better Percal volunteer the information, Uriah thought, but a piece of him clamoured to know. It scrabbled at his chest and dried his throat; he couldn't swallow. He knew Percal was toying with him, but the old man only did so when it was an unpleasant piece of work.

All of Uriah's previous assignments as Handler demanded distance, perspective. The Delaque preferred their Handlers to act for the strict benefit of the House; any personal stake in the matter was considered a threat to that interest. This was different, however, and Uriah had too many skeletons in his closet not to worry that he'd just been caught holding one of them.

To his credit Uriah said nothing, even though he prepared himself to hear a battery of potentially damning news. Instead he smiled with practiced ease and asked, 'Who is it?'

Percal nodded to the pict screen. A grainy, black and white picture appeared, at eye level, showing a man moving down an oil stained and industrial-looking corridor, towards the camera. He wore a lab frock, fairly typical to the researchers of House Van Saar. His visible implants, two eyes and an arm, were likewise of superior quality, while pinching his chin and mouth was a goatee that matched the colour of his hair. He nodded with a congenial smile before leaving the frame. The picture looped back, repeating the same four seconds over and over again.

Uriah recognized the shot. He'd filmed it over two years ago while deep undercover behind enemy lines.

'Soren?' Uriah asked Percal. 'What happened to him?'

'Our little mole has vanished.'

'Vanished.'

'He was carrying new Van Saar implants for us to examine. He never arrived at the rendezvous point.'

'Perhaps the Van Saar discovered his dealings with us. Maybe they captured him,' Uriah said, trying to maintain his professional facade. He was fighting a battering array of emotions that besieged him on all sides. On the one hand, he was relieved. This was not the secret he feared had come to light, the one that would ruin him. On the other, he was concerned. Soren was an asset, certainly, but in the process of recruiting Soren into Delaque's service, Uriah had grown to like the man. He was quirky, sharing the darker elements of Uriah's humour. Uriah would even hazard calling him a friend, despite the fact he couldn't fraternize with members of other Houses except in the pursuit of his duties as Handler.

Use anyone and everyone to further the glory of the house…

That ranked among the most cherished of Delaque commandments, and currently, Uriah was betraying that oath through his friendship with Soren.

'Captured him? Perhaps,' Percal said, 'though I have my doubts. That's where we need your skills. Locate

Soren and the implants he promised us. I need this done quietly. You mustn't alert the Van Saar about the operation. They cannot know we have a mole in their midst lest you endanger our other assets in their camp.'

'Why me?' Uriah asked. 'Doesn't this conflict with Delaque policy: no personal involvement in the assignment?'

'Soren was your mole. You befriended him. You brought him over to our side. If anyone knows how to find him, you do. If he trusts anyone, it's you.'

Uriah nodded. 'Very well. I'll find him. Anything else I need know?'

Percal shook his head. With that, Uriah stood, prepared to leave; he waited to hear the door unlock, but nothing happened. He turned and shot a questioning look at Percal.

'Forgotten something?' Percal asked, a sly grin on his face.

'Have I?' Uriah said, growing tired of this constant duelling.

'Aren't you going to ask me for something? A certain bolt pistol from the firing range? I thought you would take the opportunity to requisition the weapon from me?'

'Weapons master Coryin told you.' Uriah cursed himself for becoming so obviously distracted by the news. Perhaps he couldn't anticipate everything that was thrown his way, but in his trade, it was a cardinal sin to act surprised.

'He wounds me with his distrust,' Uriah said, adopting a cavalier attitude. 'Besides, I didn't want to disturb you with such petty details as requisition forms.'

'Requisition forms,' Percal said slowly, picking up his personal data-slate, 'of course. Nevertheless, I've granted your request for the bolt pistol. You might need it. Pick it up from the weapons master.' With that, Percal went back to examining his recorder.

The door unlocked.

Uriah left the office, a soft curse under his breath. He was already beginning the game at a disadvantage, and he didn't like feeling uncertain.

PERCAL WAITED FOR Uriah to finally leave the room before setting down the data-slate. He turned to the wall and waited for the hidden panel to slide aside on well-oiled tumblers. Standing at the secret door was a young man, no older than Uriah, perhaps in his mid-twenties. He was well dressed, his black trench coat clean and pressed; his face and scalp were Delaque smooth, while his features were sharp and angular. He wore rectangular glare-shades with wire rims.

The man stepped out of the small and surprisingly empty room and glanced at the panel sliding back into place.

'Did you miss anything, Kaden?' Percal asked.

'Caught every word,' Kaden said.

'Good, because I'd hate to think I made a mistake using you.'

'No,' said Kaden. 'And again, thanks for the opportunity. I've been–'

'Thank me by succeeding,' Percal said, interrupting the young man.

Kaden said nothing and merely nodded.

The door unlocked again, and Kaden left Percal alone in his chamber.

THE ARMOURY CHIEF was well acquainted with battle, his scars, marble eye and bolted skin plates a testament to his years in the trenches of the Underhive. They were also the cost of working in back-alley chop-shop medicine, where so-called doctors disposed of severed limbs in garbage pails and used them for unsavoury experiments – or worse. Uriah didn't care to know what exactly.

Uriah wondered whether he would one day face some disfiguring treatment; skull pump tubing, exposed steel plate for bone, pseudo-articulated gears for joints; the horrifying list of disfigurements was endless. The thought chilled Uriah, both the prospect of such pain and the physical cost.

After dutifully studying Uriah's requisition list for equipment, the armoury chief limped into the rear storerooms with their low ceilings and tightly packed shelving units, leaving Uriah to his thoughts. He was worried about Soren, but thinking about his own injuries was a sobering, and frankly welcome, distraction. He'd come close to enduring such mutilation at the hands of street surgeons, but had eventually managed to find someone with enough skill to avoid permanent disfigurement. That would have spelt the end of his career as a Handler. Uriah relied on his ability to blend into crowds and to move about unnoticed. Undercover work was crucial to his livelihood, as was the ability to alter his appearance. Any permanent fixtures upon his body would ruin one of the principle tools of his trade. He would become useless to his gang, the Handlers, and to their leader, his leader, Percal. But then, it was skirting the edge of that danger that provided the job with its thrills.

Uriah thrived on the notion of peril and he had a nose for it. In fact, Soren's disappearance promised more than was stated. Uriah had worked with Percal long enough to know there was always something more to his superior's assignments.

The armoury chief returned moments later with the standard assignment pack, the equipment satchel still flecked with dried blood from someone else's unfortunate outing. Uriah picked up the satchel and smiled at the armoury chief.

'Amateur?' Uriah asked.

'We're all amateurs when it comes to getting shot,' the Chief said.

'Not me,' Uriah said. 'I plan on bleeding like a professional Handler. All my forms signed and approved by my Overseer before one drop of blood strikes the ground.'

The Chief smirked and returned to his paperwork. Uriah checked the tools sheathed inside the heavy leather fabric, the satchel a tool belt of sorts for his crafts. More than just thieving supplies, lock picks, acid ampoules and protean metal keys, the satchel also carried small telescopes, eavesdropping equipment and other accoutrements for carrying out his role as spy.

Uriah nodded in satisfaction, at which the armoury chief deposited extra ammunition clips on the table.

'Tough assignment?' the armoury chief asked, more polite than interested.

'Subtle assignment,' Uriah answered, taking the supplies, 'but then it's the subtle ones that will cost you.'

Something in the statement attracted the armoury chief's attention. His expression changing from civil to concerned.

'Percal's boy, right?' the armoury chief asked.

'Well, not *boy*, but Percal is my Overseer, yes,' Uriah said, uncertain of the Chief's shifting interest.

'Careful with that one,' the Chief said with a casual whisper. He pointed to his marble eye with the clawed finger on his rusting metal hand. 'He cost me dearly. My first assignment too.'

'You're a Handler?' Uriah asked, shoving the ammo clips into the satchel. 'I didn't know.'

'Was a Handler,' the armoury chief said, a little pained at his own admission before he relaxed again. 'Now I'm with the Requisitioners, but then that's the nature of our craft. Nobody will ever know how good you are and they'll certainly never remember you once you're gone.'

Uriah smiled. 'In truth, that sounds glorious. I would welcome a chance to step away from it all.'

'It is glorious if you leave on your own terms,' the armoury chief said, shuffling back into the storerooms. 'But in our business, retirement is never expected or pleasant, and it often comes far too early for anyone to prepare for it.'

THERE WAS ONE last step to the process before Uriah launched into his investigation, something that fell well beyond Delaque operational protocol. The district was strictly low-ceiling and crammed with warehouses and containers. The buildings and storage cabins were mostly forgotten in the Underhive, their contents abandoned by their former owners. Still, enough were booby trapped that scavengers didn't bother pillaging the lots. Too many died in their attempts to loot, the containers electrified or coughing out some noxious gas that melted skin.

No official streets ran through here, only lot numbers belonging to the seemingly endless grid of corrugated and rusted storage units. Uriah drifted through the alleys, the rumble from his dark green bike echoing off the thin metal container walls.

Uriah turned several times, ignoring the lot numbers that were frequently switched around to lure unsuspecting travelers into ambushes. Instead, his circuit was memorized to the point of casual familiarity, and he never deviated from the path. Finally, Uriah arrived at the right section. He stopped in front of a storage container emblazoned with colourful profanities, but remained on his bike. He was centimetres from the wall. He left the engine running; he wasn't leaving its side.

There was a vox grille next to the heavy door, but no buttons, not that Uriah needed to press anything.

'State your business!' a woman's voice demanded through the scratchy vox feed.

'It's Jester,' Uriah said, using his operating handle.

'Stop revving your damn engine!' the woman shouted. 'Who is it?'

'Jester!' Uriah said, letting the engine idle. 'Or are your cameras broken again, Voice?'

'You know the drill,' the woman said.

Uriah disembarked from the cycle and turned around slowly, allowing whatever cameras that were hidden throughout the area to register his face and profile. He faced the intercom again and straddled the bike

'Happy?' he asked.

'Can you meet my price?'

'No, I came for the pleasant company, Voice.'

'Not in the mood for games, Jester.'

'Yes I can meet your price,' he said with a sigh.

'Then I'm very happy,' Voice replied, the tone more casual now. 'What can I do for you, Jester?'

'I'm on assignment and something about the mission bothers me.'

'You? Bothered? Care to share?'

'Since when do I share?' he asked, spreading his hands in feigned innocence.

'Fair enough. Same as before, then? You run your operation and I dispense my sage advice?'

'I'd appreciate that. Your understanding of the Machine Spirit is–'

'Oh, please! Not this crap again. There is no Machine Spirit. Just machine. Wires, tubes, chips and the occasional attitude. But no Machine Spirit!'

'Fine, fine,' Uriah said. 'Forget I mentioned it, Voice. I'll be in contact.'

Uriah tore through the streets, eager to reach his next objective, but his mind was still on Voice. He rarely relied on help; the nature of his business demanded self-sufficiency and it was also rife with the possibility of betrayal. Still, Voice came highly recommended from some acquaintances and she'd proven extremely useful in the past, almost trustworthy were Uriah comfortable with that sentiment. Still, it bothered him that he'd never met her face-to-face, but that was the condition of her services.

Regardless, the thought that Voice was now helping him did much to settle Uriah's mind. She was good at what she did, and she could keep up with Uriah's cavalier attitudes and humour.

Uriah reached a small tunnel barely high enough to let him through on his bike. He rode through several tunnels, taking different turns along the way, before finally reaching a locked grate against the wall. He opened the grate with a key and steered the bike deep inside the dark side tunnel, around a bend and against the dead end. Upon exiting, he locked the gate and looked back inside. He couldn't see his bike. Not the safest storage, but it served its purpose well when Uriah needed to tear through the Underhive.

Uriah made his way through the tunnels on foot and headed for a long-forgotten elevator shaft. It was going to be a long day.

CHAPTER: TWO

*Lies work best when enforced by some measure of truth…
just remember which parts are the lies and which parts are
the truth.*

– Delaque Operational Commandments
from the *Book of Lies*.

THE CEILING FOR the Saint Vibeau District was three
storeys high, but the stacked hab block containers
crammed beneath were stacked four high with uncom-
fortably low roofs. Locals claimed that millennia ago,
the district rested near the top of Hive Primus; in those
days Saint Vibeau was an affluent district that enjoyed
the patronage of the principle Houses. Hive Primus
continued growing, however, and the high ceilings
slowly sagged under the weight of the construction
above.

The last of the prosperous families moved away centuries ago, when a forgotten sump pipe burst between
two heavy load-bearing, thick-plated walls. It was
impossible to reach, so to this day the walls of Saint
Vibeau cried trickles of pollutants that afflicted many
local children with mutation and deformity. Few of
those so touched survived into adulthood between the
Goliath and Orlock gangs that occasionally swept

through on 'join-or-die' recruitment drives and the fatal nature of certain birth defects. It was also a district where nobody meddled in the affairs of their neighbours and where nobody made eye contact. It was safer that way.

The original hab blocks were sumptuous affairs until the district's principle employer, the Munitorum and its ammunition stockpiles, moved in to the district. The Munitorum administrators split the size of each hab block twice before allowing its workers to move in to the cramped quarters.

Uriah kept to the shadows of the streets, which was relatively easy considering the street lights had long burnt out and the fluorescent lichen-paint had calcified. Nobody paid him heed, but given his stained trench coat and heavy hood, he could have been a resident or another addict looking for somewhere to sleep.

Before Uriah reached the corner of a two-lane, trash-strewn street, a woman darted in front of him, her head down, her stride just short of panic as she pulled a small boy by the hand. Uriah reached the corner and peered around. Sure enough, idling on the curb were three ganger bikes with red Orlock flags hanging off heavy antennae. The bikes were nothing more than engines with large exhausts and two thick wheels; strapped on each was a heavy saddle. The bikes purred with a throaty rumble; one Orlock ganger with enough facial scars to have seen a few gang wars guarded them.

Uriah cursed softly. He knew an Orlock gang called Bleeding Iron was strong in the district. If he wasn't careful, he could easily draw the entire gang down upon his head. Uriah retraced his steps, returning back the way he had come before reaching a rubble-strewn alley. He detoured through the small corridor, finally reaching a hab block tower with a side entrance. The fortunate residents faced the outside street. The unlucky ones faced the dilapidated buildings and rusting support wall behind the block.

Uriah made his way up the rear grated stairs, up to the third floor landing. He made his way around to the building's plated front and paused momentarily to examine the street below. The Orlock ganger had yet to budge, allowing Uriah to make his way quietly to hab block #324.

The hab block's sliding door was open by a considerable gap, but the resident scavengers were nowhere to be seen despite the looting to be had through an open door. In any other situation, Uriah knew, the scavengers would have carried off anything they could carry. Peering through the half-open door, Uriah saw that the interior to his safe-house was smashed up and that whoever had made the mess was still inside, making a lot of noise.

Uriah sighed. He'd paid a foreman at the Slaughter House a considerable amount to secure this hab block for his own private use and to keep quiet. Only employees were given hab blocks, but it wasn't unusual for highly placed members of a business to profit on the side. In this case by selling Uriah the home of a dead employee who was still listed as alive.

Money lost, Uriah thought to himself as he pulled his newly acquired bolt pistol from its holster and muttered a small prayer to the weapon's Machine Spirit. The weight felt right in his hand, the engraving comfortable in his palm. He withdrew a small rectangular device from the pouch hidden inside the interior pocket of his trench coat and offered it a quick prayer as well.

Breathing slow, measured breaths, Uriah slipped through the open door and into the darkness of his safe-house. He lightly stepped over the broken glass in the entrance and ignored the frag holes in the thin metal walls. A voice, harsh and guttural, drifted from beyond the arched doorway. A woman responded. Uriah's heart skipped two beats, and he fought the urge to charge in.

Morgane is inside, he thought, but instead of rushing to her rescue and his death, he forced himself to listen to the number of voices.

'...last chance. I won't ask again,' one man said.

'Good,' the woman replied, 'I was getting tired of smelling your breath.'

Uriah grimaced, anticipating the sound of flesh slapping flesh. Sure enough, a sharp smack followed. Morgane, whom Uriah was sure had received the blow, did not sound out in pain, but neither did she say anything further.

'What?' the man's voice asked, 'nothing smart to say now?'

Morgane remained silent. Uriah knew it was time to act. He knelt down and attached the rectangular device to the power outlet. A small red light clicked on and began to blink slowly in a quickly accelerating cadence.

Uriah had thirty seconds. He remained kneeling and cleared his throat.

'Who's there?' the man in the other room demanded.

'You first,' Uriah said, congenial.

Twenty seconds and counting. The wall above his head exploded into metal shards, punched with several loud shots from heavy guns.

'That jog your memory?' the man asked with a laugh.

'Much,' Uriah said, 'thanks, but I didn't get your name over the gunfire.'

Fifteen seconds left.

'Enough with the jokes! Get out here or this woman dies.'

'What woman?'

Another shot punched through the wall, caking his jacket and hair in flakes of rust, paint and metal.

'All right, all right,' Uriah said, shaking the debris from his hair. 'Don't shoot.'

Ten seconds left. Uriah stood and entered the open archway with his arms outstretched to his sides. He held his gun in plain view. There were four men in the living room, Orlocks judging by the red bandanas, the half-plate armour and the billowing tunics that covered their compact frames. They were smaller than Goliaths, but stout nonetheless. And there were more men than Uriah had counted on, all of whom were pointing guns at him. A woman with raven black hair and bloodied lips, Morgane, sat quietly on the couch, her hands bound at the wrists, resting on her lap.

'Drop the pistol!' the ganger with multiple piercings in his nose and along his eyebrows said.

'Very well,' Uriah replied with a shrug, 'but it's not the gun you should be worried about.'

The rectangular device on the wall emitted an electrical surge that shot through the hab block's conduits, disrupting the power flow of the building's generators. The lights died instantly, but would return within moments. The last thing Uriah saw was the surprised expressions on the four men's faces. Laughing to himself, he dived to one side and fired into the darkness where he remembered the men standing. Four quick shots, each trying to score home on four different targets. The first two shots found their marks, rewarding Uriah with two grunts and the sound of someone hitting the floor. The other two shots missed, hitting wall and furniture instead. Within seconds, gunfire raked the area, illuminating the room in punched flashes of still life. Three Orlocks were firing wildly, trying to hit everything in the hopes of hitting something.

Uriah crouched near the floor, ducking behind the furniture and taking his time in firing back. He waited patiently, focusing on the muzzle flares before squeezing off another shot on the Orlock with the heavy chain pulling at his nose ring. Uriah caught a quick glimpse of dark arterial spray, the shot striking the ganger in the neck and jerking his gun upward. The remaining two gangers fired at Uriah's muzzle flash, stinging him with hot debris; he was already repositioning himself in another part of the room.

White-hot beams of green las-fire erupted from another part of the room, announcing that a new shooter had just entered the fray. Uriah caught quick glimpses of Morgane, her back against the wall, her backside on the floor, firing one of three weapons hidden throughout the safe-house. The las-beam cooked the arm of one shooter, forcing him to drop his weapon. He howled in pain and bolted for the door. Uriah, ignoring the fleeing Orlock, focused on the last gunman who was drawing his sights on Morgane. He emptied his clip into the ganger, knocking him off his feet.

Uriah raced for the hab block door, reloading a new clip into his pistol. He'd barely stepped onto the lit landing when heavy gunfire from a bolter shredded the railing wall and doorway. The Orlock attending to the bikes below was suppressing the area with cover fire. Uriah hit the ground hard, bouncing his chin off the iron floor. By the time his head stopped ringing, bike engines were revving with an angry roar – the gunfire had stopped. Uriah peered over the shredded rail in time to see the wounded Orlock and his compatriot tearing down the street. Uriah fired a handful of shots at them, more in frustration than from any real hope of hitting them.

The Orlocks had escaped.

Uriah muttered a quick curse and wandered back into the hab block through the blast-eaten doorway. Lights were returning, the device no longer disrupting the power flow. His jaw felt numb, but he was grateful to see Morgane in the living room, hunkered down behind a steel-plated sofa with her sights firmly trained on the door. She looked relieved to see Uriah, and lowered her weapon.

'The others?' Uriah asked, referring to the three bodies.

'Corpses,' she replied. 'I saw to that.'

Uriah noticed the blackened, cracked burn marks on the temples of each of the three men. 'That's a bit much,' he said. 'I could have sworn I killed at least two of them, already.'

'I guess we'll never know,' Morgane replied with a small grin. 'I'm sorry, my love. Did I steal your thunder?'

He shook his head. 'Not enough to matter.' With that he embraced her and gave her a gentle kiss. 'And thanks,' he said. 'That juicer you gave me came in handy. Are you all right?'

'As soon as you get these restraints off of me,' Morgane said.

Uriah admired the iron bindings for a moment with a devilish smile. 'Certain you don't want to keep them on?' he asked with a wink.

'Now, Uriah!' Morgane said, poking him with the las pistol. She offered him her outstretched hands, palms up.

After sheathing the pistol and removing something from his interior jacket pocket, Uriah covered the lock with his hands, his fingers moving almost imperceptibly. A second passed and a light click followed. The restraints fell away.

'One of these days,' Morgane said, massaging her reddened wrists, 'you'll have to show me how you do that.'

'And where would that leave me?' Uriah asked.

'Oh, knowing you,' she replied, drawing in close enough that he smelt the cloves on her breath, 'with still more tricks than any Handler in your industry.'

'Yes, well...' he said with a shrug, before kissing her gently. He was careful not to brush against her cut. 'What were they doing here?' he finally asked. 'More importantly, why were you here?'

'Soren,' she replied. 'The answer to both your questions.'

URIAH MOVED ABOUT the one-room hab block, collecting the few knick knacks that were valuable enough to take and shoving them into a cloth sack. They only took what they could carry. The furniture would remain, given that most of it was already bolted to the floor. Morgane sat on the couch, facing the doorway and firing above the head of the occasional scavenger that stuck his greedy nose into the hab block.

'And the Bleeding Iron gangers didn't say why they were looking for Soren?' Uriah asked.

'I didn't ask, considering I lied about not knowing him in the first place.'

'Hm. So the Orlocks didn't realise you were Van Saar. That's fortunate,' Uriah said. 'And the Van Saar only know that he's missing.'

'Correct,' Morgane replied, 'but then I'm only an inter-House diplomat. I'm not in Soren's group. They wouldn't tell me if there was more to it. I only know that they issued an Injunctus saying that he was missing, and to report his whereabouts. Since he knew about the safe-house, I came here hoping to find him.'

Uriah shrugged. 'The only people who knew about the safe-house were you and Soren. I saw to that. Unfortunately, it's compromised, so we must leave it behind.'

'Pity,' Morgane replied. 'We've made many fond memories here.'

'I'll find us a new hole,' Uriah said. 'We'll make new memories there.'

'Until then,' Morgane said, 'I must return to my duties.'

Uriah's face pinched into a small scowl. He didn't like the idea. 'Are you certain that's safe?' he asked. 'If they find out about us, your life's at risk.'

'We share that risk,' Morgane said. She stood and walked over to Uriah. 'If your Delaque masters ever realised you were in love with a Van Saar diplomat...'

'Actually, they'd try to use that to their advantage first,' Uriah said. 'I understand what you mean though. You're certain that you haven't been compromised?'

'Compromised by you? Maybe,' Morgane said with a tantalizing smile. 'Otherwise, no. I'm fairly certain. My house would have arrested me by now if they suspected anything, and the Orlocks don't know who I am.'

Uriah sighed. 'But they know me.'

'You can't be certain of that,' she said.

'I'm seventh on their most hunted list and I didn't arrive here in disguise.'

'Seventh?' Morgane asked. 'You're slipping.'

'Not after tonight,' Uriah replied. 'If the Bleeding Irons report to the House itself and they manage to connect this incident to me, you-know-who will come after me again.'

He must have looked worried, Uriah realized, because Morgane's features softened; she caressed his face. 'You don't know that,' she said, 'and if he does, you'll be ready.'

'One can hope,' Uriah said. His legs still ached at night, the pins somehow vibrating at some distant memory of his shattered bones. Slag's face darted into his mind's eye and Uriah felt the blood slip from his face.

Morgane kissed him on the lips, obviously trying to liberate him from his painful memories. 'Thank you for saving me,' she said.

'Always,' he replied, grateful for the beautiful distraction. He looked at her puffed lips. 'How are you going to explain the injuries?'

'I fell,' she said. 'That's all they'll need to know. What about you? What is your next step?'

'I have to find, Soren.'

'But?'

'But, I'm worried about House Orlock's sudden involvement. I have to find out why they want Soren.'

'They didn't seem to know very much,' Morgane said.

'They'll know enough to launch me in the right direction. You better go,' he said with a sigh. 'It won't take long before the Bleeding Irons return in greater numbers.'

'What about you?' Morgane asked, drawing a hood over her head.

'I'll escape in a moment, but I'm leaving the Orlocks a nasty surprise.'

'And the scavengers?'

'They won't have many bones left to pick clean. Now go.'

Uriah waited for Morgane to leave before activating the booby trap and slipping out of the hab block. In ten seconds, laser tripwires would activate and the explosives would destroy anyone and anything inside. The damage to the adjoining hab blocks would be minimal, but just the same, Uriah knocked on the neighbouring door.

Nobody answered, though Uriah was certain he heard movement inside. 'Hello there and well met,' he called through the door. 'Though I've never had occasion to speak to you previously, I would advise you don't go into my hab block. It's booby trapped. Big explosion awaits the interloper. Hello?'

Uriah walked away from the hab block door. 'Suit yourself,' he mumbled under his breath.

* * *

'WELL, IF IT isn't my favourite Handler!' almond-eyed Bok said with a green-toothed smile.

Uriah navigated past the five other desks crammed into the small room. 'Bok,' Uriah said, returning the smile. 'How's my favourite Cartographer?'

'Well,' Bok said, 'just returned from a mapping expedition into the Underhive. Nasty foul place, too unpleasant for a Handler's delicate sensibilities.'

'Of course,' Uriah said. 'I can still smell the stench of the place on you. Or is that endemic to all members of the Cartographers?'

Bok's smile wavered a touch, but it held. 'What can I do for you, Uriah?'

'I need to break into a location, an Orlock facility. How current are your maps?'

'Very current. Over half of our section's resources are dedicated to probing and testing Orlock assets. What do you need?' Bok asked, his smile turning into a casual, easy grin.

'Ah,' Uriah said. 'It's more like what you need?'

'The marker,' Bok said, dropping his voice into a whisper. 'I want my marker with you wiped clean.'

'I don't know,' Uriah said, rubbing his chin. He lowered his voice as well. 'That's a hefty price considering the evidence I have against you. Your taste in Escher prostitutes poses a security risk to Delaque interests. I saved you once from your pillow chats and an unfortunate slip of the tongue... though whose tongue slipped where, I'd prefer not knowing.'

'Yes, yes,' Bok replied, glancing around to ensure nobody was listening, 'but I'm a changed man. I no longer frequent the Escher's stables. And I can provide you with full schematics to one facility, a foundry, including its patrol routes and the best ways in and out.'

Uriah smiled and shrugged. 'Then who am I to stand in the way of someone's evolution into betterment. Get me the maps and, if they're as good as you claim, then your marker is wiped clean and the evidence I hold is yours.'

'Deal,' Bok said, and immediately set off to retrieve the proper maps.

'WELL, IF IT isn't my favourite Handler!' almond-eyed Bok said with a green-toothed smile.

Kaden navigated past the five other desks crammed into the small room. 'Bok,' Kaden said, returning the smile. 'How's my favourite map-boy?'

'Well,' Bok said, 'just returned from a mapping expedition into the Underhive. Nasty foul place. You'd like it there.'

'Funny, but don't you figure that's a little risky, considering what I've got on you?' Kaden said, sitting on the edge of Bok's desk.

'What can I do for you, Kaden?' Bok asked with a sigh.

'Where was Uriah heading? Which map did he want? And don't leave out any juicy details.'

'And in exchange for helping you?' Bok asked with a whisper.

'We'll call it even, and all that nasty evidence involving you and those prostitutes gets wiped.'

'Deal,' Bok said, and immediately set off to retrieve the proper maps.

CHAPTER: THREE

Harden your heart… everyone is an asset. If you don't use them to your advantage, someone else will use them to theirs.

– Delaque Operational Commandments
from the *Book of Lies*.

THE FOUNDRY FILLED the large chamber's interior. The ceiling was domed some fifteen storeys high with support struts that swept up into the shadows. Inset into the ceiling were noisy, cowled turbofans that cried a steady stream of precipitation – stained with oil – to the cement floor below. The foundry itself was a rusted block of steel, the few windows and open hangar doors lit with the magma glow of molten ores. The only entry into the dome chamber was a rolling vault door; it was three storeys high and guarded by the Steel Sentinels, an Orlock gang of considerable standing, and manned gun emplacements. Entry was strictly prohibited except to those on House Orlock business.

Uriah was sweating hard, his black clothing plastered to his skin. Despite the discomfort, he waited patiently, trying to ignore the oppressive heat that the turbofans sucked up from the main chamber into the ductwork where he sat. The heat flattened his breath, pressing his

chest with its palm; it hurt to inhale, so instead Uriah
swallowed shallower breaths and dreamed of cooler
places. He imagined himself inside a chilled Van Saar
lab, refrigerated to optimize the usage of electronics and
to prevent them from overheating. It seemed that the
Machine Spirits preferred the cold.

He also imagined the scrubbed, sterile environment
of the Van Saar facility he'd infiltrated so many years
ago. It contrasted sharply with the smelly, mildew-soft
and cramped interior of the ducts that Uriah crawled
through to reach this point. He admired the Van Saar
and its satellite gangs; to them personal hygiene was
more than an afterthought or alien principle. Certainly,
House Delaque consisted of clean and well-groomed
agents, unlike the zealots of House Cawdor, the muscle-
ripped Goliaths or the sweaty apes of House Orlock.

Admittedly, Uriah relished his undercover work at the
Van Saar labs for more reasons than their enhanced
quality of life. On one mission into the Tech-Artificer
Gang, Uriah had befriended Soren and scored a potential coup by convincing the disenfranchised engineer to
sell secrets to the Delaque. On another, into the Van
Saar's Arbiter's Guild, Uriah had met Morgane. Even
now, their tryst still felt new, passionate and dangerous,
their romance unsanctioned.

Uriah let his thoughts wander to those intimate
encounters in the biolabs, where the air was frozen;
Morgane's breath warmed his mouth. At the time, he
didn't expect much to come of their encounters. He'd
seduced women throughout his assignments – except
for House Escher women who scared the living hell out
of him – either in the course of retrieving something
valuable, or because an easy assignment needed some
additional element to spice up the challenge.

Morgane was different. Different enough that Uriah
divulged his role as spy to her. Different enough that

while initially outraged, she never betrayed his secret. They were apart for a few agonizing weeks. He returned to see her one last time and discovered she wasn't willing to let him go again so easily. She continued loving him. That was years ago.

Uriah's and Morgane's romance continued despite the physical distance between them, the physical distance they willingly imposed. Uriah could no more surrender his job or leave his house than she could hers. They both understood that revealing their relationship to either house would entail the end of their love, their careers, their lives. The Van Saar and Delaque were too ruthless and goal driven not to use Uriah's and Morgane's affair to their advantage. They would kill both parties simply because the two lovers had humiliated the houses by carrying on a relationship for four years under their very noses. Nobody liked being proven the fool.

That thought brought everything back to today's predicament and Uriah's sweltering cubby hole inside the dome's ductwork. Soren's disappearance was one thing, but that the Orlocks were also looking for the Van Saar engineer and that they had endangered Morgane's life was an entirely different beast. Uriah could not abide their actions. In nearly every previous assignment, Uriah had kept the upper hand; had remained outside the situation; the job was just a job. That was no longer the case. Uriah did not control these circumstances, he was reacting to them, trying to roll with the punches from an invisible opponent.

Uriah checked his timepiece; it was counting down to zero with a minute to spare. He opened his mouth in a mock yawn to equalize the pressure in his ears. That activated the receiver hidden in his ear and the sub-vocalizer currently lodged inside his throat. It was irritating, but he'd grow accustomed to the sensation soon enough.

'About to descend,' he said.

'Understood,' Voice responded. 'Good luck.'

Unable to stand or hunch properly in the ducts, Uriah shifted position till he was on his padded knees. He scuttled towards the noisy turbofan and steady stream of hot air. His fingers centimetres from the whirling blades, he searched the lining of the cowled turbofan; after a moment, he found a proper finger-hold. Uriah wedged a grappling hook into the small space; it was tethered with a chord that was hidden inside his belt. He pulled hard to ensure the hook held well.

The countdown on Uriah's timepiece reached zero and a collective sigh echoed through the ducts. The turbofans shut off for a few moments to cool down – the blades facing Uriah whirred to a halt. He pulled an acid ampoule from his pouch and quickly wedged it between the teeth of a large cog that connected with an adjoining gear, their teeth interlinking. They turned the fan and, the cogs still rotating slowly, bit down on the ampoule, breaking it. A sharp acrid smell filled the air, acid stripping the gear of its teeth. When the turbofans would eventually start up again, this one would remain silent and still, the toothless gears spinning, but not catching.

Testing the hook one last time, Uriah slipped backwards between two large and pitted fan blades, his feet secured against the bottom lip of the cowl, his behind dangling over the void of the long drop down. One gloved hand on the rope and the other on the vice-brake, Uriah pushed off; he fast-roped down through the steaming darkness, aiming for the foundry rooftop below. He doubted anyone could see him in the darkness of the dome, but better to be safe. The descent took seconds, Uriah on the edge of freefall, the building rooftop rushing up to meet him at an alarming rate. At the last moment, he gripped the vice to slow himself, coming to a slightly jarring, but otherwise perfect stop.

The furnaces and melted ores below radiated through the ceiling and heated the air; Uriah's feet felt hot. The smell, however, was even more uncomfortable. Smoke stacks and vents poured a noxious mix of gases and solvents into the dome, filling Uriah's mouth with an acrid medley of tastes. Worse, Uriah was light-headed, disconnected from his environment, his head feeling fixed to his body by a mere string. He fumbled for one of his pouches and withdrew a filter-cup affixed with two metallic cylinders. Uriah covered his mouth and nose with a small rebreather, grateful for the brief injections of oxygen. It wouldn't last more than a few minutes – just long enough for Uriah to act.

Untethering himself from the rappelling cord, Uriah left it hanging there for his return. From the edge of the roof, the foundry's walls were seven-storey cliffs, straight drops to the ground. No heavy-footed Orlock ever had a chance of climbing these walls unassisted, but then, Uriah was no Orlock. He was lighter of frame, nimble and blessed with quick fingers. Uriah lowered himself over the roof's edge and quickly made his way down. Hand over hand, foot over foot, he scaled down the wall, grabbing inch-wide ledges and drain pipes. Within moments, he was on the main floor in the shadow of the building, alert to all the noise around him.

It was cooler on the ground – not by much, but enough to be a small blessing. Uriah hid in a small alcove that forced him to a knee. He was draped in darkness, though he hoped the ambient heat blinded anyone with thermal vision. Uriah waited patiently, taking in all the surrounding noise, trying to familiarize himself with what passed for background noise. He

needed to understand this cacophony intimately so that
he wasn't leaping for cover at every clang and dis-
charged hiss of the great machines, conveyor belts and
supply Lorries. He needed to distinguish someone's
voice from the hiss of molten metal, and footfalls from
the piston gait of aged devices.

Uriah checked the timepiece strapped to his wrist; it
was almost time; about thirty seconds, give or take a
minute. He focused more intently on the sounds, trying
to move past the surrounding din. It was hard work sift-
ing through the clatter and thunder, but Uriah listened
for one thing alone in the sea of noise. Sure enough, he
heard voices, then footsteps in the seconds before they
appeared. A patrol that he'd spotted earlier from the turbofan vent marched by, on schedule. They were armed
with chainsaw blades and mean scowls on their wide-
jawed, stubble-eaten faces. Their circuit took them
around the building, their orbit bringing them close to
Uriah's hiding hole. They didn't linger, however, and
within a minute, had vanished around a corner.

They were gone and Uriah relaxed enough to curse
under his breath. He only heard them in the seconds
before they appeared. Not nearly enough time to react,
but maybe enough time to kill someone before they
could raise the alarm or pull their own weapon. That
would have to suffice.

Uriah checked his timepiece again and thanked the
Machine Spirit for its precision.

'Check one,' Uriah said.

'On time,' Voice said. 'Not bad. You have another ten
minutes before that patrol returns.'

'Let's call it at nine minutes, just to be safe,' Uriah
responded. By then he hoped, he'd be inside the building where avoiding guards would prove trickier. While
the schematics on the foundry that House Delaque provided offered Uriah some crucial intelligence, it didn't

offer him enemy positions or patrol circuits. Once inside, Uriah was effectively blind and on wits' edge. Then again, that was exactly how he liked it.

Certain there was nobody around, Uriah slipped out from the alcove. He padded his way to his next target, a small vent grate some ten metres along the same wall as the alcove. Upon reaching it, he pulled out a small screwdriver and worked the grille's screws, grimacing at every twisting screech and groan. It wasn't loud enough to draw attention, however, and Uriah pushed into the small hole, feet first and on his back. Not the preferred method for entering a duct, but Uriah needed to close the grate behind him.

The channel was a tight fit, the dust and soot-coated ceiling centimetres from the tip of his nose, the walls wide enough for Uriah to extend his arms over his head. He craned his head back and used a small magnetic clamp to keep the grille in place with the metal duct. Satisfied that it would hold, Uriah dug the soft heel of his boots into the floor and shimmied along while pulling with his hands. According to the building schematics, it would open up soon, but then a centimetre on the blueprints might well be a kilometre in reality.

'Uf,' Uriah grunted. 'This is tight.'

'Told you,' Voice said. 'If you get stuck, I'm not coming to help.'

'Duly noted,' Uriah said. At the very least, Uriah was thankful that he wasn't claustrophobic, though he did have to push away persistent thoughts of the passage narrowing and him getting stuck. Instead, he focused on Morgane's face until the duct widened at a large, relatively spacious junction where it split with another channel that went straight up. He switched positions, turning face forward and rolling over to his stomach so he could push forward with his legs. He continued on his way head first and proceeded to the next vent, grateful that his escape lay only metres away.

THE FOUNDRY'S INTERIOR was a honeycomb of interconnected caverns, each five to seven storeys in height. While expansive, the interior was still cramped. Huge heating engines and generators sat shoulder to shoulder with barely the room to slip through the gaps between them. Some of the equipment was rusted and useless, having died years ago; others coughed black smoke and functioned as though seized by spasms. Three-storey vats containing pools of magma-like metal bled thick ropes of steam upwards while conveyor belts carried various moulds or cooled ore ingots from one section to the next. The sky above it all was a network of catwalks and footbridges, designed around the steam columns and connected to the few offices suspended well above the foundry floor.

'I'm inside,' Uriah said. 'I see the offices, but the walkways above are well travelled and too visible for my tastes.'

'Stay on the ground,' Voice said. 'No need to climb just yet, according to the map.'

Uriah remained on the ground, hiding between the legs of gigantic engines of unfathomable purpose, darting from one shadow to the next. Traffic along the ground was light, and for good reason. The vats above rained irregular showers of molten sparks that quickly sizzled, sputtered and cooled on the pitted floors. From his vantage, Uriah could see those individuals who survived the scarring touch of the lethal rains, their skin marked and discoloured by droplets of ore. He took extra care to navigate clear of the vats when he could.

After an eternity of hiding in darkness and slowly making his way through the various chambers, Uriah reached his destination.

'Finally here,' he said.

'And only an hour to get there,' Voice replied.

'Aren't you happy you charge by the hour?'

'It depends,' Voice replied, a hint of mischief to her voice. 'Most men don't last the hour.'

Before Uriah could reply, Voice segued into: 'You see the chief foreman's office?'

'I'm standing directly below it. Or rather, it's six storeys above me.'

The chief foreman's office was a rectangular container, lined with filthy windows on its four sides, all of them dark. Only one wall connected to the catwalks; the other walls were virtually inaccessible. Virtually.

Uriah crouched in the shadow of a trestle that helped support the network of low walkways. He studied his surroundings, checking for patrols and lookouts. Most of the Orlocks were on the lower catwalks, though a few maintenance workers ran their rounds on the ground. It was his best shot, the graveyard shift running the fewest workers.

After taking a deep breath, Uriah mounted the trestle and clambered up a girder that angled upward at forty-five degrees. His foot slipped twice on the grimy beam, but he held tight despite the growing ache in his fingers. He reached the junction between the beam and the strut supporting the catwalk itself, and switched position – his fingers gripping the strut on either side and his back and feet planted firmly against the beam.

Metallic footsteps clanged directly over Uriah's head; there was an Orlock on the catwalk above. Uriah waited, acutely aware of his feet slowly slipping along the girder's greasy slope. He held on tighter, trying to remain anchored, but his fingers grew numb. The foot-steps continued their slow, plodding pace, the Orlock in no hurry to move past. Uriah cursed silently and focused on his breathing.

The dull ache in his fingers turned his hands into arthritic claws, and Uriah wondered if he'd be able to unlock them or even pull his way up through the bars of the catwalk's rails. Still, he held on and waited for the slow Orlock to walk past. Another eternity passed, and another, bringing Uriah to the edge of letting go and sliding all the way back down to the ground in a hard tumble. The footsteps above his head moved on. Within moments, the sounds of heavily booted feet against the catwalk faded away. Uriah was no longer certain if there was anyone on the footbridge above his head, but he had no choice now.

With singular effort, Uriah used the last of his guttering strength to pull himself up. He grabbed the rail's horizontal bars and slipped under the lowest one; he lay flat on the catwalk, breathing hard. His fingers now screamed in pain and it hurt just trying to unlock them from the claw-like rigour. He massaged both hands against his trousers and craned his head to look around. There were no Orlocks anywhere near him or his stretch of walkway, including the one who had delayed his ascent.

Uriah muttered a small curse against the Steel Sentinel Orlock that had pained him so, and took the extra moment to curse the Orlock's entire lineage and whatever pet he possessed. Then again, he doubted the Orlock was domesticated enough to attract a pet in the first place.

'What was that?' Voice asked.

Uriah grimaced; he'd have to remember that his throat microphone was overly sensitive. No more mouthing his silent conversations. 'Nothing,' he said. 'Just resting a moment before continuing.'

With sensation returning to his fingers, Uriah stood and carefully made his way along the catwalk. His head swivelled from side to side like a predator on the hunt and he loped close to the ground. His hand remained on the railing in case he needed to swing over the side at a moment's notice; though truthfully, his fingers ached in protest at the mere notion of repeating their last performance. Thankfully, the lower catwalks weren't as frequently patrolled as the network several metres above his head, and they remained hidden in larger patches of shadow.

Uriah was now below the chief foreman's cabin by some three storeys. Reaching the front door would require making his way up to the upper set of catwalks where the lighting was more prevalent and where more Orlocks laboured and toiled. That was not an option. Instead, he steeled himself to the inevitable climb up the adjacent support trestle of the upper walkways; with skillful navigation that would bring him eye-to-eye with one of the cabin's dark windows. After that, it would be a matter of finding a way inside, not that Uriah was worried.

Waiting until the walkway above his was clear, Uriah clambered onto the angled trestle and shimmied his way upwards again. This time, speed took precedence, and within a few seconds, he'd reached the upper catwalk precisely when nobody was close enough to see him. After confirming through the windows that the chief foreman's office was dark and unoccupied, Uriah mounted the rail and leapt for the cabin's roof ledge. Almost silently, he pulled himself up on top of the cabin and rolled away to remain hidden. With the network of hanging walkways below him, Uriah felt confident that nobody could spy on him from above. He peered over the edge of each side, trying to find the best, most discreet, way into the cabin.

KADEN SUPPRESSED A cough borne from the dusty, oily interior of the duct. The turbofans had flared to life

moments ago, dragging polluted air out of the foundry
dome, all except the one in Kaden's duct. He
approached the silent fan and immediately noted the
coppery acid smell in the air. Sure enough, two gears
had been stripped of their teeth. They spun effortlessly,
the fan blades remaining still. Kaden saw the grappling
claw hooked into the side of turbofan's cowl and the
cord that dropped down into the darkness. With a
smile, Kaden pulled Uriah's rappelling rope back up
through the blades.

URIAH DROPPED INTO the room from the vent in the ceiling and quickly surveyed his surroundings. The cabin
was a single room except for the privy, and surprisingly
neat for an Orlock's den. Still messy by Uriah's standards, but at the very least, he didn't feel like scrubbing
himself clean from proximity.

   Patches of dust and corner cobwebs coated the room.
The dusk was a clutter of work order bundles made
from recycled vellum, while a couch and small kitchen
attested to many a double and triple shift that the
Orlocks likely inflicted upon the Steel Sentinels
foundry. In one corner, piles of stripped innards belonging to various machines sat next to a small work bench.
Central to the room and thus, Uriah's attentions, was a
large work desk overflowing with data pads and piles of
parchments.

   Nearly lost in the junk heap of the desk sat an Orlock
logic hub. It was an ancient device and looked too jury-
rigged to have been touched by a Van Saar engineer. It
was also one of the few logic devices throughout the
facility, if the Orlocks remained true to form. While the
foreman likely used it for accounting and other orders
of business required to run the foundry, the device was
also connected to the primitive network shared by most
Orlock facilities. How they maintained technology of

that sophistication was a mystery to Uriah, but they must have done something right to appease the Machine Spirit.

'I found the logic hub,' Uriah said.

'Is it two cans connected together with string?'

Uriah chuckled softly. 'I see we share an appreciation of Orlock technology.'

'Cawdor, Goliath, Orlocks… they're all the same smelly breed.'

'I see,' Uriah said. 'No, the hub appears to be more sophisticated than that.'

'All right then. Start her up. I'll walk you through this.'

With little time to lose, Uriah activated the machine and prayed for a simple encryption code. The computer hissed to life, sounding as though it was on its final legs, mechanical hiccups and heavy whirrs threatening to choke it. Uriah waited for the prompt screen to begin his assault.

KADEN WORE AN ear-splitting grin as he heaved the last of the rappelling rope up through the turbofan. A click and piston sigh behind him brought Kaden to his next task. He turned to face the tiny drone, a floating child's skull with a pict-grabber in one eye socket. It hovered behind Kaden in the duct, obediently awaiting its next orders.

'Stir up some trouble, will you?' Kaden said.

The drone floated past Kaden, buoyed up by a tiny anti-grav generator, and dropped into the chamber.

'And try not to get shot this time,' Kaden whispered after it.

URIAH SLAPPED THE side of the logic device in frustration and set about coaxing it to life. It was slow, and from what Uriah could see, the Orlock's sad attempt at a user interface was a clutter of scattered files listed with no apparent rhyme or reason.

'Did you hit the machine?' Voice asked.

'Maybe,' Uriah said, puzzled. 'If I did, how would you know?'

'Tsk,' Voice replied, 'I know all. And what would your precious Machine Spirit say to such callous treatment.'

'"Thank you for awakening me" perhaps?'

'I doubt it. Keep searching for the directory.'

Uriah sighed and set about searching through the network. Finally, he found the directory he was looking for, the one that accessed the Orlock network. The logic device awaited input of a password.

'Found it!'

'Be grateful the Orlocks don't rely on Van Saar protocols,' Voice said. 'Passwords must be input within a set number of seconds. Only three mistakes are allowed before the terminal shuts down. Then the alert goes out.'

Uriah nodded. 'I know the Orlocks possess nothing of that sophistication, though its more cunning members do booby-trap their hardware.'

'Is that experience talking?'

'Perhaps,' Uriah said. 'It's certainly not ignorance speaking its mind.' Looking at this terminal with its dried lubricant tubes and exposed wiring, Uriah doubted the hub was booby-trapped.

Uriah accessed the root files, hoping to find some way to bypass the password system. His fingers danced across the input device at Voice's behest, but the system was well protected, far better then his last incursion.

With a jolting abruptness, alarms rang out across the entire facility and sent Uriah's heart straight into his throat.

'Jester, what is it?' Voice asked.

'Don't know yet. Stand by.' Uriah scrambled to the window to see outside; Orlocks were running in different directions across the catwalks. A voice boomed over the foundry's loudspeakers:

'Intruders outside. There may be more inside. Search the entire facility!'

Uriah cursed, an avalanche of questions on his lips. Did they spot his rope? Is it another intruder? What are the chances there's another thief out here, tonight? How long will it take for them to reach this office? He shook his head, trying to dislodge the cacophony of questions addling his thoughts, and returned to the computer terminal.

'The foundry's on alert. I have to move fast.'

'Pull out?' Voice asked.

'No. We continue but hurry.'

Fingers typing with furious pitch, Uriah flew through the different directories, trying to find a way past the password blockade. Voices filtered in and out of the cabin as Orlocks drifted close to, then away from it. It was only a matter of time, but that was enough to prompt Uriah to work more quickly.

Footsteps approached the catwalk closest to the cabin's windows. Uriah killed the pict screen attached to the logic hub and slid out of the chair and under the desk. The footsteps stopped and Uriah held his breath, trying to hear the conversation outside.

'Jester,' Voice asked.

There was no reply.

'Don't look like there's anyone inside,' a woman's voice said from outside the foreman's office.

'Check *inside*,' her male compatriot said.

'I haven't got the key.'

'Then get the key,' he replied.

'But it's at the security post,' she said, impatience lacing her voice.

'Good thing you've got legs, then,' he said, ending the argument.

The footsteps moved away, and Uriah braved a glimpse. The catwalks outside were empty, again, but that also meant Uriah had a few minutes at most before they returned.

Uriah was about to lift himself back up when something caught his eye. Scratched into the edge of the desk itself was a sequence of numbers: 38452.

'It can't be this easy,' Uriah mumbled to himself before setting himself back into the chair.

'What?'

'I think I found the code.' He brought the screen back to life and returned to the password prompt. Sure enough, 38452 did the trick, and the Orlock network opened. Uriah searched for the keyword 'Soren,' and was rewarded with a single entry complete with Soren's picture:

> Attention all Orlock Facilities:
> WANTED! Dead or Alive
> Soren Kaar, House Van Saar: Tech-Artificers
> Bounty: Dependent on conditions mentioned below.
> Kaar is a traitor. He has been selling technology to House Delaque and House Orlock. He must pay for that insult.
> IMPORTANT! Bring Kaar in alive OR bring his implants back undamaged! Bounty is dependent on condition of implants!

'Soren,' Uriah muttered to himself. 'You idiot. What were you doing?'

'Did you get it?'

'Yes.'

'Then leave!'

'Not yet! I'll contact you later!' Uriah said. Lost to the revelation that Soren was also selling secrets to the Orlocks, Uriah raced through more files, trying to find tidbits of information. The bounty certainly explained why the Orlocks were after Soren, but, the fact it was still active meant the Orlocks were no closer to finding the Tech-Artificer's whereabouts than Uriah was. Unfortunately, if the Orlocks knew anything further, it wasn't on their network.

Voices outside the cabin grew louder. The two Orlocks were returning with the key and headed straight for the door. Uriah quickly killed the power to the terminal and raced to the hole in the ceiling where he'd removed the grate. He jumped as the voices approached the door, and caught the lips of the vent. He pulled himself up, but his chest snagged the edges.

Uriah exhaled, forcing all the air from his lungs and contracting his chest and torso by the necessary centimetres.

The key scratched the door before dropping into the lock.

Uriah pulled himself up, scrapping his body through the opening. His belt caught on the edge.

The door lock clicked open.

Uriah pushed his belt in to clear the opening and pulled his way up.

Not fast enough! he realized when he heard the Orlocks in the cabin below shout.

'Intruder!'

Uriah cursed. They'd likely seen his legs vanish up through the hole.

A second later, as Uriah scrambled up, gunshots tore open the ceiling and shredded the rooftop beneath his feet. Wild shots hissed past him and more shouts echoed throughout the complex. It was time to move.

Uriah leapt from the roof down onto the upper-level catwalks, landing lightly on his feet. He barely caught sight of the two overeager Orlocks inside the cabin before ducking; errant shots peppered the walls and windows of the cabin, whining above Uriah's head. New shots whizzed by, pinging off metal rails and I-beams. More Orlocks were joining the battle and firing with wild abandon.

'Too many bullets! Run, run, run,' Uriah muttered to himself. Like a cat, he dived over the railing and grabbed it with both hands as he passed. He swung like a pendulum, slamming his back into the walkway with a jarring thud. He twisted to face the catwalk, and then dropped again, swiftly catching its bottom lip. The sloped trestle was centimetres from his outstretched toes, his head below the catwalk's floor, just enough to see the flurry of movement on the lower walkways and on the ground.

More shots rang out, clanging against the metal around him; Uriah nudged himself into a swing below the catwalk, towards the trestle that was angled down forty-five degrees. He let go again and fell the few centimetres to the girder. He slid down the beam, first on his feet, before falling to his backside; he grunted at the rivets that punched him on the pelvic bone and in the soft flesh of his posterior during his downward slide.

Uriah slid down toward the floor, where his angled trestle met with a vertical I-beam that shot straight up. He grabbed the edge of the girder with both gloved hands, trying to slow himself down from the near-terminal velocity slide and inevitable crash. The metal shredded the glove's padding and drew some blood from his much abused fingers, but Uriah managed to decelerate in time. His feet slammed into the I-beam at speeds less than deadly, and momentum pushed him off his ass. He struck the girder with his shoulder, the sickening pop followed by a rapier-sharp pain.

Barely functioning through the pain-laced fog of a dislocated shoulder, but reacting on instinct, Uriah slammed his shoulder into the girder again. He set his shoulder back in its joint and collapsed to the ground after nearly fainting from the effort.

Uriah fought to stay conscious, fought to remain aloft on the black waters that threatened to drown him. Somewhere in the great distance, gunshots rang out and a tiny thought nestled itself well in the back of his mind. *That's nice* he thought. *They're shooting at someone else.*

Only when one of the shots struck the concrete and peppered him with biting shards did Uriah realize he was still the prey. He rolled away, reacting on instinct, but more focused now, and scrambled to his feet. By the time sense had returned to him, Uriah was already running, darting between large pieces of equipment, none of which was spared the punishing salvoes of the pursuing Orlocks. Their indiscriminant manner brought Uriah to the mocking conclusion that the Orlocks were deliberately missing him to damage the foundry thus sparing themselves further drudgery.

As the chase continued, Uriah gained more footing with his senses; the stabbing pain in his shoulder subsided to a dull throb, but it promised plenty of aches tomorrow. For now, it diminished enough for Uriah to plan strategy.

Can't run forever, Uriah thought as the occasional round tried finding its mark. *Have to throw them off*.

The shooting stopped and Uriah realized he'd lost the pursuing Orlocks at the last jumble of machinery. It was a short reprieve. The Orlocks on the catwalks would spot him soon enough. Uriah quickly studied his surroundings, his eyes dancing over the heavy pieces of equipment, the conveyor belts, the smelting vats and the catwalks, considering every possibility.

Then he saw it.

Not the smelting vats themselves, but the suspension arms that held them in place; the same arms that tilted the vats to pour out their molten content when the ore was of sufficient purity. Uriah needed to reach a control panel despite his pursuers dogging him.

Fortunately, this time Uriah didn't need to scale trestles to reach his prize. The ceiling was covered in a network of rail tracks where hydraulic bogies fitted with spools of heavy-duty chains could lift and transport heavy equipment around the foundry. Several of the chains were long enough to scrape the floor.

Uriah kept to the shadows until he was close enough to one set of chains to make his run. He expected shots to ring out again, but neither the Orlocks in the catwalks nor those on the ground had spotted him. Uriah grabbed four chains that were almost braided together and climbed with every ounce of his strength. His shoulder and fingers protested at the burden, but Uriah had little time to lose.

He was three storeys up when a series of single shots rang out. One eager Orlock had spotted Uriah and his attention was drawing the other Orlocks into the area.

Good, Uriah thought. Makes it easier when they're all in one convenient location. Uriah was four storeys up when more shots rang out and the area became decidedly dangerous; the Orlocks, while rarely sharpshooters, believed volume was a good substitute for skill.

After nudging the chain-bundle forward, Uriah brought himself from a slow swing into a faster arc. More shots joined the chorus, a few pinging off the chains, but Uriah was focused on leaping onto the adjoining catwalk before anyone got there first. When the catwalk swung into view below his feet, Uriah let go of the chains and landed with a steady foot. He was already running before he had his bearings, shouts and shots erupting all around him. Uriah was near where he needed to be, running along the reinforced catwalks overlooking the vats.

While the heat chewed through Uriah, the vats also produced columns of steam that masked his flight across the catwalk. The barrage of shots shredded the air, this time far wilder then they had been. Uriah searched for a control panel or emergency work station. He stumbled upon one a moment later, being manned by a shirtless Orlock behemoth with as much fat as muscle. An autogun lay flat on the panel; the Orlock was obviously aware of the danger and ready for action, though the steam hid Uriah's approach. Only in the last possible second did the Orlock catch movement from the corner of his eye. By then, Uriah was already taking a running aim. He fired a shot, catching the Orlock in the face. The shot resonated with a metallic echo.

The Orlock stumbled to one knee, his face a masticated red pulp except where steel plates were riveted to his skull. His arm shot out, stumbling for the gun on the panel. 'Kill you!' the behemoth roared.

'I'm certain of that,' Uriah said, surprised at the Orlock's tenacity. 'Say, why aren't you dead? Oh never mind.' Uriah fired two more shots into the Orlock's skull, collapsing him.

'I hate Orlocks,' Uriah muttered, studying the panel. 'Seriously, who rivets plates to their skulls? Orlocks, that's who.'

On first blush, it appeared as though the five large levers on the panel controlled the five gigantic vats adjacent to the catwalk. The levers were marked in increments of three degrees, presumably for the tilt of each vat.

'Only one way to find out,' Uriah said to himself, and pulled the levers down to one hundred and eighty degrees. Giant chains affixed from the bottom of the vats to motorized chain spools on the ceiling groaned in protest as they wound back up. In the process, they pulled and tilted the vats slowly. At first a small stream

of molten ore poured from the mouth of each vat.
Then, glowing orange and yellow waterfalls of molten
ore cascaded down, flowing over the empty conveyor
belts below, warping them under their heat. The ore
turned into a deadly river that ran between equipment
and support beams, flooding the floor with instant
death. Whatever screams of pain Uriah heard were
instantly cut short. What lingered was the panicked yells
of the escaping survivors.

As Uriah turned to leave, he heard metal groan and
one section of catwalk across the way collapsed with a
loud crash. He quickly studied the carnage below him
and realized the folly of his plan.

It's only folly, he thought, if it catches me as well. The
molten metal was filled with impurities. While the pure
ore merely flowed until it congealed and cooled, the
impurities were sticking to everything they touched.
They melted the already rusting support struts and
ground equipment like globules of acid. And while they
didn't remain hot for long enough to eat their way completely through their surroundings, it was enough that
weight and age took their toll.

Still, distraction was distraction, and Uriah used the
momentum to his benefit. He ran, faster now lest his
section of catwalk fall too. The plan worked; the
Orlocks were too busy panicking or trying to contain
the damage to pursue him. Uriah used the trestles
again, jumped to the lower catwalks, and from there, to
the ground and his exit from the building.

THERE WERE FEW occasions that actually left Uriah
dumbfounded, but this was one such event. The rappelling cord he'd left behind for his swift escape was
gone. Looking up, he saw no sign of any rope, much
less the open turbofan he'd left behind; it was too
dark.

The dome itself was alive with noise of machines and the screams of enraged Orlocks. The molten rivers had done their damage, collapsing catwalks and a portion of the ceiling, and partially crippling the foundry. If the Orlocks caught Uriah, he knew they would rip him apart. Now the rope was mysteriously missing, stranding him on the roof and suggesting that something more was at play. Well, nearly stranding him at any rate. There was always the chance during this mission that someone would discover the rope, or that Uriah would be cut off from the roof for whatever reason. So, as with any of his plans, there were always contingencies. In this case, two remaining exits, one of which was convenient, if not pleasant. It was an old sewer-pipe access, and while reaching it was not an issue, travelling through the stink of Orlock waste was a hazard in itself.

Uriah shook his head at the prospect and headed out.

THE ORLOCKS SWEPT through the dome numerous times, but there was no sign of the intruder. Part of the building was ruined and at least five men were dead. The Orlocks did not accept defeat well and fistfights broke out among the search parties over puerile matters or simple misunderstandings. Still, four Orlocks had seen the intruder proper, and one could even identify him from the wanted list. The name Uriah Storm went out to all Orlock strongholds and gangs, and within an hour, the bounty on his head increased by a handsome figure. So too did his ranking.

More importantly, it also drew the attention of Slag.

Slag's arrival was like that of a flood that silenced all conversation in his presence, and it spread outward. Soon, the only words spoken were whispered, and they echoed the same words: *Slag's here.*

The strong Orlocks, not easily cowed, stepped aside as Slag approached; they made eye contact and nodded to show their respect. Slag, however, rarely returned the courtesy. Still, the foundry workers could not help but stare at the impressive, bald man. Wide shelves for shoulders, muscle fibres stitched in perfect detail against his skin, black jagged tattoos that spiraled up each massive arm and cradled his thick neck, all these were impressive, but not the most telling of Slag's features. It was his face that was unmistakable, the wash of heat from a foundry accident twisting his flesh into a waxen parody; the splash of metal droplets that burnt through skin and muscle to fuse to his skull; the spherical eye-implant riveted roughly into the bone surrounding the socket. And still, Slag's reputation was beyond that of stature or features. His reputation was made in the displays of his ruthless cunning. He was among the smartest of the Orlocks in the way they respected most.

Slag was their saint and their devil, and he walked among them tonight.

A few Orlocks tried offering Slag a summary of the evening's events, but he seemed more interested in where Uriah had been rather than the damage he'd caused. That led him to the office, where a nervous Steel Sentinel foreman plinked away at the logic hub.

'I have it,' the Foreman said, grateful that he'd found the information. 'The intruder called up this file.'

Slag leaned in close to study the screen. 'The Van Saar engineer? You after him too, Uriah? ' he asked, mumbling. He threw a quick glance over his shoulder to one of his own men. 'Firefight earlier today,' Slag said. 'The boys were lookin' for Soren at some hab block. Someone dropped in unannounced. I'm thinking Uriah Storm. See if the survivors can confirm that.'

'Do you need to see anything else?' the foreman asked, indicating the screen.

'Yes. Remove Uriah from the hunted list. Here's the authorization,' Slag said, leaning in to type the password himself.

'But–'

'Now,' was all Slag said. Without a further word of thanks or otherwise, he turned from the office and walked outside to the catwalks. He surveyed the damage below him, waiting for the foreman to rejoin him.

'I've done as you asked,' the foreman reported.

'How many dead?'

'Nine, likely more. Three men are still missing. A dozen burned, but we know how he came in. A turbo-fan was–'

'I don't care,' Slag said. 'Security was pitiful. Hundreds of Orlocks and one Delaque. The odds were in your favour, not his.'

'I know,' the foreman said, his voice betraying a slight tremble. 'And I will take full responsibility for–'

Slag was already walking away, already planning his next steps. His entourage of five, well-armed and beefy Orlocks quickly fell in line. The foreman caught up with the rearmost Orlock and slowed him down enough to ask a whispered question.

'Why did Slag have me remove Uriah Storm from the hunted list?'

A smirk crept up on the Orlock's lip. 'Because,' he responded, 'he wants no interference when he goes after Uriah himself.'

SLAG AND HIS five men had barely exited the dome when he turned to face them. 'Find Storm,' is all he said.

'We'll put out word for Uriah's head–' one Orlock said before he noticed Slag's almost spite-riddled scowl directed at him.

'Anyone less stupid want to answer?' Slag asked.

'We find Uriah by going after the Van Saar engineer?' another Orlock offered. 'That way, Uriah comes to us.'

'Smart man,' Slag said, walking away.

CHAPTER: FOUR

*Plan your strategies in advance and consider all outcomes,
no matter how unlikely. The game should be won before
you ever set foot on the field.*

– Delaque Operational Commandments
from the *Book of Lies*.

'UGH! YOU SMELL!'

Uriah smiled and nodded to the female Delaque clerk
in the hallway. It was hard acting so cavalier about the
foul reek when Uriah himself wanted to retch, but he
had to admit he was deriving some pleasure from the
experience.

'Thank you, yes,' Uriah said, walking down the hall
and addressing everyone whether they intended to listen or not. 'I discovered the stench recently. It's my
newest disguise designed to ingratiate myself with sewer
scavengers, Orlock plumbers, Cawdor prisoners, the
incontinent as a whole. Tell all your friends. Better yet,
let them smell the experience themselves!'

With a sigh, Uriah opened the lock on his door and
pushed into his small living quarters. Almost immediately, the itchy, damp clothes came off and found their
way into a disposal receptacle, never to be used again. A
chemical scrub came next, not exactly normal Delaque

procedure, but the ingredients came courtesy of Morgane and were designed to eliminate harmful bacteria. The Van Saar were particularly fussy when it came to hygiene.

Uriah exited the bathroom and went to his desk. He removed the drawer, revealing a false back, and retrieved a small teardrop-shaped pendant. The pendant was a black diamond, cradled in a lattice web of fine gold and hung from a delicate chain. Uriah watched it twirl, and smiled at Morgane's beloved gift. She'd given it to him as a symbol of her love, and Uriah lost himself in that perfect moment where nothing in the world mattered; when everything felt right. He eventually put it away, feeling sore but far better than he had earlier.

The message light blinked on Uriah's pict screen. He punched in his access code, thanked the Machine Spirit for its diligence and replayed the scratchy image. The face that greeted him was familiar, nose crushed flat and beady eyes. He spoke and sucked in air through his mouth, breathing as though drowning on his own congestion.

'Uriah. Heard you lost yourself a Van Saar agent,' the image said with some satisfaction. 'I got the information on his whereabouts if you can meet the price…'

THE RENDEZVOUS SPOT was a Fumes Bar. Situated near an active industrial complex, and often sharing the same owners, the bar was one of several that piped in low concentrations of filtered gases from nearby factories. The fumes produced a cheap high in the bar's clientele, a constant sense of euphoria at the mere expense of one's brain cells.

Uriah avoided such establishments, but business brought him to these places frequently. Fortunately, it wasn't uncommon to see clientele wearing rebreathers for whatever reason, so nobody batted a sluggish eye when Uriah arrived wearing one.

The bar was a small, comfortable affair, with no more than a dozen small tables scattered across the open floor, and a bar set against the back wall. The air was hazy from a noxious cocktail of smoke and various gases. Uriah adjusted his heavy duster and surveyed the bar for any suspicious behaviour before finally making his way to the table nestled in the shadows.

'Hale,' Uriah said, taking a seat.

Hale, the man with the crushed nose, studied Uriah for a moment, as though trying to place him. He blinked twice, his bloodshot eyes heavy with the fumes, his tongue dragging his speech into a numb drawl. 'You look different,' Hale said. 'You cut your hair?'

'You ask me that every time we meet. It's the mask. I look different because of the mask.'

'That can't be it.'

'Fine,' Uriah said, 'I cut my hair.'

'That must be it,' Hale said before he returned to his drink.

Uriah waited a few moments before sighing. 'You called me?' Uriah said, trying to prompt the conversation.

'Oh, yeah. Soren, I know what happened to your Van Saar spy.'

'And how did you know I was looking for him?'

'C'mon!' Hale said, his eyes sober for a moment.

'I'll admit,' Uriah said, 'that despite your choice of diversions, you are surprisingly sharp. How you manage to function in this environment is beyond me.'

'Think of it as a test of will,' Hale said with a smile. 'If I can operate in this environment, just think how dangerous I am when completely lucid. I'm so dangerous that I keep myself in this state for the safety of everyone around me,' Hale said, sweeping his hand to indicate the whole room.

Uriah shook his head. 'Magnanimous of you, but your logic is entirely suspect. That made no sense!' he said with a laugh.

'True enough,' Hale admitted and returned to nursing what was now his dry tankard.

'So what about Soren?' Uriah asked.

'My throat,' Hale said, squeezing his oesophagus for good effect. 'Terribly parched. Couldn't possibly talk.'

Uriah turned to the bar and nodded to the thin man with a full face gasmask tending drinks. The bartender walked over with another tankard and a bottle of Ratbile.

'Leave the bottle,' Uriah said, dropping coins into his hand and sending him back to the bar. The Jester poured a glass for himself and Hale, offered a silent toast and lifted his rebreather before downing the searing rotgut in a shot. 'Better?' Uriah asked, his throat torn.

'Oh yes,' Hale said with a grimace. 'And for that, you get this little tidbit of information. Soren's dead. They found his corpse somewhere deep inside the metal guts of the Underhive.'

THE BOTTLE OF Ratbile was nearly empty before Uriah finally spoke. 'So what is it you're holding back?'

'You brought me my merchandise?'

Uriah reached into his duster and slid the small black cloth packet across the table. 'Careful,' he said before Hale could examine the contents. 'That's enough to stupefy an entire gang.'

Hale opened the cloth flap and counted the forty green pills. He smiled at the sharp smell that they produced and was about to pocket them when Uriah placed his hand on Hale's wrist.

'The information, what is it I'm buying?'

'Soren wasn't just shot, y'know. He was savaged, butchered!'

'That buys you ten pills,' Uriah said, never releasing his grip.

'All right, then. Someone stripped him clean of his pretty implants.'

'At best that's another five pills,' Uriah said. 'Scavengers steal implants off corpses all the time.'

'Scavengers don't remove implants with surgical precision, do they? The wounds were cut with real skill.'

'All right, that's worth another ten pills. That's fifteen shy of what I figure is worth the cost.'

'How about this, then?' Hale said, obviously saving the best for last – if Uriah read him correctly. 'I don't know how he got them, but a black-shop bio-surgeon – goes by the name of Cantrall – was selling Soren's implants. Cut-throat rates for premium Van Saar tech.'

THE LEAD WAS thin, but Cantrall was all Uriah had for the moment. As the tram rumbled along the ceiling track suspended high above the streets, Uriah pondered the matter. He knew Cantrall through reputation only, but that was sufficient to launch him in the proper direction. Why the bio-surgeon would have Soren's implants was a question Uriah was keen to ask Cantrall – followed, of course, with, 'Who murdered Soren?'

The tram coasted along the ceiling rails before ducking into a roof tunnel that separated this district with the one above it. Uriah's stomach lurched as the tram soared on an elevated track angled straight for the ceiling of the next district. It levelled out moments later, slowing at a suspended platform attached to a tall tower. Uriah disembarked at the station and followed the exiting mob to the lifts. Within moments, he was on the street, approaching the area where Cantrall operated. The tram lumbered above his head, gaining speed to its next destination.

The district was a warren of tight alleys and low ceilings that added to the claustrophobia. It was a garment quarter of sorts, the workers living and working in their one-room hab blocks, each one an independent contractor for a consortium of interests. Here, the House loyalties blurred with several entrepreneurial – but minor – gangs forging a non-aggression pact to ensure the flow of commerce.

As Uriah approached the stretch of road where Cantrall's business lay, he immediately noticed locals fleeing in his direction. The irregular sounds of gunfire rose to meet him. The area was besieged, and Uriah was of the growing suspicion that it was centred on Cantrall's business.

'Voice,' Uriah said. 'I need your help.'

'Voice here,' Voice responded, crackling in Uriah's ears. 'What's happening? Where are you? This wasn't on your itinerary.'

'Yes, yes,' Uriah responded with a chuckle. 'Call it a necessary detour. You're being paid well enough. I have a lead on the assignment. What can you tell me about Cantrall?'

'Cantrall? Hm. Black market surgeon and pricey too. He has an ego to show for it.'

'So he isn't one to normally offer discounts?' Uriah asked.

'Normally? Try never.'

'Thank you. Can you stay with me in case I need help? I think I'm walking into a firefight.'

'Hold your hand, as it were?'

'If that means finally meeting you face to face, why not?' Uriah replied. After checking his bolter and rounds, Uriah headed towards the sound of gunfire. He paused long enough to grab one mousy looking man by the arm as he tried running past.

'What's happening?' Uriah asked.

'What d'ya think! Orlocks and Cawdor blastin' each other ta bits!' With that, the man wrestled free and continued his mad scramble to safety.

Uriah continued on his way, hugging the building's shadows closely and ducking behind bits of cover on his approach to a T-junction. The sounds of gunfire grew more heated, more furious. It was an all-out battle, with screams, curses and endless volleys the punctuation of the fight, and it was growing worse. Angry and armed neighbours poked their heads out from windows long enough to contribute to the skirmish. They threw objects or fired the occasional shot with autoguns. Uriah could not see the main combatants.

'Unbelievable,' Uriah said with a mutter.

'What?' Voice asked.

'It's like trying to get someone to shut up by yelling louder than them.'

The firefight was unfolding right around the corner, though Uriah saw the occasional local denizen chance a shot from a window. A ricochet punched a hole in the plascrete wall above his head. Uriah ducked and approached the building corner while throwing the occasional glance to the neighbours. He peered around the corner, and sure enough, amid the dead and dying who littered the streets, a gang of Orlocks had entrenched themselves behind all available cover. They shot at a facing building, exchanging heated fire with the Cawdor hidden inside.

Uriah was in the process of assessing the situation when one figure caught his eye. Slag was directing fire and issuing orders in his usually clipped manner. Uriah froze, the bones in his legs suddenly aware of the cold pins that held them together. He could still hear the sound…

…the crisp snaps… bones broken… blinding anguish… vision warped by the delirium of agony.

Cold sweat washed over Uriah, soaking him in seconds. He ducked back around the corner, muttering a soft curse.

'What was that?' Voice asked. 'I didn't catch it.'

'Slag,' Uriah said, feeling punched in the chest. 'Slag's here?'

'The Orlock ganger. What's his gang called?'

'Soulsplitters, and he's more like a butcher.'

'Encountered him, have you? Does he know you're there?'

'No,' Uriah said. 'He hasn't seen me yet.'

'If he bothers you that much, maybe it's time to pay him an ill courtesy. You're a good shot. A bullet to the back of the head should do it.'

'Right,' Uriah said, trying to clear the painful memories from his head enough to function. 'You're right.'

'Of course I am.'

Uriah peered back around the corner. The fight was nowhere near abating, not with both groups so well entrenched. Uriah took careful aim, lining up the iron sights of his bolt pistol with the back of Slag's head…

…bones broke, heavy boots pressed down on his femur and tibia, snapping them under casual weight…

He could still hear the crack and the screams that followed, his own screams. The memories of the past were too powerful to reconcile here and now. His iron sights danced, unable to remain fixed on the back of Slag's head. Uriah's vision blurred and the pistol's grip felt greasy in his sweaty palms.

'I can't,' Uriah said, his heart beating so fast that he felt breathless.

'What's wrong, Jester?' Voice asked, concern in her tone.

'I… I don't have a clear shot,' Uriah said.

There was a pause on the other end, as though Voice was stripping the lie apart and weighing it. 'Is there a way around him?' she asked.

'I don't know yet,' Uriah said, grateful that Voice didn't challenge him further. 'Likely.'

'More than likely,' Voice said. 'Under the best conditions, surgery isn't a certainty. Patients die or are frequently disfigured.'

'Right,' Uriah said, trying to focus on other matters. 'So Cantrall, like all experienced surgeons, likely has a rabbit hole to escape through.'

'Sewers?' Voice asked.

'No,' Uriah responded. 'A little beneath someone of Cantrall's standing, I'd warrant. Too much like groveling for a man who holds himself so highly. I'm checking the adjoining building.'

'WHERE TO START?' Uriah said, navigating the pock-marked hallways of the building. The metal sliding doors to the various hab blocks were closed, the heated battle still being waged outside.

For Uriah, it felt good to have that distance between him and Slag. Each wall between them felt like another world removed, though Uriah knew Slag. The Orlock was tenacious, determined. He would find his way into Cantrall's business sooner or later, and knowing Slag, it would be sooner.

'Jester,' Voice said, 'if Cantrall has an escape route through this building, then he likely owns property here.'

'Or,' Uriah added, 'he knows the building prefect. In either case, the prefect is the one we want.'

'But…' Voice hesitated. 'What if he's escaped already?'

'We'll see when we get there.'

The building prefect was easy enough to locate; they generally chose the most defensible position in the building, which was the basement in this case. The basement looked like a secured bomb shelter with heavily barred windows looking out. It could likely shoulder the building's collapse – a frequent occurrence in Hive Prime – with no damage to the occupants. Uriah knelt in front of the prefect's door, so marked by the obscenities scrawled across its face, and fidgeted with an open security panel with all the earmarks of jury-rigging.

'What do you see?' Voice asked.

'Thirteen wires leading to the number pad,' Uriah whispered. 'Three are burnt at the contacts. Looks like a poor soldering job.'

'Aren't they all? The thirteenth wire is the problem. It should lead to a small bank of capacitors.'

'Right it does. Booby-trap?'

'Electric discharge. Enough to shock you and possibly burn a few implants. Clip the wire and strip the insulation.'

Uriah followed Voice's lead, but offered the Machine Spirit a silent apology for the intrusion. 'Done,' Uriah said.

'Use the capacitor wire to short out the security panel itself but be ready to move.'

Sparks of electricity erupted when Uriah dabbed the live wire across the contacts. An acrid, burning smell filled the air and the metal door slid open. Uriah was inside the hab block hall quickly, bolt pistol at the ready. The building prefect was standing at a bedroom doorway, facing into the room with an autogun in hand. The prefect didn't even see Uriah until he was on top of him, the bolt pistol pressed against the back of his balding head.

'Hello, I'm looking for a friend,' Uriah said with a grin.

'That's the best you can come up with?' Voice asked in his ear.

Uriah was grateful that only he heard her.

'Who're you? What d'ya want?' the prefect asked.

'Drop the gun and I'll tell you. Don't drop it and…' Uriah tapped the back of the man's head. A moment later, the autogun hit the floor.

It was then that Uriah realized why the prefect had been staring into the bedroom. Piled against the closet door were stacks of furniture: mattress, bed frame, nightstand and dresser. Beyond the closet and adjoining wall, gunfire continued its stuttered chorus.

Uriah started laughing, and while his gun never wavered, he couldn't stop for a good moment.

'What?' Voice asked, crackling in his ear.

'I think I found Cantrall's emergency escape route,' Uriah said, regaining some composure despite the random slip of giggles.

'What's so funny?' Voice asked

'You talkin' to me?' the prefect asked Uriah.

'So let me see if I understand this,' Uriah said for both the prefect's and Voice's benefit. 'Cantrall pays you for an escape route, and at the first sign of trouble, you barricade his only way out?'

'Ahh…' Voice said while the prefect muttered something Uriah couldn't hear. 'I understand, now. That is funny.'

'So Cantrall hasn't escaped?' Uriah asked the prefect. He nudged him with the pistol when the prefect didn't answer.

'No.'

'You've actually helped me,' Uriah said, 'and for that, my good man, you get to live… with a headache for your efforts.'

One blow to the back of the head and the prefect slumped to the thinly carpeted floor.

It took a moment for Uriah to dislodge the furniture and shove it to the side. Pistol in hand, he cautiously opened the closet door and peered inside. It looked typical of a bachelor's walk-in closet, with junk piled against the walls and scattered across the floor. The back wall, however, was ajar, revealing a sliver of light from another room beyond. Somewhere beyond, in the floors above, the gunfire continued, though far more sporadically. The firefight was drawing to a close. Uriah knew he had to act fast.

Beyond the hidden door rested a surgeon's bay – an operating slab with restraints, an assortment of butchering surgical tools, metal cabinets, cold units and waste bins. Despite a decent calibre of equipment, blood and machine-oil spatter still stained the walls and floor. On the operating slab rested the corpse of a Cawdor ganger. Two more corpses, one Cawdor and the other in filthy operating garb, lay on the floor.

Uriah entered the room in time to see someone slip away through the only set of double doors. He followed through, bolt pistol at the ready, and entered into a short hallway ending at a staircase, with doors on either side. The trench-coated quarry was already taking the steps two at a time. Uriah fired again, missing by centimetres.

Up the stairs, Uriah stared down another hallway. He had bare seconds to register the scene; the dead Cawdor gangers in the corridor; his bald-headed prey darting through another door while cradling a machine arm; the Orlock gangers, led by a confident-looking Slag, marching down the hall.

The stranger was quick enough to have avoided the attention of the Soulsplitters.

Uriah wasn't as fortunate.

He stopped in his tracks. Slag locked eyes with Uriah and smiled at the unanticipated gift. In that moment, Uriah realized he was in trouble. Whoever the stranger was, he'd stolen an implant from the surgical bay – likely Soren's implant – and was now beyond pursuit.

Worse yet, Slag had his sights set on Uriah, and that was one bone which he would not release. Uriah practically dived down the stairwell as the walls and ceiling around him disintegrated under a blistering onslaught of bolter and las fire.

Uriah tumbled off a couple of steps before hitting the basement floor. He rolled to his feet and ran for the surgical bay.

'Damn it!'

'What is it?' Voice asked.

'Someone stole the implant from under my nose and now Slag's here.' Uriah reached the surgical bay and quickly tossed a round, flat object down the hallway. 'Oh, and remind me to get more explosives!' he said, diving through the double doors.

'Explosives? Why–?'

Voice's question was answered by the loud explosion. The grenade detonated at the foot of the stairs and shook the building. It was more for effect than actual harm, but the blast was enough to damage the stone stairs and to slow the advance of Slag's men. Uriah was back on his feet and at the secret door. He quickly surveyed the surroundings, but there wasn't much to salvage. He needed to speak with Cantrall and Cantrall was dead. Whoever the thief was who'd stolen the implants, he'd done a professional job of executing all three men.

'Pull out!' Voice said.

'Not yet,' Uriah said, suddenly noticing the spherical ocular implant in Cantrall's left eye. Uriah pulled out his knife and began prying at the edges of the implant, cutting skin and muscle.

'What are you doing?' Voice asked, hearing Uriah's grunts.

'Playing a hunch,' Uriah responded. He removed the implant from the eye socket, ignoring the wet shucking noise it made, and pulled on the ocular cable till it popped loose. He ignored the bits of grey matter stuck to the cable's receptor plugs and shoved the bloody mess into a belt pouch.

The double doors swung open as Uriah came to his feet and he found himself staring down the barrels of a half-dozen guns as well as into the sly stare of Slag.

'Uriah Storm,' Slag said, almost purring.

Uriah's throat went dry, but only for a moment. He wouldn't die here, and he certainly wouldn't give Slag the satisfaction of acting scared in his presence.

'Please,' Uriah said with a smile. 'People I've made fools of call me Jester. I insist you do the same.'

'You're funny. But corpses usually are.'

'Ah!' Uriah said, 'banter from an Orlock that doesn't involve gunfire and grunting.'

'You're half right, there,' Slag replied, raising his heavy bolter up into Uriah's face.

'What do you know?' Uriah said, shrugging. 'I was wrong, I *do* have more explosives.'

The Orlocks only noticed the grenade in Uriah's hand when it dropped and hit the floor. Slag's eyes widened. Almost everyone dived behind cover or back through the doors. Uriah, however, was running for the secret exit while Slag threw one of his men atop the puck before diving clear.

The explosives were on a six-second fuse, and Uriah was already counting down from when the grenade left his hand; one second spent in falling; another second lost waiting for the Orlocks to realize they were dealing with an explosive so they didn't shoot Uriah when he ran; three seconds running for the hidden door that was slightly ajar, and pushing through it.

The remaining second evaporated in the blast that shoved the secret door shut, sparing Uriah from the brunt of the explosion. After spending what felt like minutes recovering from the head ringing, Uriah stumbled through the closet door and out of the prefect's hab block. It was only when he reached the street that he heard Voice through his earpiece.

'…all right?'

'I'm fine, I'm fine,' Uriah mumbled. He stumbled down the street, losing himself in the crowd of people brave enough to satisfy their curiosity. 'I can't hear you properly. I'll check in with you later.'

Uriah stumbled away on shaky legs.

Slag rose to his feet in the hallway and ignored the groans of his men. Several looked dead or severely injured, though they were easily replaced. The doors had shielded Slag and a couple of his more able men from the blast, but the operating bay was ruined.

'You two. Find the implant,' Slag told his men. 'The rest of you find Uriah!'

'What about the injured?' a subordinate asked.

Slag pulled his heavy bolter and blasted one of the injured Orlocks lying near his feet. His moans died as quickly as he did.

'Couldn't hear you over his groans,' Slag said, drawing nearer to the man who'd questioned him. 'What about the injured?'

'Nothing, Slag. We'll find the implant.'

'Good idea,' Slag said. He holstered his weapon and examined the wall Uriah had slipped through. A small smile snuck past his lips in anticipation of a worthy hunt.

CHAPTER: FIVE

Choose your fights before your fights choose you.

– Delaque Operational Commandments
from the *Book of Lies*.

URIAH WAS AGAIN disheveled and sporting additional cuts and scrapes from his most recent altercation. His muscles ached from their ordeals, though Uriah knew that age was taking its slow toll on him. Fortunately, he rather enjoyed the soreness that spread through every corner of his body. It made him feel alive and kept his mind sharp.

That was a necessity in his line of work, especially when two men were gunning for Uriah's head. The first was Slag, and the thought of the Soulsplitter bruiser turned Uriah's sweat cold. The second person, however, was perhaps a little more troubling. The second was the man who had stolen the implant.

Uriah walked down the familiar corridors of Shadowstrohm; he came to Percal's plain door. He knocked in code and waited a long moment before the familiar click and whirr sounded from the door's hidden mechanisms. The door opened.

'What is it, Uriah?' Percal asked, not looking up from his data-slate. 'I have work.'

'Then you'll have to accommodate me this once,' Uriah said, entering the room. He touched the uncomfortable metal chairs, feeling the lingering warmth of someone else's presence. 'You can tell him to come out,' Uriah said.

'Pardon?' Percal asked, looking annoyed as he glanced up from his work.

'Whoever was sitting in this chair. The one who is currently hiding in the little room beyond that hidden door,' Uriah said, nodding to the adjoining wall. 'You know, the *other* Handler you sent on the Soren job. Percal, you trained me better than that.'

'You're quick to accuse,' Percal said.

'But never wrong in my accusations,' Uriah responded.

'We'll see. Never wrong and never *been* wrong are two different issues. What is the basis of your allegations?' Percal asked.

'Please' Uriah responded with a laugh. 'The next time you send a second Handler to ensure the mission's success, send someone who won't get caught as they're escaping with the implant.'

'You saw a face?'

'No, but I'd recognize another Delaque Handler anywhere.'

'That's the basis of your accusation?' Percal asked, the stump of his nose twitching. He went back to studying the datapad. 'I have work, Uriah.'

'I'm surprised at you,' Uriah said. 'You've never tolerated failure before. Why are you protecting someone who so obviously led me right back to you?'

'Assuming your accusations have merit.'

'Fine,' Uriah said, standing. 'I'll assume you have Soren's arm, then, and continue with my investigation.'

'Soren is dead,' Percal stated while remaining focused on his work. 'Someone stole the implant from under your nose, and yet you accuse me of tolerating failure?'

'Who says I failed?' Uriah said, a steady, mean smile cutting across his face.

Percal looked up. 'You have something?'

'Question your second Handler,' Uriah replied, heading for the door. 'And maybe you can figure out what he missed when he stole Soren's implant.'

'Uriah,' Percal said. 'The implants. I still want them. Find them at all costs.'

THE SECRET PANEL slid open and Kaden stepped out, shaking his head. 'He's lying,' he said, waving his hand through the holograph pieces on the regicide board.

'Is he?' Percal asked. 'He saw you escaping. Be grateful he didn't see your face.'

'Uriah Storm doesn't scare me,' Kaden said, smirking.

'He should. I trained him.'

That drew a momentary, uncomfortable silence from Kaden.

'Did you miss something? At Cantrall's surgical bay?'

'No,' Kaden replied. 'I searched it top to bottom. There was nothing there. Well, other than the arm I took.'

Percal thought on the matter a moment before shaking his head. 'No, you missed something. Uriah is not one for idle boasts.'

'I swear there was nothing there,' Kaden protested.

'Sit down. Recount every detail of your mission. Leave no description vague.'

'All right,' Kaden replied, sitting down. 'But I'm telling you, it's a waste of time. There are more implants that need recovering. Uriah's gaining ground and I'm not there to keep an eye on things.'

'Then you'll have some catching up to do,' Percal said, stroking the scar on his lip. 'Now, from the beginning...'

THE WORK BENCH waited, but Uriah was distracted by one thought. He went to the desk and pulled out the small pendant hidden in the drawer. Uriah brought it to his nose and smelled Morgane's sweet perfume that still lingered on the keepsake. It brought a warm smile to Uriah's lips and washed away his recent concerns. Slag grew distant in his thoughts and Soren's death was easier to manage. Uriah missed Morgane, but he was grateful for her gift.

Satisfied with the moment's peace, Uriah kissed the pendant before returning it to its nest. He went over to the work bench.

Uriah surveyed the tools awaiting his touch. The lights in his hab block were dim, the sole illumination a bright circle at his table from an overhead spotlight. Centrepiece to the light was Cantrall's ocular implant, all it biological bits cleaned off. Uriah closed his eyes and muttered a wordless prayer.

'What? I didn't catch that,' Voice said.

Uriah finished his prayer before answering. 'Nothing. I was merely praying to the eye's Machine Spirit to forgive us for the intrusion.'

'You're just like the Van Saar, praying to machines.'

'Given their proficiency with devices, I thank you for the compliment.'

'Not much of a compliment,' Voice said, grousing. 'Has anyone ever accused you of being a Van Saar?'

'How do you know I'm not?' Uriah asked.

'Because no Van Saar would ever ask for outside help – my help – in handling technology. You know there is no Machine Spirit. It's just circuits and relays, nothing more.'

'That's heresy to some,' Uriah replied.

'And music to others. The more we treat machinery as mysterious, the less we'll truly understand mechanics. Do you know I actually saw some poor fool praying to a keypad. He forgot his code – he was begging the Machine Spirit to open it up.'

'Some people don't want to understand machines, Voice. They find solace in believing in the spirit of the device. For them, communion and prayer is wearing implants.'

'Ah yes, fleshworks,' Voice responded. 'But that's not really true of you, is it? Certainly, you give the Machine Spirit its undeserved due, but you know your way around the guts of the machines.'

'Enough to stumble. That's why I need your help here.'

'Modesty? From you? How uncharacteristic of the Jester,' Voice replied, chuckling.

'Seriously, Voice. You do know why I stole Cantrall's implant?'

'I do,' Voice replied.

'So you know what I need?'

'Enough to guide you through it. Do you have a pict screen and input device nearby?'

Uriah patted the small black monitor with its bubble screen, sitting at the table's corner. The screen displayed the chaotic spatter of static. 'Yes, and they're ready.'

'Very well, time to walk you through this,' Voice responded, and proceeded to guide Uriah through the process slowly.

The first course of action was to connect the implant's sensory micro-bundles to a data plug that was promptly jacked in to the monitor. The static fluctuated, but otherwise remained the same.

'I still see static,' Uriah said.

'That's because the data plug can't interpret the implant's signals. It wasn't designed for that.'

'But how–?'

'Have faith,' Voice said.

It took Uriah a moment to understand the joke. 'Funny,' he replied, 'for a heretic...'

'Ah, flattery,' Voice replied before continuing with her instructions.

Delicately, Uriah slowly pried open the implant's outer casing, revealing its innards. Another fine example of Van Saar technology – the implant's lining having prevented vital fluids from leaking into the pristine-looking device. Uriah examined the interior and finally located his quarry, a small circuit board connected to wires. He used tweezers to pinch what Voice called 'optic bundles.'

'Is that it?' Uriah wondered aloud. 'Pinch the bundles?'

'Careful now. Pull the wire out, it's socketed.'

'Now what?'

'Look for a green chip near the circuit board. It's delicate work, but there's an empty socket for the bundle there. Push it in and that should do it.'

'Moving wires around seems a bit crude for Van Saar technology.'

'Actually, the Van Saar have machines that do this for them without ever cracking open the implant's casing. We don't have the same luxury. That leaves us to cheat the device into working.'

'Done,' Uriah said after a moment. The screen flickered and displayed a menu system. At the press of two buttons, Uriah was replaying the eye's video-logs. He could see everything that Cantrall had seen through the artificial eye, recorded in scratchy, but otherwise clear, blacks and whites.

'I have it!' Uriah said, practically chirping at his success. He studied the images. 'Is this how Cantrall saw the world? In black and white?'

'For Cantrall, likely no,' Voice replied. 'Only the recordings are in black and white, I suspect. He likely had live colour input. But now you see the first reason why I dislike sensory-implants. It's like living inside a monitor, with screens for eyes.'

'And the second reason?' Uriah asked.

Voice paused to think about the matter. 'Fleshworks,' she said.

'You mentioned that before,' Uriah said. 'But what does it mean?'

'It's when the implants, the surgery itself, become more valuable than the individual who uses them. The flesh becomes tool for the machine, not the other way around. It's when we mutilate our flesh to *improve* ourselves, but demean ourselves in the process. Fleshworks.'

'You don't approve of implants.'

Voice sighed. 'You are paying me by the hour, Jester,' she replied. 'Don't you want to know something more relevant to your case.'

'You're right,' Uriah said, sensing Voice's impatience. 'How many hours of recordings does the device contain.'

'Try weeks.'

'Impressive,' Uriah said, focusing on the various files stored by date. 'The Van Saar are crafty spies.'

'They are. Van Saar implants sold to outsiders often contain recording devices. That way, they'll never bother interrogating someone for information. They'll just retrieve the implant and take the data they need.'

There was a pause in the conversation as Uriah examined the videos, opening files at random and watching them with a voyeuristic glee. It was Voice who broke the silence.

'Jester, you were right about it being Van Saar tech. How'd you know about their hidden protocols?'

Uriah smiled. 'You're not my only friend with knowledge of such things.'

URIAH PLAYED BACK the recordings, using Soren's missed rendezvous as a rough benchmark for the starting date. Even then, they comprised several days' worth of material. Thankfully, the implant was smart enough to stop recording when Cantrall closed his good eye to sleep, and Uriah ignored the other dead spaces and procedural moments when the bio-surgeon operated on patients or worked on implants. Instead, Uriah searched for faces; faces of those who received Soren's implants; faces of those who sold them.

After several hours of searching, Uriah's lids were growing heavy. His eyes stung from the work and he was ready for a deep, comfortable sleep.

He almost missed the image that flashed across the screen.

The recording was from the day of Soren's disappearance, several hours after his missed rendezvous. Cantrall was working in his office, one likely gutted during the fire-fight, when he answered the door. A young man stood there – black hair, plain face, no gang markings – with several packages strapped into a heavy-frame dolly.

Delivery boy, Uriah realised.

The delivery boy deposited the boxes in Cantrall's office and left. It didn't look like he said much during the exchange.

Cantrall was expecting the delivery, Uriah thought to himself. Which means he received a call or he made the arrangements.

Uriah watched as Cantrall unpacked a total of six implants: Two eyes, an arm, two internal organs of undetermined nature and one leg. All were replacements for body parts that Soren had lost in a lab explosion.

Cantrall began his examination of the implants, cleaning them off in the process, but Uriah had stopped watching. Despite his normally strong constitution, it felt too grisly, even for him.

Instead, Uriah returned to earlier portions of the recordings, searching for more clues.

SEVERAL MORE HOURS passed, but Uriah had assembled some more pieces of the puzzle. Cantrall received several calls in the time of Soren's disappearance, but without an audio-feed, Uriah couldn't be sure if any of them were related to the delivery of the implants. With that lead seemingly dead, Uriah had moved on to the next related task, that of the implants themselves.

Six faces stared back at Uriah from his monitor, six faces in still frame from the video playback. Five men, one woman – each a different client of Cantrall's; each a ganger or street-mover of different affiliation; each earning one of Soren's scavenged implants. The last one Uriah already knew; it was the Cawdor ganger who lay dead on Cantrall's operating table, his promised arm in the hands of his executioner and thief. Thankfully, Uriah recognized another two, one by firsthand experience and one on description alone.

Cantrall had been quick to sell the items, but then most good bio-surgeons had a waiting list of clients and preferred stock. That's when Uriah slapped himself in the forehead. If Cantrall did keep a list, then it was at his surgical bay. Worse, Uriah had to assume that Slag might have already found the list while searching the office, meaning that they likely shared the same remaining five targets. Whoever possessed the list definitely held the advantage since Uriah only recognized two of the five people who received the implants from the images.

At least he had two new leads to pursue.

But which to pursue first, the implant or the list, which might already be taken? Steal the implant first,

Uriah thought, and I could lose the list – I can't identify the other three gangers. Go after a list, which may
not exist or is already gone, and I may lose the only
implants whose locations I do know...

Uriah sighed. So much for sleep. He grabbed his
trench coat and headed out.

THERE WAS NO decision, really; at least not for Uriah.
The two implants, while valuable, were short-term
victories; finding the list was critical to the long-term.
Unfortunately, while the scavengers had yet to strip
Cantrall's operation of its equipment, it was because
of the Orlock presence that they stayed their hands.

'Killing Orlocks seems to be a hobby with you,
Jester,' Voice had said as he approached the same
building where he'd foiled Slag's attempts to kill him.

'It's a job,' Uriah replied. 'I don't derive pleasure
from killing them, though I do seem to be killing
quite a few of them these days.'

THE GUNFIGHT WAS furious, bolter shots and muzzle
bursts imprinting the rooms with quick lightning
flashes. Uriah had walked in on the Soulsplitters as
they were searching Cantrall's place of business.
Maybe Uriah had been encouraged when Slag's heavily armoured bike was nowhere to be seen. Maybe it
was just stupidity. All that mattered now was that
Uriah had entered the corridors unseen, until turning
one corner to find Soulsplitters heading his way with
plastic containers filled with data-slates and files.

'Thank you, you shouldn't have,' was all Uriah
managed to say before the Soulsplitters dropped their
boxes and reached for their weapons. Uriah was
faster, however, drawing his bolt pistol with blinding
speed, and firing through the brain pan of the lead
Orlock. The others dived through adjacent doors,

firing and screaming as they leapt. Uriah ducked to his right, back around the corner. Unfortunately, the firefight now raged full pitch.

'Problems?' Voice asked.

'Nothing that a few clips couldn't solve,' Uriah responded before unleashing several rounds down the corridor.

'What's your situation?'

'I have several Soulsplitters trapped down a dead-end corridor. That's the bad news,' Uriah said, firing a flurry of shots through the walls in the hopes of hitting an Orlock.

'Is that bad?' Voice asked, her questions being cut off by gun battle.

'Yes, it is,' Uriah said. 'They're trapped, but they're well protected. I can't get to them without charging down the corridor.' Almost in response, a blistering hail of gunfire shredded the corners of Uriah's wall, as well as the wall facing the corridor.

Uriah immediately knew what the Soulsplitters were trying to do, and crouched down. He peeked around the corner and fired two shots into the chest of the red-headed ganger trying to sneak forward under cover fire.

'I neither have the clips nor the patience to hold out in a sustained gunfight,' Uriah said.

'So you're going to retreat? Wait, I forgot, look who I'm talking to. What about the list?'

Still crouching, Uriah peeked back around the corner and eyed the boxes lying in the no man's land between him and the Orlock nest. 'I'm working on that,' he said.

Before Uriah could act, there was movement in the corridor behind him, someone's feet scraping the floor. Uriah spun around and landed on his back. Two shots ripped the air above his head. He fired into an advancing Soulsplitter covered in heavy rags, dropping him.

'That settles it,' he said. 'I can't stay. They're advancing on two sides now.'

'Can you escape?'

'Yes,' Uriah said, pausing long enough to fire down both corridors. 'But I'm not terribly happy with what I'm about to do.'

'Which is?' Voice asked, sounding wary.

'It's a surprise,' Uriah said. With that, he tossed a grenade down the corridor, lobbing it straight into an open container. The explosion shredded the boxes and their contents, destroying the data-slates and setting alight the vellum-imprinted files.

'Done!' he said, racing down the remaining corridor. A few shots rang out behind him, but he was already rounding corridors and making his way outside before anyone realized what had happened.

'You destroyed the lead?' Voice asked.

'Tsk, tsk. That's the "the glass is half-empty" observation,' Uriah responded. 'I prevented Slag from gaining the advantage. It's half-full to me.'

'How do you know he doesn't have the list?'

'I don't. But if he did, why bother ransacking Cantrall's office?' Uriah asked. He slipped into a room and headed for one of the bullet-shredded windows. 'Slag's men stayed behind to find something, and if they'd found the list, they wouldn't have bothered with the other boxes.'

'Seems plausible. I hope you're right.'

'So do I,' Uriah said, slipping out through the window and into the darkness of the surrounding buildings. 'I suppose I'll find out soon enough.'

'Where to then?'

'My original target. One of the men I recognized from Cantrall's clients. A Goliath thug named Jaffa Hur.'

CHAPTER: SIX

*Commit with conviction or prepare for a short life filled
with failures.*

– Delaque Operational Commandments
from the *Book of Lies*.

THERE WAS A district in this portion of the Underhive once,
but the city above grew too heavy. The tallest, warren-like
buildings were the first to collapse, buckled under by the
crushing ceiling. More buildings followed until the area
was half its height and scavengers and gangers had the run
of the streets. When a fuel fire finally gutted the major caverns, only scored and blackened rubble remained
standing. People couldn't even bother to preserve the
name of the place, and that too fell into disuse.

The ceiling continued sinking at the rate of an inch each
year, and now rested some three storeys above the ground.
That wasn't counting the huge piles of rubble that
plugged entire caverns and brought the ceiling within
touching distance. Where the pockets remained lay a
shanty town of flimsy shacks and tents crammed together
shoulder to shoulder. Pathways had been cleared between
the different enclaves and tent cities, but even then, some
trails required travellers to traverse through them
hunched over.

The area was dark, the only lights coming from poles in the ground holding glowing radioactive fluid suspended in thick, filthy glass globes. This marked the Goliath territory of the Lords of Ruin.

URIAH SCRAMBLED UP the rubble slope, far from the lit paths and the Goliath patrols moving from one camp to the next. The darkness enveloped him in anonymous comfort, and his black clothing and thermal cloak added to the camouflage. His goggles amplified the ambient light, allowing him to see more clearly. His feet were light on the ground, but still tripped the occasional trickle of rubble. Uriah paused after each misstep, drawing the cloak around him tighter to shield him from thermal optics. Nobody investigated the disturbance, however, either because the local boar-rats had heavier feet than Uriah or because the Lords of Ruin didn't care.

Finally, Uriah reached the lip of a debris crater's slope. Below, the crater was shallow – three storeys deep – but wide enough that the outskirts remained hidden in shadow. Covering the surface of the crater was a community of well over one hundred tents of different sizes, colours and fabrics. The largest were pavilions that easily housed a dozen people, while the smallest were intimate affairs for two people. At the centre, the Goliaths had cleaned the rubble down to the district's original floor. The centrepiece was a large ring over a dozen metres in length, lined with a half-wall of rubble. It was well-lit, the wall lined with glow-liquid. Overlooking it was a platform – a huge slab of rock that was once a building's wall, complete with torn rebars jutting out from the sides.

Uriah recognized the design of the ring. It was a combat circle where the Goliath fought and maimed one another for fun and bragging rights. Tonight it was packed with auctioneers trying to bid on the latest items.

'Wonderful…' Uriah said, mumbling into his radio set.

'What?' Voice asked.

'It's a slave auction,' Uriah replied, looking at the line of broken slaves anchored in their chains and wearing rags that threatened to disintegrate at a touch.

'WAIT!' URIAH SAID, watching the different groups. 'This may actually work to my advantage.'

'How?'

'I can blend into the crowd of people gathered for the slave auction. Who'll notice one more buyer moving through the streets?'

'Could be dangerous,' Voice said. 'What if it's invitation only?'

Uriah smiled. 'A risk, admittedly, but a small one. Somehow, I don't see Lords of Ruin slavers printing out invitations for the evening.'

'True. Good luck, then.'

Uriah cleared the lip of the crater and slowly moved down to the first clusters of tents. He lifted the goggles over his forehead and pulled his hood tight over his head. Satisfied, he stepped into the light and walked down the sloped, rubble streets. The tents grew thicker around him as Goliath men, women and children cooked, bathed and ate dinner in the open. Some possessed hulking frames ripped with muscles, but most local denizens were of normal stature; they likely paid the Lords of Ruin for protection or provided services like cooking and mending.

A few people watched Uriah walk the streets before other outsiders caught their attention. It was obvious that this lot distrusted strangers, only tolerating them for the auction. Uriah kept his eyes open, trying to distinguish the different makes of the tents. He suspected that those marked with paints belonged to the Lord of Ruin's foot-soldiers, a supposition supported by the well-muscled women and children around the tents.

Uriah continued his slow trek through the crater's streets, growing more comfortable with his surroundings. As he approached the bottom of the crater, he passed a fence of twisted girders pointed outward like pikes. From the two rotting corpses impaled on the girders and painted skulls hanging from the bent metal, Uriah knew it served as a warning. The bottom of the crater was for Lords of Ruin only, a suspicion made likelier by the larger tents and more intricate markings painted on their sides.

The tents at the bottom of the crater served as part of the slavers' compound. Metal pens lined the street with every variety of human misery caged within, and the Goliaths patrolled the area with heavy weapons and mean scowls. The crowds were likewise thicker here, with people bumping into one another to reach the auction. Despite the noise of the crowd, a barker's voice rose above the others, selling a steady stream of slaves to the hungry crowd. Uriah felt a twinge of sadness for the sorry lot on stage, the men bound for back-breaking physical labour and the women for domestic work or to satisfy someone's carnal pleasures.

'Anything?' Voice asked.

'Nothing yet,' Uriah said, his voice no stronger than a whisper. He brushed past several wealthy buyers attired in a rich array of clothing. He finally stopped at the edge of the street, near an open sewer trench, and allowed people to rush past him. The smell was horrible; nobody was willing to stop and wait under the weight of the stench. Uriah persevered because hardly anyone paid attention to him as they rushed by. It allowed him a few moments to survey the area.

'I can't locate Jaffa Hur's tent,' Uriah said with a whisper.

'Well? Are you sure it was him in Cantrall's recordings?'

'Yes,' Uriah said. 'He was one of the five who received an implant. I've seen his face before.'

'Has he seen yours?'

'Not this face,' Uriah said with a smile. 'He saw another one. He won't recognize me.'

'One would hope,' Voice replied. 'Actually, I have an idea. Jaffa is likely holding court tonight. To impress all these visitors.'

'And where would that be?' Uriah asked.

'Could be anywhere,' Voice said. 'He could be at the auction. Or in a private tent.'

'So, how does that help me?'

'He'll expect his rich guests to pay their respects.'

'You're saying follow the rich buyers till they gravitate into his orbit.'

'It's an option. Otherwise, stumble around in the dark. Pray for luck.'

'Already did,' Uriah said, scouting the people entering and leaving the noisy auction ring. He chose a cluster of three men and two women, all well-dressed despite their surroundings, and followed them back up the slope until it was obvious they were leaving the crater. Uriah headed back down.

Uriah waited until another two men left the auction. The pair were cloaked, but their boots were rugged and crafted with the kind of care only the rich could afford. He followed them on their slow saunter through the streets. They spoke in low voices and studied their surroundings carefully. The pair turned down one street, then another, seemingly without purpose. Finally they cleared the corner of a tent and Uriah followed.

The sword was level to Uriah's chest, and he almost impaled himself on its tip upon rounding the tent.

'Well, it looks like we have ourselves a thief,' the swordsman said, his face full with beard. His compatriot, wearing a blond moustache and golden locks, nodded.

Uriah realized they'd spotted him following them, though they obviously misunderstood his intentions. 'Hardly,' Uriah said. 'I thought you were going to Jaffa Hur. I was following you so I could offer him my respects.'

'And why would he want the respect of a guttersnipe?' the swordsman said. 'Likelier, you thought us easy marks for robbing.'

Uriah glanced around. The street was relatively empty, though at least one Goliath with twin Mohawks watched the exchange with cruel interest. 'How could I, one man, rob two men of such skill?' Uriah said. 'I was seeking Jaffa Hur. I'm sorry for the confusion.'

Before Uriah could turn to leave, the swordsman lashed out with his blade, cutting Uriah across the cheek. It stung fiercely. Uriah's hand went to the wound, trying to catch the blood that dribbled between his reddened fingers. He met the two men's gazes, but there was only malicious humour in their eyes. They were going to hurt him regardless. Uriah returned their smile and pulled his bolt pistol, his movement a blur.

The smile remained carved on Uriah's face; he spun past the blade, his cloak momentarily blinding the swordsman, before punching the pistol's barrel straight into the man's gut. Uriah pulled the trigger twice, the shots muffled by the swordsman's body.

The swordsman slumped to the ground before his friend even reacted. Uriah wasn't going to give him that chance either. He spun again, this time catching the second man with a spin kick in the gut. The gun followed the kick, and Uriah emptied another two muffled shots, this time into the man's chest.

Uriah looked around again, locating the Goliath who'd been watching the exchange. The Lord of Ruin ganger was still there in the shadows, but his expression had changed from one of cruelty to one of animal caution. Uriah leaned down and took the money purses off both bodies. He tossed one to the ganger who caught it without ever drawing his gaze away from Uriah.

'Jaffa don't like dead bodies on auction night. Ain't good for business,' the ganger said.

'Then best make sure nobody finds them,' Uriah said, tossing the Goliath the second money purse.

The Goliath weighed both bags in his large hand and nodded. Uriah walked away.

URIAH SQUATTED BEHIND a dark tent; he was hidden in the shadows and free from the prying eyes on the street. The medical adhesive strip he'd attached to his face stung, but it kept the wound closed. After a few moments, he applied water from a bottle to the strip and felt it bubble against his skin. A few seconds more, and the strip dissolved, leaving him with a wound glued shut and, hopefully, no scar.

More wonders of Van Saar technology, Uriah thought; he'd have to remember to thank Morgane for her wonderful gifts.

Low voices approached Uriah's position from an adjoining alley. Uriah quickly pulled himself deeper into the shadows, behind a rack with drying clothes, his cloak pulled tight around his shoulders.

'...saw them, all bleeding' a woman's voice said. 'Ducked in here, he did. Up to no good, I reckon.'

Uriah readied his bolt pistol and waited for whoever it was to appear. There were two of them. The speaker was a large woman with the well-muscled body of a

Goliath and a long ponytail on her otherwise shaved head. Her companion was equally built, with a roadmap of scars on his half-naked body and a high green Mohawk. Neither of them had eye implants, for which Uriah was grateful.

'Don't see nobody,' the man said.

'He came through here. I saw him!'

'He ain't here now.'

'Maybe that way,' the woman said, walking down another alley. The man followed, shaking his head.

Uriah waited for the footsteps to fade away before emerging from his hole and ducking down another alley away from the two Lords of Ruin.

'Not good,' Uriah said to himself, stepping back out into the streets with his hood drawn down.

'More trouble?' Voice asked.

'I've drawn too much suspicion.'

'Well you're in luck,' Voice said. 'I spoke with a friend. Someone who's been to the area before.'

'He knows where Jaffa Hur's tent is?' Uriah asked, watching his surroundings carefully. He headed back down the crater, where the crowds were thickest.

'Go to the auction ring and face the stage.'

Uriah slipped through the crowd at the slave auction, under the raised arms of those bidding on the current lots. It was hard ignoring the shouting to gain the auctioneer's attention, but Uriah found himself facing the stage.

'Done,' he said, and fought hard to hear the instructions.

'Turn right,' Voice said, nearly muted by the surrounding crowds, 'until you see a street with a high pole mounted with a skull.'

'Ah! I see it and I think I see Jaffa Hur's tent,' Uriah said, his gaze halfway up the crater. He stared at a grand black pavilion, which was slightly larger than those around it.

'If it's marked with red paint, then that's it.'

'I don't think that's paint,' Uriah said, heading for the street.

Uriah was a few yards from the street slope when he caught movement out of the corner of his eye. A Lord of Ruin, more compact in frame than his companions, was walking parallel to Uriah and watching him carefully.

'I've been spotted,' Uriah whispered to Voice. 'I believe the ganger who saw me kill those two men has given me up.'

'Be careful. Might be time to pull out. Call it a lost cause.'

'My dear Voice. Gambles require risk,' Uriah said, before steering back into the crowd. Faces flashed before him, but in between the gaps, he saw another Goliath trying to follow him. This was certainly a hunt, though Uriah had no inclination of remaining the prey.

The throng of auction-goers was thickest closest to the slave podium, and the gangers were waiting in the wings. Uriah manoeuvred himself into the heart of the crowd. He affixed his trusty re-breather to his mouth and drew down the goggles to protect his eyes. He dropped a smoke grenade.

Uriah stood there as the ashen cloud enveloped him. Screams and angry voices followed as the smoke spread out, bringing those caught within it to choking, hacking coughs and fits. The crowd scattered in different directions, and Uriah moved with the panicked mob, straight for the Goliaths who were maintaining the perimeter.

Uriah's path took him past one of the large gangers. He was hoping to slip by unnoticed, but the tattooed Lord of Ruin spotted him.

The Goliath brute muscled his way through the crowd and reached past people to grab Uriah by the hem of his cloak. Uriah allowed himself to be pulled in, close enough that the ganger didn't see the bolt pistol until the barrel was pressed into his ribcage. A single muffled shot, further drowned out by the growing stampede, was all it took to drop the brute.

Escaping auction-goers quickly filled the sloped streets and Uriah allowed the mob to carry him towards Jaffa's pavilion. When the crowd lost some of its momentum, Uriah ducked into the alleys between the tents. He made his way up through the back ways, confident that the commotion was drawing everyone to the main streets.

APPROACHING JAFFA'S TENT proved less of an issue than Uriah's initial attempts to find it. The crowds still milled about in the streets while the Lords of Ruin tried weeding through them to find Uriah. It wouldn't be long before they moved into the side streets and tent alleys to find him. Uriah hadn't much time left.

Jaffa Hur's tent was a pavilion with a three-peaked canopy. Plastic and sheet-metal plating stitched the walls while dripping red marks offered crude warnings to rivals. Uriah, however, wasn't fluent in Goliath-tongue, and ignored the messages with a smile. He crouched down and cut a small v-shaped slit between two plates. Careful not to push against the tent wall, Uriah peered through the slit.

The room beyond was dark, lit by three or four candles. The pavilion was sectioned by a heavy curtain five feet away from the wall. That was all Uriah could really see except for the corner of two pieces of furniture; a trunk covered in stitched leather and a scavenged cabinet complete with scratches and worn lacquer. There was also the rhythm of laboured breathing, as well as whispered voices.

'Best you not disturb him,' a woman's voice said. 'Infection set in.'

The news was met with two grunts and people moving away, their candle-cast shadows dancing against the wall.

Uriah waited until the noises inside the pavilion had died away completely before speaking with Voice.

'I believe Jaffa Hur is still recovering from the operation. Something about an infection.'

'He did take an internal organ. Heart accelerant, was it?'

'I believe so. I'm not an expert.'

'That's major surgery. He needs time to recover. And frankly transplant rejections and infections kill more patients than the operation itself.'

'Indeed.' Uriah said. 'Going dark.'

Uriah cut a vertical gash in the fabric with his knife. A quick glance inside confirmed his suspicions; it was a bedroom of sorts with the mighty Jaffa Hur in bed and unconscious. Blood-soaked bandages covered his otherwise bare chest and abdomen, and his skin glistened under a thick sweat. An empty chair stood next to his cot for whoever watched over the ganger brute.

Slipping through the slit was easy. Uriah stayed low to the ground, below the flickering candle lights. He could still hear hushed voices toward the pavilion's entrance, again a woman speaking of Jaffa's care. She was probably the local midwife. Unfortunately for Uriah, this meant he had the caretaker to neutralize as well as any of Jaffa's personal guards who were inside the pavilion.

One step at a time, Uriah thought to himself. He hid to the side of the cabinet; it shielded him from the curtain. It was poor cover, but anyone entering the room wouldn't notice him at first glance. In fact, with luck, they'd have turned away from him as they headed for the chair. He unsheathed his knife for the quiet kill.

Uriah waited until the voices in the next room finally said their farewells; two women and at least one man,

Uriah realised. He cursed under his breath. Footsteps approached and Uriah's fears were realised. Jaffa Hur's caretaker was a local woman. Not as well-built as the Lords of Ruin themselves, but well-defined and scarred enough to have seen combat of her own. Uriah had heard of such men and women, those within the gang who refused to inject themselves with the chemicals to add obscene muscle mass. The Goliaths considered them to be inferior, but never enough to treat them harshly. Still, a woman was a woman and Uriah was rather squeamish about killing her. He had killed women in the past, but preferred avoiding it when possible.

The woman didn't see Uriah as she entered and turned for the chair. He rushed up behind her with his drawn blade. She sensed the rush, but didn't turn in time. Uriah struck her against the back of the head with the knife pommel, rendering her senseless. She collapsed with a muffled grunt; she was dazed.

'Jezra?' a man's voice demanded from the next room.

Uriah poked the woman hard in the ribs with two fingers. She groaned at the pain. There was movement from beyond the curtain.

It took a second blow to knock out Jezra. Uriah flipped the knife and caught it by the blade. When the pug-nosed ganger entered, Uriah threw the weapon with practiced aim, catching the Goliath in the neck. Blood spurted from the wound in thick rivers and the ganger grunted, his face contorted by shock. Uriah rush forward and grabbed the knife's bloody pommel. He sliced it out sideways, severing the vocal cords and jugular. The Lord of Ruin fell to the ground, gurgling, but Uriah had already entered the main pavilion in time to see another ganger with dreadlocks running forward.

Uriah launched the blade with an underhand flick. The knife sank into the man's chest through a thick vest.

Uriah shut the man's mouth with his hand, preventing him from screaming, and grabbed the knife again to stab him several times in rapid succession. The Goliath struggled for a moment before his eyes went dull. He slumped to the floor.

Uriah paused long enough to wipe his blade on the ganger's vest and to confirm that the exchange hadn't alerted others. There was no such misfortune, leaving Uriah with one last unpleasant task to complete.

Jaffa Hur remained unconscious despite the grisly scene played out in his tent. Uriah had already bound and gagged Jezra, leaving the two Lords of Ruin dead where they lay. Uriah wasn't one for cruelty despite the brutality of his action. He took a pillow to muffle the sound and placed it over Jaffa Hur's face before firing twice. Hur twitched before falling still.

It was grim work, but Uriah had little choice. He cut away the bandages to reveal an ugly chest gash stitched together with black thread; it was purple from the bruising. With little thought, Uriah cut away the stitches with his knife and spread the wound open with his gloved hands. There was no heartbeat, so little blood to spill. Uriah cut through the thick ropes of pectoral muscles to reach the sternum and ribs. Cantrall had swapped six ribs as well as the breastbone with titanium replacements. Uriah examined where the bone ribs gave way to metal, and proceeded to crack the bolted seams. He tried not to grimace and focused on other things instead, any other things.

Uriah removed the skeletal plate of titanium, revealing the exposed organs; he instantly spotted the octagonal heart accelerant that was fused against the grey-red heart itself. With his knife, Uriah cut away the blinking Accelerant and dropped the mess into a pouch.

'I have it,' Uriah said. 'I don't even know what it does.'

'It has several functions,' Voice replied. 'It can boost the heart rate, oxygenate the blood more easily and deliver an electric charge to stimulate the heart.'

'I have no idea what all thats means,' Uriah said, sighing.

'Doesn't matter now. Can you escape?'

'Not easily,' Uriah said, looking down at the unconscious woman. 'But I have an idea.'

'Don't you always…'

IT WAS QUICK work. Uriah placed the candles near the pavilion's different walls and hanging partitions. It took a quick moment for the fabrics to catch aflame and faster still for the wildfire to spread up the walls and across the ceiling.

Uriah marched back into Jaffa Hur's bedroom and found the woman, Jezra, struggling against her bonds. He cut the ropes around her wrists, his bolt pistol at the ready and his face covered by the hood and goggles. Jezra stood, eyeing Uriah warily; he nodded for her to escape outside. She hesitated and the fire bellowed its heated roar around them. It spread quickly, driving up the heat. Jezra turned and darted past the flames, screaming for help as she fled.

There was no hesitation in Uriah's step. With Jezra's escape, Uriah slipped back through the slit in the tent's fabric before flames claimed it as well. The roaring fire was joined by the concerned screams of the Goliaths trying to reach their leader through the pavilion's front flap. Uriah, however, looked back only to confirm that no one was pursuing him.

Walking through the back alleys of the tent city, Uriah directed himself up the crater's slope. He moved against the rush of curious onlookers, all of whom were too interested in the blaze to pay him any heed.

Moments later, Uriah had reached the top of the crater's lip. The fire had spread to several other tents, for which Uriah was genuinely sorry. He wasn't interested in anyone except Jaffa Hur, but that was the nature of his work; death and carnage were random and often most effective when indiscriminate.

'Done,' Uriah said.

'You escaped?' Voice asked.

'Almost.'

'Then what are you doing there. Run!' Voice said, annoyed by her own tone.

'Just admiring the view,' Uriah said. The blaze was enough to light the entire crater. Uriah watched the slopes of the bowl-like basin glow red with the flames.

'Isn't that risky?' Voice asked.

'Normally, yes,' Uriah responded. 'But considering I just sank my hands into someone's chest to remove an implant, I think I earned a moment's reflection.'

'Something's bothering you. What's the matter?'

'None of this makes sense,' Uriah said. 'Soren's life meant nothing to anyone. It's the implants they want. But why?'

'Bring the implant to me. I can examine it,' Voice offered. 'See if it's truly unique.'

'I – I'm not certain,' Uriah admitted.

'You don't trust me?' Voice asked.

Uriah could hear the surprise in her voice, perhaps even hurt.

'What quality of trust do you expect when you don't offer it yourself?' Uriah asked.

'Meaning?'

'Meaning I know nothing about you. I don't even know what you look like.'

'It's a game we both play. And yet you trust me enough to bring me along on your missions,' Voice said.

'I like mysteries,' Uriah said, a faint smile on his lips.

'So, are you bringing the implant?'

Uriah thought about it for a moment. 'Very well. But I want something in exchange.'

'Excuse me,' Voice said, 'but you're the one who needs the help.'

'Please,' Uriah said. 'You love a mystery as much as I do. You want to see the implant, perhaps more than I need to understand its importance.'

'Perhaps,' Voice said in her typically succinct manner. 'But can you take that chance?'

'Indulge me one question,' Uriah said.

'Only one?'

'For now,' Uriah responded.

'Very well, state your question. I may not answer it, but if I do my answers will be honest.'

'Which House did you belong to?' Uriah said. 'You're too well-spoken and too well-learned to have been raised outside of a Guild school.'

There was a pause on the other end. Uriah was about to press the matter when his answer came.

'Escher,' Voice said. 'I was born into House Escher.'

Uriah smiled. 'I'm coming to deliver the implant.'

After absorbing the sight for a moment longer, Uriah left the area and vanished into shadows beyond the burning crater.

CHAPTER: SEVEN

'Expect the Unexpected' is the credo of distracted fools.
Anticipate, prepare and when all else fails, strike first.

– Delaque Operational Commandments
from the *Book of Lies*.

IT WAS LATE into the night when Uriah finally returned
to his hab block in Shadowstrohm. The hallways were
empty, most good Delaque quiet and asleep. Uriah's
steps grew heavier each footfall. Fatigue overtook him
swiftly.

It had been a busy day, between his misadventures
with Slag and Jaffa Hur, and taking a side-trip to
deliver the implant to Voice. He had never seen Voice,
and tonight was no exception. She'd left a slot open in
the reinforced door of her hideout. He slid the implant
through and waited. Nothing. There was no more to it
than that. He left, more tired than curious.

Uriah entered his hab block with no other thought
than falling into a fast dream, whether that meant
sleeping on the couch or making it into his bedroom.
He switched on the lights and was immediately jolted
awake. His hab block was in ruins. Sofa and chairs
were gutted of their stuffing, drawers tossed to the

floor and spilt of their contents and the monitor on his workbench still smoked from its shattered vid-screen.

The workbench was in a state with tools thrown and broken. Looking at the mess, Uriah realised that this was more than someone searching his dwelling. It was someone with a grudge, someone who took particular delight in ruining his possessions. The artificial eye was gone, as were the recordings of Cantrall's implant. Uriah cursed himself for not protecting those better, though he did have extra copies hidden elsewhere. Now he had lost his only advantage.

It was only on second glance that Uriah's heart went cold. The desk where he kept Morgane's pendant was overturned. He raced to it, hoping against fear that it was still there. The drawer had been pulled out and the hidden compartment was empty. Morgane's keepsake was missing.

PERCAL HEADED DOWN Shadowstrohm's corridors on his way to his office. Nobody wished him a good morning. They knew better than to bother the master of the Handlers, the chieftain spy of House Delaque. Percal wore a filter mask over his nose slits to filter out airborne particles. Once in his hermetically sealed office, he would remove the mask and allow the room's filtration system to do its work.

The last thing Percal expected to see upon opening the door and stepping into his office was Uriah seated there waiting for him to arrive.

'What are doing in my office?' Percal asked in more of a growl than a question.

'Admiring your furniture,' Uriah said.

'Tread carefully, Uriah. I don't take intrusion well.'

'A coincidence, then. Neither do I.'

'What are you talking about?' Percal asked, going over to his desk. He examined it, ensuring nothing was out of place.

'Someone ransacked my hab!' Uriah responded. 'Practically gutted the place with their heavy hands.'

'And you think I did it? You're a far poorer judge of character than I expected.'

'I think not. Playing regicide I see,' Uriah said nodding over to the holographic board.

'What has that to do with anything?'

'I don't believe you robbed my hab block. I think you sent one of your pawns into my home to do the deed.'

'To what end?' Percal asked, sitting behind his desk. By the looks of it, he was regaining his composure.

'To whatever end prompted you to send another Handler on my assignment.'

'This again? Your paranoia knows no bounds.'

'And again you insult me,' Uriah said shaking his head. 'I don't know which of your slights is worse. The fact that you sent a Handler after me. The fact that you tolerate his sabotage when I'm doing the house's bidding. The fact that you continue to lie to me about it. Or the fact that you actually believed Kaden could best me.'

'Kaden?' Percal said. 'Why do you say Kaden?'

Uriah studied Percal for a moment, trying to fathom his motives. Percal wasn't questioning the accusation. In fact, he was calm and intrigued. He seemed playful, in as much as a predator was playful with his intended meal. Uriah, of course, knew it was Kaden. Kaden was the only Handler with enough of a grudge against Uriah to ransack his hab and destroy his belongings for the sheer pleasure of it.

He's playing the game, Uriah realised. And suddenly everything clicked into place. Percal was the oldest surviving Delaque Handler. He'd been playing the game for so long that Uriah doubted he knew how to interact normally with people. He would never speak in direct terms, and he'd evade straightforward questions as a defensive measure.

No, Uriah thought, *he wasn't being dishonest. He was playing the game, the game which required its own set of rules and its own language.* Uriah returned the smile and switched tactics. 'How long has it been?'

Percal's smile broadened. His body language shifted, becoming more relaxed – casual. He was shifting tactics as well, synchronizing himself with Uriah.

Uriah understood what was happening. The nature of the conversation was about to shift into the dou-blespeak of the Delaque, into the give and take that said everything and nothing in equal strokes. What was about to be said had to be ignored. What wasn't being said was more important.

'Been?' Percal asked, shrugging. 'Since what?'

'Since you engaged in field work. You were quite good at playing the game.'

Percal smiled. 'You're embarrassing me. I survived through sheer luck, nothing more. I'm certainly not the Handler you are.'

'You exaggerate, I'm sure,' Uriah said. 'But you must miss the game.'

'Not really,' Percal said. 'I'm quite comfortable here, still doing my part to serve the House.'

'I don't know if I could give it up so easily,' Uriah said.

'Oh, eventually it becomes boring. You crave risks that few can provide. You almost wish others would offer you greater challenges in the course of your duties.'

'You mean your opponents?'

'Among others,' Percal responded. 'Did I ever tell you about my mentor?'

'Only in name. Liam the Grey, correct? His reputation speaks for itself.'

'He was a good mentor. Always pushing me harder than the assignment demanded.'

'Cruelty?' Uriah asked.

'No,' Percal said, his eyes distant. 'He thought the assignments I received were beneath my skills. So he elevated the game to challenge me.'

'How so?' Uriah asked.

'Small tricks. Starting me off with the barest of intelligence. Giving me a few hours to resolve the issue. Alerting enemies of my position–'

'Sending other Handlers after the same prize?' Uriah asked.

'I can't remember all his tricks. Quite possibly, yes,' Percal said, shrugging. 'He thought it best to keep me challenged.'

'What happened?' Uriah asked. 'With that kind of adversity, why did you grow bored of the game?'

'Because Liam died early in my life. And my new mentor, Genadine, was only interested in results. So she sent me on assignment after assignment, never asking for anything more than my quick success.'

'So it grew boring,' Uriah said, nodding, half-listening while stitching the pieces together.

'Without Liam to challenge me, yes. He wanted a worthy successor.'

'Are you sure that's all?' Uriah asked.

'How so?' Percal asked, suspiciously.

'Liam, I mean,' Uriah said. 'Are you sure he was challenging you? Or was he playing the game through you?'

Percal hesitated. Uriah could see him wrestling with his patience. He'd struck a nerve.

'Liam was a great Handler,' Percal said, measuring his words carefully. 'Greater than you or I. What he did was for my betterment. You would do well to have a mentor like him.'

'Who says I don't?' Uriah asked with a smile.

'Perhaps,' Percal said. 'But what of you, Uriah?'

Ahh, Uriah thought. *Here's where he goes on the attack.* 'Me?' he asked.

'Surely the game isn't your sole ambition?'

'The game?' Uriah said. 'No. Surviving the game is perhaps worthier.'

'Good, good. A man like you can hardly afford other distractions.'

'Distractions? Such as?'

'No, no. I'm merely speaking in the greater sense. I've seen Handlers strive for other goals, only to have such distractions cost them their lives. Better the game serve as your sole mistress. Better nothing divert you from your duty.'

'Seems like a hollow existence, doesn't it?' Uriah asked.

'We live alone, we die alone,' Percal said. 'There can be no other way.'

'And whose truth is that? Yours or Liam's?'

Percal shrugged. 'It's a truth I've come to accept. The game doesn't allow for distinction in our lives. We play the game. We always play the game. We are in it whether in the arms of those we love or fighting the enemy. Once you realise the game is your reality, everything else is superfluous. Friends, family, all assets to be used against you. To have none of those is to have no weaknesses.'

'No friends? No family? Sounds like it means to have no strength,' Uriah said.

'If they are your strength, then they are your weakness to exploit.'

'What are you saying?' Uriah asked. The comments were strange and could be understood in any number of ways. Did Percal know Uriah was friends with Soren? Did he know about Morgane? Or perhaps Voice? Uriah wasn't sure, but Percal would play it vague enough to keep Uriah on his toes.

'Saying? Nothing, of course,' Percal said. 'I'm merely trying to help you free yourself. Someone broke into your hab, you say? Well, they might not have done so had they not considered it a weak link – fair game and all that. You have no privacy. Everything you are and everyone you know is committed to the game.'

PERCAL SAT IN his chair for a few moments after Uriah had left. He knew Uriah was good at what he did, but he was also cocky about it, and the stakes were too high for such allowances. Unfortunately, Percal had to admit that using Kaden might have been a mistake. Kaden was out to prove himself at Uriah's expense; it was becoming personal for him. That meant he would lose.

The regicide board flickered. Percal went to the board and saw that the hologram piece for his opponent's Ecclesiarch had been moved. It was about time his opponent committed himself. Percal was prepared for it. He smiled and touched the base of one of his Citizens before touching an empty spot on the board. The Citizen slid across the board into position.

Percal returned to his chair. He activated the black pict screen and entered in three separate code sequences to access his logic hub. A quick scan indicated it had remained inactive since the night before, when he'd left it. Uriah hadn't tampered with his network. A moment later, six images manifested on screen. All Cantrall's customers as captured by his ocular piece – all recipients of Soren's implants – all data stolen from Uriah's logic device.

Percal reached into the hidden pocket and pulled out a tear-shaped pendant hung from a delicate chain. He examined it, bemused curiosity in his expression.

'So, Uriah,' he said to himself. 'Who are you hiding from me? Nobody is spared from the game.'

URIAH HAD SENT the message less than an hour ago. He was sure he'd caught Morgane sleeping, but she'd never admit to that.

The message was more a signal – a pict call with static drowning both voice and sound. The static burst in pitch every four seconds, thanks to Uriah's playing with two exposed wires in his own pict screen. To anyone else, it meant nothing, but to Morgane, it said: meet me in a pre-arranged location. Had the static bursts emerged every eight seconds, Morgane would have rendezvoused with him at his no-longer safe house. Four second bursts meant a different place altogether.

The inn was crushed between two larger buildings that loomed over it and appeared to sweat oil stains; thankfully, the inn itself was relatively clean and well maintained despite its hourly rates and the constant stream of prostitutes and their clients. It was anonymous.

The knock at the door was almost timid, a mixture of the quiet of the morning and uncertainty. Uriah checked the eye piece and opened the door quickly. Morgane slipped through and was immediately in his arms, her lips pressed against his. They kissed, taking comfort from one another and making up for long absences. Then again, any night away from one another was a long absence.

'I missed you,' she said between gasps of air.

'I know,' Uriah responded. 'I missed you too.'

'Pleasant place. How long do we have here?' Morgane asked, peering around.

'They rent by the week, the day and the hour. Offer them a rate on minutes and I'm sure they'd take it. We have it for a few hours at best.'

'Is that all?' Morgane asked, saddened.

'Sorry, love,' Uriah said. 'It'll have to do for now. Best not get comfortable with one place regardless of its qualities. It'll get better, I promise.'

Morgane smiled and nodded. She understood what was at stake. That didn't stop her from tightening her grip around his waist. Uriah grimaced and tensed. Morgane studied him with a worried look.

Uriah smiled. 'I'm a bit tender. It's been a rough few days. I've been put through my paces.'

Morgane nodded. 'I'll have to work around the pain then. Just tell me where it hurts.'

'Everywhere,' Uriah said, laughing. 'If you're trying to work around the pain, maybe you should wait outside.'

'Not a chance,' Morgane said. 'You'll adapt. You always do.'

With that, Uriah swept her off her feet and carried her towards the bed.

'SOREN IS DEAD,' Morgane repeated, more statement than fact. She leaned back into Uriah's chest; he draped his arm over her shoulder and kissed her on the back of her head. 'I suspected as much. What happened?'

'I'm not sure yet,' Uriah admitted, pushing another pillow behind his back. 'It's a messy affair and I'm afraid it's about to get messier. Whoever murdered Soren sold his implants to a black-market bio-surgeon named Cantrall. Cantrall, in turn, sold the implants to six others – gangers by the looks of them.'

'He operated on them?'

'On four, yes. The fifth one bought the implant and left. The sixth and last was killed before the implant was grafted on.'

'Maybe the fifth one has his own bio-surgeon.'

'Or maybe he's a broker, I don't know,' Uriah said. They lapsed into silence, both lying in bed. Uriah, however, was distracted by all the things he had yet to tell her.

'What else did Cantrall say about his customers?' Morgane asked. 'I know you can be quite persuasive.'

'No, it's not like that,' Uriah said with a sigh. 'I went to question him, but he was dead, as was the last ganger. There was another Handler there. He made off with Soren's arm.'

'Another Handler? Operating on his own?'

'Unfortunately not. He was officially sanctioned.'

'Meaning?'

'Meaning I can't eliminate him. As much as he deserves it.'

'Do you know him?'

'It's a man named Kaden, I'm certain of that.'

'Why would your House assign two handlers? Don't they trust you?' Morgane shifted out of Uriah's arms and turned to face him. She was concerned.

'I think so.'

'But you're not sure?'

'The House trusts me,' Uriah said, 'I'm certain, but I'm not sure about my Overseer. He's playing at some game. He says he's testing my skills by challenging me with a rival, but I'm not certain yet.'

'What do your instincts tell you?'

Uriah laughed and shook his head. 'I'm afraid my instincts are preoccupied at the moment. This thing with Soren – with you – has me so turned around.'

'I can take care of myself,' Morgane said.

'I know you can, my love, but there's something else. When Kaden killed Cantrall and stole the implant, I still came away with the better prize. I stole Cantrall's eye implant. It was a Van Saar model.'

'Ah,' Morgane said with a large smile. She pushed a strand of black hair from her face. 'Did you remember what I taught you about the hidden protocols?'

'I did,' Uriah said. 'I accessed the eye's memory archive and came away with the faces of the five remaining customers.'

'But?' Morgane asked, sensing Uriah's hesitation.

'Kaden broke into my hab and stole the data. I have backups, but that wasn't all he stole. He took your black diamond pendant – my keepsake.'

Morgane's expression of shock quickly subsided. 'That doesn't mean anything,' she said.

'Or it could mean everything. Whether he knows about you or not, both he and my Overseer know I have someone in my life. Someone they can use against me. I was careful in coming here, but my life is now under scrutiny. That is why I only took this room for a day.' Uriah hesitated; he looked away. 'That's why I think we should–'

'Stop right there,' Morgane said. Her face was a storm of emotions, a mixture of indignation and anger. 'If you're about to suggest we keep our distance–'

Uriah turned to face her. 'Morgane, love, it might be for the best.'

'No,' Morgane said. 'I appreciate your concern, but I will not allow anyone to come between us. I love you too much.'

'And I love you too much to see you hurt.'

'I am not some timid flower to be crushed under someone's boot.' Morgane cupped Uriah's chin in her hands. 'Let them come – the Delaque, the Van Saar, the Orlocks, all of them. I will not be bullied and I will not leave your side.'

'Morgane–'

'My decision is final,' she whispered before kissing him on the lips.

'So be it,' he whispered back. 'You do realise this will end in both of us becoming fugitives.'

'Likely, but an eventuality I'm prepared for.'

'As am I,' Uriah said.

'There's something else, though, isn't there? Something you're not telling me.'

'There's nothing, love. I'm—'

'Stop,' Morgane said. She pressed her finger to his lips.

Uriah, in turn, took her hand and kissed her finger. 'I'm sorry,' he said. 'It's difficult. I've been a part of this for so long, that it's easy to lie.'

'I know,' Morgane said. 'But you don't have to, not around me. Whatever it is, I'm strong enough to hear it.'

'All right. Slag is after me. He saw me at Cantrall's. He has my scent. This won't end until he kills me, or I kill him.'

Morgane smiled and nodded. 'It never ends with you, does it?'

'Never,' Uriah said.

'Well then,' she whispered, drawing into a kiss, 'end him before he pays you in kind.'

The lovers sank back down to the bed, in one another's warm embrace.

'HER NAME IS Corval,' Uriah said, studying the mammoth building across the narrow street. It appeared as though it had been built inside the level's support pylon. A lattice of the pylon's I-beams and girders covered the building like a scabbard covers a sword.

Uriah stayed in the shadows of an alleyway, one of many in this tight maze. The other buildings rose up several storeys around him like dirty, crooked fingers. All of them were home to squatters or the gangs that could hold them.

'Name's not familiar,' Voice said.

'Really? She's a member of your house.' Uriah counted the number of angry, well-built women walking through the various streets and alleys. A couple kicked the scrawny, rag-wearing men scouring the refuse piles for food.

'I'm no longer Escher,' Voice said, her tone laced with an annoyed lilt.

'Of course,' Uriah said. 'Do you still have the physique of one?'

'Uh-uh,' Voice replied. 'You pay for those kinds of questions.'

'Indeed,' Uriah said. 'Something to keep in mind. Anyway, Corval is matriarch for the Cybilline Sisterhood.'

'Heard of them,' Voice said. 'They're well placed in House Escher. What was their poison, again?' she seemed to be asking herself.

'You mean, how do they choose to denigrate men?'

'Drugs,' Voice said, suddenly remembering.

Uriah nodded. 'Rotting Fetter Injections and Acidyne Spinal Taps.'

'Vicious, even by Escher standards. Her clients must be desperate to ride those rushes.'

'I wouldn't know,' Uriah said. 'Gasser Bars are as far as I go to ruin my health.'

'Smart. Though I wouldn't call your lifestyle *healthy*.'

'Ah, the lifestyle is thrust upon us all. I merely choose to play it well.'

'All right then, Jester. How will you play this? I suspect you can't blend in this time.'

'You're right. I'm not downtrodden enough as a man or *gifted* with your attributes to play the woman.'

'You'll manage,' Voice said.

'That I will,' Uriah said, peering around. 'This time, I think I'll start from the top and work my way down.'

'Any particular reason?' Voice asked.

'Corval is likelier to be at the top of the building than at the bottom. And the lower floors will be too well guarded to sneak or bluff my way through.'

'Get to it then,' Voice said. 'Contact me when you need help.'

With that, Uriah waited silently until two muscled and pony-tailed women walked past his hiding spot. After another moment of lurking in the shadows, he darted across the street and reached a tight alley along the side of the building. A thick layer of detritus and rubble covered the floor.

Corval's den and the buildings next to it were built with age-pocked and crumbling plascrete. Uriah removed his gloves and slowly crawled up the side of the building, pulling himself up along the pylon's slanted girders, occasionally shifting over to the building's façade to climb one handhold at a time. His trench coat fluttered freely behind him. Fortunately, the wall was relatively easy to scale between the small craters and the narrow ledges separating the floors.

Uriah came to rest on a narrow ledge some three storeys high. The structure continued for another storey above his head before melting into the ceiling. The building and its pylon carapace served as a support column for the level above it, and when age finally crumbled one or the other, the section above would collapse as well.

The nearby window was one of the few without furniture or metal sheets covering it. In fact, the lower floor windows were better covered than those on the upper floors. Something about heights made people feel more secure, which always worked to Uriah's benefit.

Uriah sidled up close to the window and peered inside. Despite the building's dilapidated exterior, the Escher provided better treatment for its interior. The room was respectable – despite the humidity-stained walls – with a made bed, a worn dresser and a porcelain rinse bowl. By the looks of it this was likely a woman's quarters or one belonging to a house trustee; the Escher did not offer men the same consideration.

Quietly, Uriah entered through the window, his foot testing the floor before he settled his full weight inside. The building was quiet, but the floors were solid beneath Uriah's feet – they did not creak or groan; it would be difficult to hear him move about. Once inside, Uriah crept to the door and listened. Silence beyond. That, more than anything else, played on his nerves. Sound could have painted his expectations and warned him what to expect next. Without sound, what lay beyond this door was an absolute mystery.

Uriah opened the door a crack and peered through the slit into the corridor. It was empty and silent – enough so that Uriah waited a few moments in the hopes of hearing something. Not even a shuffle or muted conversation greeted his ears. The building felt abandoned. Uriah didn't like the feeling.

Rooms flanked either side of the corridor, but no sound came from them when Uriah pressed his ear against their doors. From one end, the corridor met wall, but from the other, it intersected another corridor with more of the same. Uriah tested the occasional door, his fingers light on the handle; some were locked, but others opened into silent rooms. Beds half-made, yesterday's clothing still heaped on the dressers. Those rooms that Uriah found open seemed caught in transition.

Uriah equalized the pressure in his ears, opening the transmission with Voice.

'What is it?' she asked.

'The floor is empty,' Uriah said, keeping his voice near sub-vocal.

'What's on the floor?'

'Bedrooms. I suppose this is where the Escher sleep.'

'Escher don't sit around in their rooms, you know. They're highly motivated. Perhaps the building matriarch runs a tight ship.'

'Meaning?'

'Meaning she doesn't like dawdlers. She keeps her daughters busy. Or maybe, they're at a gathering.'

'The last thing I need,' Uriah said, 'is for all the Escher to be in one room.'

'The gatherings were fun,' Voice said. 'But you're right. You would stick out.'

'Suggestions?' Uriah asked.

'Investigate the lower floors. If Corval operates a drug den, the Escher are likely below, tending to their male clientele.'

'I'm curious,' Uriah said. 'Why denigrate men in this fashion? With drugs I mean.'

'The drugs keep the men pliant, breaks the will of stubborn individuals and break down potential recruits.'

'Recruits? You mean the men who come here are willing Escher slaves?'

'It's a hard life for many out there,' Voice said. 'The Escher demand subservience in exchange for shelter, food and protection. For some men, that's a small price to pay.'

'But Corval also sells drugs. To other clientele, I mean.'

'Some recruits don't know they're candidates yet,' Voice replied. 'This is likely how Corval recruits. From among the stock of already broken men. If someone cannot pay, the Escher extend drug credit... with interest. Eventually, the poor bastard is in so deep, he becomes gang property. What difference does it make to him? He was a slave, already.'

'Well,' Uriah said, shaking his head, 'the sooner I'm done with this unfortunate mess, the better. This place disgusts me.'

'And yet you didn't blink twice when you were inside the Goliath slave camp,' Voice said, irritation flecking her tone. 'Just because the Escher enslave men–'

'Now's not the time to debate politics,' Uriah said, cutting her off. 'But, if you want to know, it bothers me the same. Unfortunately, I'm not here to liberate slaves or house property. I came for Corval. And considering Corval is the only other face I recognized in the archives, I have no other leads.'

Well, not entirely true, Uriah thought. Kaden was also a lead in this sorry affair, but Uriah wasn't ready to tap him yet. It wouldn't have taken much effort to eliminate Kaden as a threat, but Uriah didn't believe in wasting potential assets.

'Voice,' Uriah said after neither of them had spoken. 'Can we return to the moment at hand?'

'Agreed,' Voice said, having regained her composure. 'Head downstairs. Just be careful of the gate.'

'The gate?'

'Few Escher actually sleep with their mavants–'

'You mean slaves,' Uriah said.

'To an Escher, the difference is negligible.'

'So, what's the gate?'

'It's what separates the Escher from slaves and clients. It's likely a heavily reinforced door, with at least two guards. The slaves themselves maintain a second gate.'

'Let me guess – to separate slaves from the addicts or clients.'

'Correct,' Voice said.

'Thank you,' Uriah said. 'Jester out.'

FURTHER INTO THE floor and still no signs of life. Uriah moved through the hallways of the enormous building, looking for any hint that would tell the story here. Finally, he found it in one corridor where bullet holes and blood spatters painted one of the walls. Uriah touched a droplet of blood and smudged it. It was partly wet; whatever had happened had been violent and recent.

Uriah crept from door to door, studying each for something new. Further down the corridor, he noticed a small blood smear on the floor that vanished under a door. He listened carefully before finessing open the lock with picks. Uriah opened the door carefully, his body low to the ground and to the side. Only silence greeted him, so he peeked inside.

Five bodies had been dumped inside the room, three strong-looking women and two scrawny men; all shot or hacked with large blades – probably machetes. Uriah quickly studied the three women's faces, but Corval was not among them. Their wounds still appeared wet and the flies had yet to find them. They were fresh, too fresh for Uriah's comfort.

The little voice in Uriah's head screamed for him to leave, but that thought flickered for as long as it took Uriah to crush it. Being a Handler meant entering unfamiliar and frightening waters. Being a Handler meant committing to the unpleasant.

Uriah closed the door, now forewarned and, hence, forearmed. Something had happened here in this building, and it was likely linked to recent events. All that was left to do was to find that link.

THE ESCHER GATE was located at the stairwell where the corridor widened. It was a trapdoor over the stairs, a huge slab of grey iron pinned to the floor with a pair of greasy hydraulic arms. The blackened joints hissed and popped sparks and the slab of iron was partly open, enough for someone to slip through the crack. More bullet holes riddled the nearby walls. The hallway appeared smeared in blood.

The gate was over thirty yards down the corridor, but Uriah had yet to move from his hiding spot. He studied the gate through the crack of the partly open door. Nothing moved, nothing breathed.

'Not good,' Uriah said in a whisper.

'Still no sign of life?' Voice asked.

'You could say that. The gate looks badly damaged.'

'Maybe they abandoned the building.'

'Again, you could say that.'

There was a pause on the other end before Voice spoke again. 'What did you find?'

'Two rooms filled with dead bodies.'

'A fight?'

'Yes,' Uriah said. 'No survivors thus far. I'm looking at the gate. It looks damaged from here.'

'Time to leave, perhaps?'

'And disappoint my hosts?' Uriah asked with a smile.

'Hm?'

'Someone hid the bodies,' Uriah replied. 'Gunplay and death isn't so uncommon as to require hiding the bodies. Not unless killing everyone here was the first of two plans.'

'You're thinking trap?'

'Yes.'

'All the more reason to leave,' Voice said, sounding concerned.

'If I wasn't a Handler, then yes,' Uriah said. 'But someone has gone to the effort of laying a trap. I want to know why, and for whom.'

'Why?' Voice asked, startled. 'If it's obvious they're expecting someone, why play into their hands?'

Uriah's smiled deepened. 'I do appreciate the concern, Voice, but the fact is I still retain the upper hand.'

'You do? Care to explain that.'

'I entered through the top floor – something they wouldn't expect or the trap would have been sprung upstairs. If there's a trap to exploit, it'll be mine to play.'

'You are a dangerous man,' Voice said with some appreciation. 'Anything I can do?'

'Not at the moment. At least not until I find Soren's implant.'

'Understood. I'll stand by, Jester.'

'Thank you,' Uriah said.

Quietly, Uriah entered the corridor and moved to one of the doors. He pulled a rectangular matchbox-like container from his pouch and fixed it inside the door frame, at knee height. It stuck to the metal, clinging with magnetic grip. A second later, a tiny burst of air sounded from the matchbox and Uriah caught the glint of the silvery flechette firing into the opposite wall of the corridor.

Sixth door down, Uriah reminded himself, *knee-height*. He then headed for the gate, darting from door frame to door frame. At every second door, he affixed another matchbox to the door frame and waited for the puff of air to follow. Each time, he placed the matchbox at a different height and reminded himself of its location.

At the last door before the corridor widened, Uriah stopped and listened. He noticed that the gate was heavily damaged, the trapdoor's edges crimped and indented from something or someone strong enough to force the hydraulics open.

Uriah then caught the hint of something, a shuffle of someone moving. It had come from the door right next to him. Quick whispers followed. Uriah moved away from the doorframe, but it was too late. Whether he'd brushed against the door inadvertently or they'd seen his shadow beneath the door's bottom edge, they knew he was there.

'Someone's upstairs,' a muffled voice cried.

Noise erupted around Uriah, from the rooms next to him as well as several downstairs. Uriah understood their game, now. They were waiting to catch someone crawling through the trapdoor, hoping to snare them at a disadvantage.

Uriah bolted back the way he'd come; behind him feet stampeded up the staircase and two doors opened in the corridor, unleashing a handful of Orlocks from each.

'It's Uriah!' someone shouted.

Uriah cursed and ducked beneath the first matchbox. The trap was meant for him, which meant Slag was nearby. He heard someone scream and glanced back long enough to see that someone had run into the first micro-wire that he'd strung across the corridor. It looked like it had cut an inch into his nose, slicing cartilage, before snapping. Uriah continued running and ducked to avoid another strand at neck level. He leapt over the third wire and pretended to duck under another one before a voice caught his attention.

'Uriah!'

Uriah slowed and turned, despite himself. Slag stood there with his men who looked too scared to advance on him. They now realised the hallway was strung with micro-wire filaments.

Next to Slag was a behemoth, someone of Goliath stature with pistons and mechanical claws for arms and hands. His shoulders, and spine, were also plated implants. The behemoth drooled and giggled to himself. Uriah now knew who had broken open the trapdoor.

Slag looked to the behemoth and nodded. 'Get 'im,' he said.

The behemoth tore into a fit of childish giggles and stumbled forwards half running, half-lumbering. Uriah backed away, surprised. The behemoth reached the second wire trap and snapped it a quarter inch inside his flesh. He never slowed; he never reacted to the pain or the cut that stretched across his muscled chest. Instead, he giggled harder. The voice in Uriah's head screamed for him to run, but he was caught off guard. It was only when the third tripwire snapped against the behemoth's artificial legs that Uriah tried running. By then it was too late.

The Orlock behemoth lunged forward with a burst of speed that belied his size. He caught Uriah by his collar and lifted him clean off the ground. Before Uriah could slip free of the trench coat, the behemoth shoved him face first into the wall, twice. Uriah barely had time to turn his head and avoid a broken nose.

Spots of blinding white light peppered Uriah's vision and the sound of rushing blood almost drowned his hearing.

'Hurt more?' the behemoth asked somewhere in the distance.

'Not yet,' Slag said, his voice further away.

Uriah fought to regain focus, to see through the pain, but he was slipping out of consciousness…

URIAH TRIED TO *scream, but the steady jolt of electricity sealed his jaw shut and filled his nostrils with the smell of burning flesh. He went rigid with the spasms and rattled the bolted chair, nearly tearing it loose from the floor. He was strapped in, but his arms were free.*

Percal loomed, holding the mechanism that controlled the flow of electricity burning through Uriah. He placed the device on the table in front of Uriah, taunting him with it. The message was clear:

Salvation is a foot away.

'Focus,' Percal told the young Uriah. 'Your life will depend on it.'

Uriah tried to scream 'I can't,' but all that came out were grunts and squeals.

'Quit,' Percal said. 'Only the best can be Handlers. You're obviously not cut out for it.'

Uriah managed to shake his head from side to side by throwing his entire body into the motion.

'If you seek mercy from me,' Percal replied, 'then you'll be disappointed. Turn the device off yourself, or die here and now.'

And with that, Percal walked out of the room, leaving the device on the table, leaving Uriah to the pain and the smell of burning flesh.

URIAH FORCED HIS way through the pain, forced his fingers to move, forced his senses to come to bear. He was still dangling from the metal fingers of the behemoth, but his back was to Slag and the others; he still had a chance.

The movement was automatic, Uriah's fingers reaching into the right pouch without thought or hesitation. There were two types of memory in Uriah that coexisted with one another; the first was conscious thought; the second was muscle memory born from repetition and practice. Uriah pulled out another matchbox and quickly palmed it before the behemoth swung him around to face Slag.

'Time you died,' Slag said, raising his heavy bolter.

'No gloating?' Uriah asked, trying to sound disappointed.

'Only idiots gloat,' Slag said, taking aim.

'Hm,' Uriah said. 'I thought idiots shot prisoners before questioning them about the implants. I could be wrong.'

'You're stallin',' Slag said.

'Of course I'm stalling,' Uriah said with a laugh. 'But that doesn't mean I don't know anything.' Uriah paused a moment when a thought occurred to him. 'I'm curious. How exactly did you know to ambush me here?'

Slag said nothing. He never lowered his gun, but Uriah could see him deliberating matters.

'Let me guess,' Uriah said. 'You're well informed. Someone told you I'd be coming.'

Slag lowered his bolter. 'Drop him Gordo. You two; search 'im, strip 'im and bring 'im,' was his response before walking away.

The behemoth dropped Uriah with a dissatisfied rumble of a sigh and lumbered after Slag. Uriah smiled at the two men advancing on him. He pressed a small button on the matchbox's side. The near-invisible flechette fired into the nearby wall, but neither man noticed. They searched him and removed his pouches while he raised his arms in mock surrender, bringing the matchbox and micro-line well above their heads. Slag, however, turned around long enough to notice Uriah's action.

'Search everywhere!' Slag said with a growl. 'Up his sleeves, too. He's tricky.'

Uriah brought his arms back down, and in one quick flick of the wrist looped the wire around the first Orlock's neck. Before either ganger could react, Uriah punched the second ganger in the nose with the matchbox still in hand. That pulled the wire tight around the neck of the first ganger, cutting deep into his flesh. The filament sliced through both jugulars and the throat, enough to send arterial spray everywhere. The second man reeled back, momentarily blinded from the pain of his shattered nose.

It was enough for Uriah to drop the matchbox and run down the corridor. He turned the first corner before bolter-fire shredded the walls behind him. Uriah dodged and weaved around the corridors, trying to stay one step ahead of the Orlocks.

'Voice!' Uriah said, trying to keep his fleeting breath.

'Here! What's the matter?'

'Trap,' Uriah said, dodging around another corner, 'for me. Pursued.'

'What can I do?'

'Not sure!'

'I have an idea. Keep your head down.'

Uriah kept his bearings despite twisting and turning through the corridors of the large building. Throughout his tour of this floor and the one above it, he'd found three rooms with unprotected windows. He navigated for the first room, but upon turning the corner, found himself face-to-face with two surprised Orlocks. Uriah reacted far more quickly than they did; he elbowed the first in the face and pushed him into the second man before running past them both.

More shots rang out, but Uriah remained one corner ahead of impending death. He relied on pure instinct to push himself forwards. Another corner turned at the intersection of two corridors and Uriah came up behind an Orlock search party. He turned to avoid them and headed for the nearby stairwell. Angry voices erupted behind him; Uriah darted up the stairs.

'Done,' Voice said.

'What?' Uriah asked, trying to keep his sentences short.

'You'll see. Just get out.'

The Orlocks had yet to spread upstairs, allowing Uriah to run straight for his next exit. Uriah's pursuers had dropped further behind, following several successful feints, and he reached what he hoped was the right door before they spotted him again. He shouldered his way through as a new volley of shots rang out and punched the wall around him.

Uriah slammed the door shut and heaved the metallic cabinet against it. Something in his back twinged at the heavy weight, but Uriah added it to the mental tally of the week's exhausting damage and pushed it out of his thoughts. He crawled out of the window and was on the ledge when the Orlocks lacerated the door with shredding gunfire. It would only take them a moment to realise Uriah was no longer inside.

With a pained grunt, Uriah leapt to the support pylon girder, and from there, to another building ledge across the very narrow alley. He dived through the broken window. The building was derelict, save for the odd transient and addict. Uriah fled down the stairs, hoping he'd make it out the front door before the Orlocks could alert Slag that he'd escaped into an adjoining building.

Uriah neared the ground floor when shots rang out on the streets and the rumble of heavy engines shook the walls, dislodging trickles of dust. A quick glance through the window revealed Cybilline Sisterhood gangers on bikes, besieging Corval's building. The Orlocks were locked in a pitched battle with the Escher, and the fight had spilled out into the streets.

'You called in your old House?' Uriah asked.

'Nothing like the murder of sisters to draw swift retribution. The first wave consists of those Escher already mobile or in the area. More will come. The Escher gangs are tightly knit against outsiders.'

'Thank you,' Uriah said. 'I don't know what that cost you.'

'Not nearly as much as letting you die. I am charging you by the hour.'

'Duly noted,' Uriah said with a grateful smile. 'And worth every Guilder credit I can scrape together.'

'Did you find the implant?' Voice asked.

'No,' Uriah said. 'And I lost my new bolt pistol. I was rather fond of that piece.'

'What's your next step?'

'Not sure yet,' Uriah said. He was heading down the refuse-cluttered hallway to a side exit. 'Someone betrayed my position to Slag. The Orlocks were expecting me.'

'Someone? From inside your House?'

'Yes,' Uriah said. 'But the only person who knew my exact location was you.'

'I didn't betray you,' Voice said.

'I know,' Uriah said, stepping into the alley through a door hanging off one hinge. 'It was one of my own, but I helped him, stupidly enough.'

'I don't understand.'

'Someone broke into my hab block and stole Cantrall's implant and the recordings.'

'You didn't mention that to me,' Voice said, sounding annoyed.

'I didn't want to worry you,' Uriah said. 'And it was embarrassing, frankly, that someone in my House, my gang, would do this to one of his own.'

'I'll give the Escher this,' Voice responded. 'They are loyal to their sisters.'

'Then why did you walk away?' Uriah asked, trying to ignore the gunshots and screams echoing through the streets. He stuck to the back alleys and took the long way to the tram.

'A subject for another time. Cantrall had five patients, how did your betrayer know where you'd be?'

'I tell you what,' Uriah said, pausing. 'I'll answer two of your questions if you answer one of mine.'

'Jester…' Voice said, 'I'm trying to help you work this through. And you're not exactly safe yet.'

'Actually, who betrayed me and how they did so is not vital to your work. You're curious, plain and simple. And besides, it'll help me keep my mind off the pain. Two questions – within limits – ask away,' Uriah said, grimacing against the slow creep of ache that permeated his body.

'Fine,' Voice said. 'But you get one question for my two, within limits.'

'Agreed.'

'All right, how did Slag know where to find you?'

'My stupid fault,' Uriah admitted. 'When I was studying the pictures of the gangers, I identified two of them
by name and placed question marks next to the other
names. That list was taken.'

'Ah,' Voice said. 'And with news of the attack on Jaffa
Hur spreading–'

'That left Corval as my only remaining lead.'

Uriah reached the edge of the street. Several blocks
away, the Soulsplitters were trying to escape, but more
Cybilline Sisterhood Escher were arriving. Uriah darted
across the street to the next set of alleys.

'Your second question?' Uriah asked once he was
safely inside the alleyway.

'Your question first,' Voice said. 'I'm still thinking.'

'Very well. Why did you leave the Escher?'

There was a pause. Finally, Uriah stopped and rested
his back against the alley wall.

'Too painful?' Uriah asked.

'I helped a mavant escape slavery,' Voice said.

'Ah, a secret lover?'

'Not so secret,' she said. 'They quartered him rather
than kill one of their sisters. There was supposed to be
a lesson in that, but I never saw it.'

'I'm sorry,' Uriah said, embarrassed. 'That was insensi-
tive of me.'

'My question,' Voice said. 'Do you have a lover in your
life?'

It was Uriah's turn to consider the question. He hesitated before finally continuing down the alley. The
sounds of gunfire grew more distant. 'Yes,' he said. 'And
I love her dearly.'

That drew a pause from Voice.

'You best be on your way,' Voice said. 'Just remember,
you owe me four more questions.'

'What?' Uriah asked. 'How'd you figure that?'

'You asked me two questions, not one. Don't think I didn't notice. You asked me why I left the Escher and you also asked me if I had a secret lover. Two questions hidden in one. You owe me four more questions, Jester.'

'Damn,' Uriah said, laughing. 'I didn't think you'd noticed that.'

'Go,' Voice said. 'Sounds like you could use the rest. We'll talk later.'

Uriah paused long enough to catch his breath before continuing his escape. He desperately needed sleep, but the day was not yet won. Three implants were still up for grabs.

'PULL OUT!' SLAG ordered, striding for his bike while his men provided cover fire. If Slag was worried, he showed no sign of it.

'We lost Uriah!' one of his men shouted, ducking from the return fire.

'Noticed,' Slag said, unflinching. He swept one leg over the carriage of his bike. 'The leg?'

'The implant? Right here!' another man said, holding a wrapped cloth with a blood stain at one end.

Slag paused and held out his hand. The Soulsplitter holding the stump stayed low to the ground. He passed the stump to Slag, who promptly fitted it under his own arm.

'We're leavin',' Slag said, his demeanor calm.

'What about them?' another man shouted from behind the cover of his heavy bike, shooting at several Escher.

'Not them you gotta worry about,' Slag said, gunning the engine. Two shots ricocheted of the bike's chassis. Slag didn't blink. His men look confused.

Slag kicked his bike into a screeching fit, his rear wheel fishtailing, his heavy tires gouging the street. As the remaining Soulsplitters raced for their bikes, an

armoured truck swept around the corner; Slag, unde-
terred, released the brakes and hurtled straight for it.

'Enforcers!' a Soulsplitter yelled, referring to the local
authorities.

The heavily-plated armoured car turned and spun
into a bootlegger one hundred and eighty degrees,
bringing the back end forward. It screeched to a halt on
the street, bullets ricocheting off its skin. Before the rear
doors swung open, Slag knew what was coming. He
pulled away, off to the side and gave the rear door a
wide berth as he was about to pass by.

Sure enough, the rear doors swung open, revealing a
shielded turret bolter manned by someone in scuffed
chain-armour. The Enforcer squeezed the trigger and
unleashed a barrage of high-velocity rounds. In seconds
the armoured car was pacifying the street, ripping walls
to shreds, causing bikes to explode and killing Cybilline
Sisterhood Escher and Soulsplitter Orlocks alike.

Slag flew by the armoured car and turned a street corner before the roof turret could lock on him. He headed
for one of the shuttle elevators, the implant still under
his arm, the sounds of gunfire fading in the background.

CHAPTER: EIGHT

War is the absence of reason. But then, life often demands unreasonable responses.

— Delaque Operational Commandments
from the *Book of Lies.*

THIS HAD GONE on long enough. Between the loss of the first implant to Kaden in Cantrall's building, the ransacking of his hab and the information leak that had allowed Slag to ambush him, Uriah was tired of being on the defensive.

It was time to act. This was something he should have dealt with at the outset.

The first step was acquiring new tools, since the Orlocks had stripped him of this old ones. What hurt him the most was the loss of his beloved bolt pistol; he was fond of that weapon and would be hard pressed to replace it with something of equal worth. He doubted Weapon's Master Coryin would offer him another chance on that front.

'You lost the pistol?' Coryin asked, disbelief stretched high on his eyebrow. The bald man was unhappy, that much was obvious.

'I know,' Uriah said, trying to soothe Coryin's rising temper, but too tired to actually care. 'It was a fine weapon, but I had little choice.'

'So you've said,' Coryin responded. He went back to work along the range, bucket in hand, collecting shell casings from the stands. 'The truth is that weapon was worth more than your hide.'

'Well of course you'd feel that way,' Uriah said, snapping. 'Believe it or not, your precious weapons are here to serve us, not the other way around.'

Coryin spun around and stormed to within a nose hair of the smaller handler. 'Don't you speak down to me, boy, don't you ever! I didn't say my equipment was worth more than a Delaque's life. I said it was worth more than yours.'

The comment caught Uriah off guard. 'So that's the game. Where's this spite coming from, eh Coryin?'

'The great Uriah Storm,' Coryin said. 'Always laughing in the face of danger.'

'That's what this is, jealousy?'

'No,' Coryin said. 'I'm tired of your cavalier attitude. I'm tired of you treating everything – everyone – around you as a joke. Like it's all beneath your notice. Worthy of nothing but your contempt. So typical of Percal's Handlers, but none more so than you.'

Uriah paused. 'All right,' he said. 'Maybe I am cavalier with those around me, but that's nothing to do with contempt.'

'You don't act like it.'

'Why this sudden rush of animosity? You've never been one to hold your tongue, before. So why am I hearing this now?'

'Like you don't know,' Coryin said, returning to his errands.

'Enlighten me.'

'You were protected, Uriah. Percal's shining protégé. He said you were to want for nothing and though you were not of the Requisitioners we provided for you as per the terms of our alliance, even when it meant holding our tongues.'

'But you're no longer holding your tongue. Why? You no longer scared of Percal? Or are you saying I no longer hold Percal's favour?'

'It doesn't appear so, no.'

'What have you heard?' Uriah asked.

Coryin sighed and stopped. He didn't turn around, but neither did he ignore Uriah.

'Please,' Uriah said. 'What have you heard?'

'Nothing specific,' Coryin said, putting down the bucket. 'But you know Percal. He never speaks in specifics. He leaves it to you to interpret his statements and act accordingly. So long as he doesn't dirty his hands.'

'Then the implication?'

'The implication is *no more special treatment*. The implication is you are no longer the favoured son. It's as though you're not even a Handler any more. At least in his eyes.'

Uriah listened, but his tired mind raced at the thoughts. He enjoyed Percal's support, but he never saw the reach of it. This was a new element in his life, one to which he was blind. Was he really that privileged that the other gangs in Shadowstrohm were forced to heed his concerns? If he was, everything made more sense. He had no true friends among the Delaque, but always seemed to find them outside the House, outside Percal's influence. Was this Percal's doing, to alienate him from his peers? Or was this inter-House jealousy for his position as Percal's protégé.

'Who is, then? Who is the new favoured son?' Uriah asked.

'I'm – I'm not sure,' Coryin admitted. 'I don't think there is one.'

'What of Kaden?' Uriah asked. 'Could it be him?'

Coryin laughed. 'That fool? As much as Kaden would like to believe he's Percal's favourite, he isn't. Or at least,

Percal hasn't offered him the same preferential treatment that he gave you and the others.'

'Others?' Uriah said.

Coryin studied him, searching his face hard with a mixture of surprise and pity, Uriah realised.

'He's really kept you on a tight leash, hasn't he,' Coryin said.

'What others?' Uriah asked.

Coryin looked around, as though sharing in some great mystery. 'Before you, Percal had other protégés. Very few lasted long – a few months here, a year there. Killed in duty, you know. A couple, though, a couple possessed your skill.'

'What happened to them?'

'One retired and vanished. Talented lass, she was, and popular. Percal didn't like that, so he pushed her harder than most. Finally got to her. At first, we thought Percal had a thing for her and was jealous that he had to share her. But it was his way of keeping his Handlers from getting too close to anyone else. His way of controlling them.'

'Why didn't anyone tell me?' Uriah asked, shocked.

'Nobody wanted to cross Percal. After her, it was understood that you left Percal's protégés alone. It was difficult to ignore some, and easier for others.'

'Like me?' Uriah asked.

'You're good at what you do, Uriah,' Coryin said, 'I'll admit that. But you're arrogant, and if you aren't, then you act it. That little stunt on the firing range a couple of days ago was typical of your behaviour and it did nothing to ingratiate you with your Housemates. Percal had his work cut out with you. Stroke your ego enough for you to drive others away.'

'That's not fair,' Uriah said, but his comment felt feeble on his lips.

'You're a student of Percal. Enough to know that nothing is fair,' Coryin said.

'So noted,' Uriah said. He pitched his back against one of the metal firing stands and sank to the ground. He felt exhausted, but worse, defeated. 'You mentioned Percal had another protégé, someone of my skill?'

Coryin nodded. 'He was executed. For betraying House Delaque. I never knew the specifics. Percal kept that matter internal to his gang.'

There was a moment's silence as Uriah absorbed the full impact of the news; Coryin stood there, studying him.

'Percal's kept me close to control what I hear,' Uriah said, his own voice distant and numb to his ears. 'And everyone knew?'

'Not everyone. Only those of us who've survived our service knew Percal's game. A handful really. No, most people believe you're privileged or spoiled or both.' Coryin waited for Uriah to say something, but Uriah was quiet, absorbing the news. 'Wait here,' Coryin said, finally.

Uriah sat in the comfortable dark of the quiet shooting range, reflecting on everything that was happening. Coryin returned a short time later, holding something wrapped in cloth. Uriah took it and unwrapped it. It was another slender bolt pistol with silver engraved siding, two extra magazines and a box of rounds.

'And for the Machine Spirit's sake,' Coryin said, about to walk away, 'don't lose her too.'

'Thank you,' Uriah said. 'Wait, you believe in the Machine Spirit too?'

'Most Requisitioners pay some lip service to the Machine Spirit, but yes, I do believe. It's hard working with devices without seeing the miracle in them. I'm more surprised that you do, however. Never seen a Handler thank the Machine. Percal isn't the type to encourage faith in anything but himself.'

'It was something I picked up on assignment,' Uriah said.

'I'd be more careful about talking to the Machine Spirit in public. I saw you doing it on the range.'

'There's nothing wrong with paying it thanks.'

'Not for some folks. Others think it's a Van Saar streak – they might question your loyalties.'

'I'll keep that in mind. Thank you, again,' Uriah said.

Coryin nodded and left Uriah alone to his thoughts.

SLAG KILLED THE throttle on his bike and coasted to a stop next to the snub-nosed truck. An Orlock ganger, a small man with a soft stomach and sagging features, was leaning against the vehicle; he stood when Slag stopped.

'You got it?' the ganger asked, eyeing the wrapped and bloodied cloth in Slag's grip.

Slag pulled Uriah's bolt pistol from his waistband and pointed it at the ganger. The Orlock immediately brought his hands up.

'Hey! Whoa! Why you pointin' that thing at me?'

'Go ahead,' Slag said. 'Ask me another dumb question.'

'Okay, okay,' the ganger said, lowering his hands. 'Sorry.'

Slag casually tossed the wrapped implant at the man with one hand. It nearly bowled the ganger over.

'Heavy,' the ganger said, eyeing Slag and getting a better grip on the implant.

'Yeah,' Slag said. 'Get the leg to Stainstrip Research Facility. They're expectin' it.'

'Yeah, I can do that,' the ganger said.

Slag levelled the pistol at the ganger, whose eyes widened.

'And no detours,' Slag said. 'No takin' it to other suppliers first. No borrowin' components. You got thirty minutes to reach Stainstrip. At thirty-one minutes, you're a dead man and I'm the killin' stroke.'

'All right,' the ganger said, not daring to move a muscle, his brow slick with sweat.

Slag didn't break eye contact, nor did he lower his pistol.

After a moment, the nervous ganger blurted out with 'What?'

'You have twenty-nine minutes,' Slag said.

'All right, all right,' the ganger replied, getting in the truck. 'I'm going.'

SHADOWSTROHM FELT LIKE a different place. Uriah examined his surroundings with a new awareness; he studied the people with a new wary appreciation. He'd always interpreted their stares as those of jealousy for his skills or for the favour the Handlers enjoyed in Shadowstrohm. Percal had taught him that lie; better with which to alienate him. Now he saw the cold edge to their eyes – the dislike, the disinterest, the loathing in some cases. This was a barren hostility, one he'd never recognized before.

He was an unwanted stranger in his own House.

Uriah recounted and questioned everything he remembered Percal telling him. Use people before they use you; falsehood is more comforting than the truth; there are no friends, only assets. Everything seemed designed to alienate him from his peers. Uriah even found himself questioning those lessons found in the Book of Lies, a tome of advice partly written by Percal himself.

Then, like all emotions left to fester, Uriah's sorrow turned into indignation and then anger. He was being used, nothing more than a pawn in a game. Uriah thought himself above that, above the board itself, setting the pieces into motion rather than being manipulated by them.

Uncertainty was also playing on his nerves. If he was a piece to Percal, which piece was he? A Citizen, an Ecclesiarch or perhaps even the King? Uriah wasn't sure, if only because of recent events. Was Percal using Uriah for a feint, sacrificing him for a more important play? Or was he still needed on the board?

Actually, Uriah realised, it didn't matter. The regicide player loses his power to control and dictate the game when the pieces gain autonomy or self-awareness. They are no longer restricted to a strict range of movements determined by extended laws. Uriah realised that was exactly what was happening to him. If he was a regicide piece, then perhaps it was time to play the game his way.

Control the board, or leave it entirely.

The thought stopped Uriah in his tracks. The disadvantage shared by all regicide pieces, even with autonomy, was that their scope remained limited. They couldn't see the entire board from their vantage; only the player could. Then, as someone who controlled the pieces, you were locked in an entirely different game, one where the board consisted of two adversaries. At that point, the rules of the game changed, because you didn't play to win, you played to engineer your adversary's downfall. It wasn't about playing the game itself, it was about playing the other person.

That's the trap Percal set for himself, Uriah thought. *He went from being a piece to being a player without realising there was no real transition. And if I'm not careful, it's the trap I'll fall into as well.*

Uriah entered his hab block using his new key and checked the laser tripwire he'd set under the sofa. It hadn't been activated. Nobody else had entered his sanctuary. Uriah collapsed onto the sofa and allowed the aches of the day to soak into him. He was tired, on the verge of exhaustion.

I can no longer play the game. I must survive on my own terms. I have to force my rivals to keep pace with me.

Uriah chuckled at the irony of the last sentence and fell asleep.

SLEEP WAS A pitched battle that Uriah was losing. He woke up with a start, the last buzz of the pict screen ringing in his sleep. The light was flashing. Someone had left him a message.

Uriah checked the time, and then regretted doing so. Less than an hour's sleep; just enough to remind him of his exhausted state. The fatigue seemed to accentuate the pain in his joints and the bruised stings.

Uriah replayed the message on the pict screen and caught only bursts of coded static. Morgane needed to see him.

THIS WASN'T AN opportunity for an intimate tryst, as much as Uriah and Morgane wanted it to be. Instead, they stayed on opposite sides of a wall with no easy way to reach one another; their only conduit was a metal grate. The wall was in a relatively unused portion of an abandoned Underhive transport station. Anyone trying to see who either person was speaking with would have to follow a long set of tunnels to the other side. Uriah and Morgane had this place timed to the minute. They could speak for two-and-a-half minutes before they endangered one another.

'Are you all right?' Uriah asked. He stayed near the grate with his back against the wall. He was trying to seem casual even though the station appeared empty.

'I'm fine, my love,' Morgane said. 'I heard something interesting that I think you should know.'

'What is it?'

'A maker by the name of Rot-Tongue spoke to my House today. He wanted to sell us one of Soren's implants. He was hoping we'd have a bounty for the return of Van Saar property.'

'And did they?' Uriah asked.

'No. That's the reason I wanted to speak to you. The House refused to buy back Soren's implants.'

'Is that unusual?'

'Yes it is,' Morgane said. 'We're so territorial with our technology that we offer substantial rewards for the return of intact Van Saar tech, if it's advanced enough.'

'Wasn't Soren sporting some of your newest models?'

'He was,' Morgane said, 'which is why this is so strange.'

'How did you hear about this?' Uriah asked.

'Unlike you Delaque,' Morgane said, 'we Van Saar delight in rumour, especially in the failings of another gang.'

'Rumours can be disinformation, you know,' Uriah chided.

'I know,' Morgane said. 'Which is why I spoke directly to the House representative who dealt with Rot-Tongue. He's an intermediary of my guild. He said the orders to refuse the implant came from high within the Van Saar hierarchy. It came from the House proper.'

'So this Rot-Tongue still has the implant?'

'I believe so, but for how long? I don't know. He was making noise about selling the implant to one of the other Houses.'

'Which means I have to move fast,' Uriah said with a sigh.

'Before you go,' Morgane said, 'there is one other thing.'

'Hurry, we have to leave soon,' Uriah said, checking his timepiece.

'The representative who spoke with Rot-Tongue saw the implant in question... an eye. He's not a technician, but Uriah, he says the eye looks like an older model.'

'So maybe Rot-Tongue was trying to swindle you? Pretend he had the right property.'

'The representative didn't think so. He's dealt with this maker before, and says the man is a professional. He's as close to a House asset as possible without being in our full time employment. Rot-Tongue even provided us with Soren's genetic material from the implant to confirm the owner's identity.'

'So at the very least, something is afoot and Rot-Tongue has some connection to the implants or Soren's death. Thank you, love. You've renewed my faith in this ordeal.'

'Be well, love. I miss you,' Morgane said before Uriah heard her walk away.

Uriah walked away as well, contemplating the turn of events. That House Van Saar refused to buy back the implants, much less even entertain the thought, was troubling in itself. Unfortunately, rather than revealing any truths, it clouded matters further and added another layer to the mystery. Were this the only ordeal facing Uriah, he might have been better suited to handling it. Now Uriah contended with battles on multiple fronts, with Percal playing his own version of the game and Soren's death taking a stranger turn.

Uriah felt exhausted, but he couldn't quit now. There was too much at stake and if he paused, for even a moment, events would spiral beyond his control. It was time to handle both situations and damn the consequences. The first step would be to find Rot-Tongue.

Fortunately, Rot-Tongue was a maker, meaning he dealt with the sale and distribution of illegal or hard-to-obtain products. That meant he'd be easier to find than most, and Uriah knew where to start.

Uriah reached his cycle, its green chassis housing a massive engine and two thick wheels. He hated the fact that he couldn't use this cycle anywhere outside the Underhive. Unfortunately, the Underhive had been lacking in public transportation for Helmawr knows how many millennia but was also a place where Uriah really needed to get around. He mounted the bike, gunned the throttle and tore through the near-abandoned streets. He activated his throat communicator.

'Voice. You there?' Uriah asked.

It took a moment for a groggy-sounding Voice to respond. 'I'm here. I'm here.'

'Sleeping?'

'I don't sleep,' Voice said with a yawn. 'I take small naps to invigorate myself.'

'That's called sleep,' Uriah said with a grin.

'If that's what you call it,' Voice said. 'What do you need, Jester?'

'Two things. First, what's the prognosis on Jaffa's implant? The heart accelerant.'

'I – I haven't dared touch it.'

'What? Why?' Uriah asked, surprised.

'Well, it's a complicated piece of equipment,' Voice said. 'Far superior to the components I'm used to handling. I'm afraid I might damage it if I tamper with it.'

Uriah paused a moment, waiting for something else to follow. He felt a gap in Voice's reason. 'What else?' Uriah asked finally. 'You're holding something back.'

Voice sighed into her transmitter, flooding Uriah's earpiece with a brief wash of static. 'It'll sound strange,' Voice said.

'I won't judge.'

'Very well,' Voice said, obviously steeling herself. 'It feels wrong.'

'What does?' Uriah asked, uncertain.

'The heart accelerant. Every time I set about examining it in-depth, I have second thoughts.'

'You feel strange around it?' Uriah asked. 'Is the Machine Spirit trying to warn you?'

'I don't believe in the Machine Spirit,' Voice said. 'That's a Van Saar thing.'

'Not always,' Uriah said, 'but you feel strange around it.'

'I can't explain it. I don't feel like I should be tampering with the implant. And neither should you.'

'That's remarkably… cryptic.'

'You said you wouldn't judge me,' Voice said, snapping.

'And I'm not,' Uriah said, still zipping through narrowing streets. 'I find it strange that you feel this way. I trust your instincts.'

'Thank you,' Voice replied. 'Should I return it?'

'No,' Uriah said after a moment's consideration. 'Hold on to it. Maybe you can determine why the implant makes you so uneasy.'

'Thank you,' Voice said again. 'I – appreciate your trust. You said you had another question?'

'Yes,' Uriah responded. 'Rot-Tongue. What can you tell me about him?'

URIAH FOLLOWED VOICE's instructions, contacting Rot-Tongue through the appropriate channel. The channel, in this case, was Rot-Tongue's associate and manager, who then forwarded the request for the meeting and potential purchase of Soren's implant. The response came within fifteen minutes. Rot-Tongue was willing to meet.

The meeting spot was an old sewer network, two centuries dry and taken over by the poor, the down-trodden and the mutated. Filth stains still painted the cylindrical corridors and raw sewage still ran down the central trough. People had carved their homes into the walls or taken residence in natural niches, but for the most part, the dwellings were rarely more than three metres deep inside.

Why Rot-Tongue chose to reside in this district was a mystery, but Uriah surmised it was the big fish, small pond syndrome. Rot-Tongue's estate was located in an old pumping hub. Three tunnels converged on the six storey high hub. Crushed within the chamber were several hundred residents perusing the stock of enterprising merchants whose wares were laid out on carpets.

Above, the air extended three-storeys high before reaching the first thick grate that covered half the ceiling like a wide balcony. Six desiccated corpses hung from the metal ceiling, a reminder to those below never to draw the ire of Rot-Tongue for any reason. Above the grate was Rot-Tongue's two-storey sewer mansion, one floor separated from the other by another thick grate. The balcony's ledges for both levels were covered in thick banners of hanging fabric, providing Rot-Tongue with some privacy.

Uriah waited for his turn to speak to the stair guards. When he finally announced his presence, the guards patted him down. They found the knife that he wanted them to find and missed the pistol he wanted them to miss.

The metal stairs were enclosed within a chain-linked cage, and they followed the curve of the cylindrical room. Uriah mounted the stairs to the second floor, where more guards awaited.

The so-called mansion extended over thirty metres along the diameter; gossamer fabrics hung from the grate above and undulated at the barest hint of movement; carpets covered the floors, as did mounds of cushions that served as chairs and sofas; columns extended to the grated ceiling above. Oil-lamp globes, as well as a haze of smoke from water-bubble pipes added to the exotic nature of Rot-Tongue's pavilion.

Rot-Tongue sat on a throne of pillows while four guards – dressed in heavy leathers – flanked him. He was a big man, even without the body fat dripping from his frame. His straw coloured hair hung loose at his shoulders and the moustache did little to hide his baby-face; he wore billowing robes and walked barefoot. Rot-Tongue was aptly named, though Uriah was at a loss to identify what malady was capable of turning someone's tongue into a masticated, rotting piece of flesh. Half of it looked bitten away, and when he spoke, he spoke with a slur. Uriah did not recognize him; he wasn't one of Cantrall's customers.

'You're the Choir, I presume?' Rot-Tongue asked, his voice lazy and imperious.

'Jakob the Choir. Jakob is fine,' Uriah replied, slipping into his false identity.

'What brings you to my home?' Rot-Tongue asked.

'I was told you had an implant for sale, an eye purchased from the bio-surgeon Cantrall?'

'Told? By whom?'

'I can't say,' Uriah said, shrugging.

'Which House are you with, then?'

'I freelance for the Van Saar.'

'They didn't want the implant.'

'Officially, you're right,' Uriah said, slipping into his prepared story. 'Unofficially, the House has been having problems – scavengers poaching Van Saar agents for their implants and selling them back to the House.'

'So?'

'The Van Saar have been refusing to purchase back implants to curtail the trade against them. They hire me to make the transactions on their behalf.'

'Why are you telling me this?' Rot-Tongue asked, looking unconvinced.

'You're still in good favour with the House and you have supporters. I also think you might have scared the Van Saar when you threatened to sell the implant to another House.'

'Is that so?' Rot-Tongue asked, looking bored again. His eyes wandered about the room.

'I am curious, though.' Uriah said.

'Hm?'

'How is it you obtained the implant? I thought Cantrall implanted it in a client.'

'He did not,' Rot-Tongue said.

Uriah realised it must have been the client who took the device rather than having it implanted.

'He took it to have it grafted on by someone cheaper and I took it from him. He owed me money.'

'And this man?' Uriah asked.

'He doesn't owe me money, anymore.' With that, Rot-Tongue looked down at an exposed portion of the grate. A piece of chain was tied to the edge of the grate's hole; from it dangled someone's corpse.

Uriah couldn't identify the man through the grate, but his hair colour and style looked similar to the ganger who had walked away with the eye.

Rot-Tongue sat forward and raised his arms. Immediately, two guards grabbed him by his elbows and gently lifted him to his feet. The rotund maker walked to the pavilion's balcony, where the two guards rushed to draw aside the curtains; Rot-Tongue studied his domain. The remaining two guards stared at Uriah.

'Do you like my kingdom?' Rot-Tongue asked, leaning against the railing and watching the people below.

'Most impressive,' Uriah said, standing.

'Down here, I am a God,' Rot-Tongue said, stretching out his arms. 'By my word, men live and die.'

Uriah said nothing.

'Some men, though, some men would like nothing more than to kill a God eh, Jakob?'

'I wouldn't know,' Uriah replied. 'I'm a businessman.'

'Really?' Rot-Tongue asked, turning to face Uriah. He rested against the railing. 'You know, I wouldn't take you for a Van Sarr.'

'I only freelance for them. Much like yourself,' Uriah said. He wasn't sure where this was going, but he knew it was going somewhere. Uriah prepared himself, slowly drawing the pistol from the sleeve of his coat.

'No,' Rot-Tongue said. 'I wouldn't call you a Van Saar. You strike me more as… an assassin.'

The two guards were expecting to get the drop on Uriah, but they weren't fast enough for the nimble Handler. They brought their autoguns up at the same time Uriah drew his pistol and emptied a round into each of their skulls. The gunshots echoed through the pavilion with a sharp snap. Uriah knew he was counting his life in the seconds. Were the guards below expecting to hear gunfire? It didn't matter; Uriah was in for a fight.

Rot-Tongue looked horrified at the sudden speed at which events turned against him. He froze. His two bodyguards, however, reacted far quicker.

Uriah dived behind the nearest column, shots whining past him and dinging off the metal grate. He

exchanged a few shots with the guards, switching
from one side to the other to prevent them from
flanking him. Uriah was certain all this gunfire would
draw the remaining guards upstairs. There wasn't
much time left. He looked around in between snapping off shots at the two guards. It took a quick
second to register the oil lamp globes and hanging
fabrics.

Muttering a quick prayer, Uriah fired at a nearby
globe. The shot splattered oil and ignited it; the hanging fabrics nearby caught fire. Uriah shot again,
hitting another globe and spraying another curtain
with flame.

Rot-Tongue shrieked at the inferno spreading along
the web of fabrics like a lit fuse. The carpets covering
the grates upstairs caught fire as well, spreading the
blaze further.

'Do something!' Rot-Tongue cried with a hysterical
shriek.

Uriah fired again at the guards, keeping them
pinned down, before directing his attention to the
stairs. The two guards from downstairs had just
arrived, their heads level with the grate. Uriah shot
the first in the temple; the other guard retreated fast,
out of sight.

The blaze spread far quicker than Uriah anticipated. Waves of flame sheathed the ceiling and the
fire was spreading fast along the curtains. Still, if
there was one lesson that Percal had taught him –
one lesson Uriah could trust – it was that victory
belonged to the calm. A flurry of erratic gunfire
proved Percal correct; the guards were panicking, no
thanks to Rot-Tongue's hysteria, and rushing Uriah's
position. Uriah fired around the column, catching
both men in their sprint. One guard fired a shot that
struck him.

The round nicked Uriah in the left arm, cutting across his bicep. It was a white-hot explosion of pain. Uriah stifled a cry and the sudden wave of nausea. He continued firing, catching both men in the open. They both dropped; the pistol clicked without the accompanying thunder; Uriah was firing blanks. He was out of shots.

Rot-Tongue continued shrieking and was trying to find a way past the flames and the wounded Handler. Uriah raised his pistol, praying Rot-Tongue didn't realise he had spent his ammunition. The rotund maker, however, was in no state for rational thought.

Despite the stabbing pain in his arm and the accumulating smoke that made his eyes water, Uriah rushed up to Rot-Tongue and pushed him up against the railing with the gun barrel to his forehead. People below were running and screaming.

'Don't shoot! Don't shoot!' Rot-Tongue shrieked.

'The implant!' Uriah said, 'where is it?'

'I sold it!' Rot-Tongue said, crying. 'Don't shoot!'

'To who?'

'The Delaque, one of their Handlers!'

'Kaden!' Uriah said, snarling. 'Was it Kaden?'

'Yes, yes!' Rot-Tongue replied. 'Now please, I don't want to burn.'

'Not yet!' Uriah said, shouting over the din of the roaring blaze. 'Why did you attack me? Who said I was an assassin? Was it Kaden?'

'Yes! He said you were sent to kill me!'

'What else?' Uriah asked, pressing the gun barrel into Rot-Tongue's temple.

'Nothing! I swear! Just–'

'Just? Just what?'

'He said to open the curtains on the balcony. So he could see me shoot you!'

Uriah's head whipped up. His eyes darted across the wall opposite the balcony. Only he was too late.

A skull-probe floated in the air, lazy and watching Uriah with its bionic eye. Beyond it, in an old drain pipe that was three storeys above the ground, Kaden was kneeling and staring down the scope of a sniper rifle aimed right at him. Uriah winced as the gunshot echoed through the chamber; he felt certain of the outcome. It took Uriah a quick moment to realise the shot wasn't intended for him. Rot-Tongue slumped forward, the back of his skull a rose of exposed brain and skull, his eyes emptied of life.

With a broad grin, Kaden gave Uriah a casual salute before vanishing into the darkness of the drain pipe. The skull probe followed, bobbing lazily behind.

Uriah let Rot-Tongue drop and uttered a small curse. Fire engulfed the floor, cutting him off from the stairs. His only hope was a three storey drop over the balcony railing. After tucking away the pistol, Uriah manoeuvered his way over the railing and lowered himself until he was dangling. Despite himself, Uriah waited until the heat of raging flames threatened to eat at his fingers. Then he let go.

The ground rushed up faster than Uriah expected, barely giving him time to fall properly. It still didn't prepare Uriah for the shock of feeling his legs hammered up into his body and his jaw slammed shut with a jarring crack. Uriah hit the ground, stunned from the fall. A moment later, the numbness dissipated and Uriah's body screamed its cacophony of complaints. Screaming people ran past him, oblivious to his pain.

Uriah tried to stand, but his legs failed him. Someone grabbed his trench coat and began pulling it off him. Uriah reached for the gun with blind instinct and waved it in the face of a female scavenger dressed in rags. She ran.

Through the din, someone shouted. It sounded like orders, though Uriah couldn't hear the barking man clearly. The intention was clear to the Delaque Handler. They were after him. Uriah stumbled forward, suddenly pressing into the backs of the frightened mob. More people surged in around him, holding him up in the rush of bodies, pushing him forward and through one of the tunnels.

Uriah didn't stop running, even after he was lost, even after he careened off several walls in his mad escape. It would take him another couple of hours before he finally found the surface.

CHAPTER: NINE

*If war must be fought, then ensure it's being fought
between your enemies and not with you.*

– Delaque Operational Commandments
from the *Book of Lies*.

THE NEWS SPREAD quickly. The Orlocks had besieged an
Escher stronghold and murdered its matriarch, Corval.
The resulting street battle claimed dozens of lives and
sparked gang skirmishes across Hive Primus.

Activity in Shadowstrohm had increased substantially
as a result; not for the reasons most people suspected,
but Kaden was enjoying his ringside seat to the event
nonetheless.

Kaden sat across from Percal, watching quietly as the
man issued orders to various agents. Most of his instructions were issued quickly, using the vox. Seeing Percal in
person was a privilege few people actually experienced.
Kaden felt smug in that regard.

'Utopia, dear,' Percal addressed someone over the vox
caster, 'the Escher are stretched thin. It's the perfect time
to ingratiate yourself into their ranks. Say the Strong Sisters or the Billie-Clubs?' Percal switched channels. 'Is
the strike team ready? All women? Good. Hit the
Orlock's Meltpile facility by tonight and make it look

like an Escher attack.' Percal switched channels again.
'Roedai, I need those updates! Where are the other
Houses in this conflict?'

Kaden had never seen Percal this purposeful before.
He looked like he was actually enjoying himself. Kaden
waited until the master Handler was done with his current batch of assignments before bothering Percal.

'So why hit Meltpile?' Kaden asked.

'Think,' Percal instructed, checking incoming messages on his private monitor.

Kaden considered it for a moment before shrugging.
'Are you trying to prolong this? Take advantage of the
situation?'

'If that's your guess, then it must be right,' Percal said,
still distracted.

Kaden waited in silence, but quiet was never his thing.
'You need somethin' done?'

'How about sitting quietly?' Percal said, engrossed in
his reading.

'Okay,' Kaden said. The silence lasted another
moment before, 'but you did call me, right? Figured you
needed something.'

'Kaden,' Percal warned.

'Because I should be out there, you know? Gettin' the
implants. Kickin' Uriah around some.'

Percal sighed and pinched the bridge of his missing
nose. Kaden suppressed a shudder.

'Fine,' Percal said. 'You wish to talk. Let's talk. Why did
you let Uriah see you?'

'What, at Rot-Tongue's place?' Kaden shrugged. 'I had
Uriah dead to rights–'

'I told you I didn't want him harmed.'

'I didn't do nothing. Just made him sweat a little. Let
him know I had the best of him.'

'Handlers are supposed to work quietly behind the
scenes,' Percal said, impatiently.

'Well, yeah,' Kaden said in agreement. 'Most times I do. But with Uriah it's different, right? It's part of the game. Sportsmanship, right? Tends to get bloody.'

'Be very careful,' Percal said. 'You and Uriah are playing entirely different games.'

'That's right. I'm winning. He isn't,' Kaden said, laughing.

Percal leaned forward. 'I thought the goal was to strengthen the House? Strengthen the Handlers?'

'Sure,' Kaden replied, unabashed. 'But if there's personal glory for the taking, then why not. So long as it don't hurt the House or Handlers, right?'

'I wonder…' Percal said.

'Wonder away,' Kaden said with a grin.

'I doubt Uriah would make the same mistakes that you're making.'

Kaden shrugged. 'Are you paying me for style or for results? So far, I've got you two implants.'

'Actually,' Percal said, 'the way I see it, you've failed to secure the four remaining implants.'

'And I like to think that I haven't got them for you yet.'

'Then shouldn't you be out looking for them instead of pestering me?' Percal asked.

Kaden stood up with a heavy sigh. 'That's what I've been saying! You're the one who called me in.'

'Yes,' Percal said. 'I wanted to tell you to stop attracting attention.'

'You don't want me pushing after Uriah?'

Percal sighed. 'No. But stop being so flagrant about it.'

Kaden shrugged. 'Whatever you say, boss.'

It wasn't until he'd left Percal's office that he muttered to himself. 'Stop being flagrant about it? Where's the fun in that?'

THE CHAMBER WAS relatively spacious, big enough for the large man and his assistant. One wall was covered with all manner of optographs, from grainy ones taken at range to full-colour jobs. Each shot was the picture of someone, their name inscribed or their face occasionally crossed out with red. None of the subjects ever realised they were being shot.

'Well met, Uriah,' the large Information Culler said. Despite his congenial smile and bright green eyes made more brilliant by his red hair and beard, he never offered his hand.

Uriah nodded instead and smiled despite the numbing fatigue and joint pain flaring throughout his body. He sat on the comfortable couch and almost melted in relief. His loud groan drew a smile from the assistant, a black-haired girl barely old enough to be out of the House scholam.

'Derrik, you have good news, I hope?' Uriah asked.

'Depends. Is one out of three good news?' Derrik asked.

'Only if the one out of the three isn't Rot-Tongue.'

'Who's Rot-Tongue?'

'Perfect,' Uriah said, satisfied.

Derrik looked perplexed and flipped through the optographs on his desk. 'No, seriously. Which one is Rot-Tongue?'

Uriah smiled. 'You can't stand not knowing someone's name.'

'It's my job. If I didn't know names, you'd be lost.'

'True,' Uriah said. 'You managed to identify one of the pictures I sent you?'

'I did. This man,' Derrik said, pushing an optograph toward Uriah.

Uriah leaned forward and studied the picture. It was a Goliath ganger, a small compact man with all the muscle of that House, but shorter by far. 'Does he have a name and affiliation?' Uriah asked.

'His name's Rival. He lairs in the Anachrolis District, fifth level.'

'What does he do?' Uriah asked, already dreading the answer.

'He's the head of a gang. The Black Rats.'

Uriah threw his arms in the air. 'Why is it every one of these fools leads a gang? Couldn't I find a toadie or a minion?'

'Well,' Derrik said, 'they were all clients of Cantrall, correct? Cantrall was expensive. Not many toadies could afford him.'

'Yes,' Uriah said, his eyes narrowing. 'How'd you know about Cantrall?'

'Kaden,' Derrik said with casual aplomb. 'He brought in the same exact optos a short time after you. Only, he was far more "generous" with his information.'

'Does he know about Rival?' Uriah asked.

'No,' Derrik said, smiling. 'Not yet.'

'You saved it for me first? To what do I owe the pleasure or is it a favour?'

'A bit of both. I don't like Kaden,' Derrik said. 'And favours are never a bad thing to have.'

'But you've already offered me the information,' Uriah said, grinning.

'Only because you're an honourable man. I've dealt with you enough to know that. Besides, unlike Kaden, you've always kept the Information Cullers current on your intelligence. We appreciate that.'

'Fair enough,' Uriah said. 'Respect, a favour and our mutual dislike of Kaden it is.'

'Now,' Derrik said with a sigh. 'Which one of these chaps is Rot-Tongue?'

Uriah leaned forward and tapped the picture of a ganger with greasy brown hair. 'Well that's not actually Rot-Tongue. This man owed Rot-Tongue money, Rot-Tongue collected with interest. Besides, Rot-Tongue's dead now,' Uriah added, sitting back. 'Courtesy of Kaden.'

Derrik frowned. 'Doesn't make sense. If Kaden knew how to find him, why give me the picture?'

'Kaden didn't know. Rot-Tongue contacted us. That's not important right now. I'm hoping you can help me with something.'

'With what?'

Uriah glanced at the assistant who was hard at work. Derrik smiled. 'I'm grooming her to replace me eventually. She'll need to know everything I know. Besides, she doesn't much like Kaden either.'

The assistant turned her head and raised her eyebrows, as though agreeing.

'Very well,' Uriah said, 'but this has little to do with Kaden. I want to know about Percal's former protégés.'

Derrik inhaled softly and leaned back. 'Tricky matter that,' he said.

'Please. I seem to be following a path that Percal's already laid out before me. I don't know where it's going, but I suspect Percal's former students travelled further along that same road before their circumstances changed.'

'You want to know if there's danger ahead?' Derrik asked, glancing at his assistant's back. She'd stopped working and was listening. 'What I say doesn't leave this room, that goes for the both of you,' Derrik said.

Uriah nodded, as did the assistant who swivelled around in her chair to face her mentor.

'I have enough problems with Percal without this getting out,' Derrik muttered.

'Problems?' Uriah asked.

'I sweep my office for micro-transmitters on a frequent basis. Percal eventually gave up eavesdropping on my conversations, though he still tries on occasion.'

'He spies on you?' Uriah asked, shocked.

'He does it to everyone here. The Seductresses, the Information Cullers, the Cartographers – even his own

Handlers. Only a handful of us know about it. Those of us with enough connections to remain safe.'

'But,' the assistant said before hesitating. She didn't intend to intrude. Derrik smiled his encouragement, and she continued. 'But we're part of the same House.'

'Percal is loyal to the House, but we, my dear are outside of his gang and therefore below his notice. I know of no man or woman whom he holds in equal esteem to himself.'

'So he spies on you?'

'On everyone who barters in information.'

'But why trust me with this?' Uriah said. 'I'm not of your gang and everyone here thinks of me as Percal's lackey and they think me arrogant.'

'The arrogant bit, I can believe,' Derrik said laughing.

Uriah returned the laugh, grateful that someone was comfortable enough around him to joke about the matter.

'I trust you with this,' Derrik said, 'because most of the other protégés were truly arrogant. You're certain and perhaps cocky, but you're also questioning Percal's role for you. The others didn't, and they suffered for it.'

'Tell me about them?'

'I can't remember them all,' Derrik said.

'Then tell me about the most promising ones. The woman who retired and the man who was executed.'

Derrik grimaced. 'Ugly affairs. The woman was called Bettyna. A real beauty she was, with skin a luxurious brown. She was friendly and liked by many in Shadowstrohm.'

'I thought Percal liked his protégés kept isolated,' Uriah said.

'Didn't work, not with her,' Derrik said. 'She was too vibrant for Percal to contain. But he tried. Gods how he tried,' Derrik said, shaking his head at some distant tragic memory.

'What happened?' Uriah asked.

'Percal sent her on errands, never giving her a full accounting of what she faced. Thought he was challenging her or some such nonsense. Some of us, those who liked her, tried softening her rigours. We helped when we could, digging deeper into her assignments, trying to warn her of any pitfalls we uncovered.'

'But you didn't always succeed,' Uriah said.

'No. We didn't. Make no mistake, Bettyna was competent and quick on her feet. She survived situations that would have killed Percal at his best, but she didn't emerge from all unscathed. It's difficult enough playing the game without also counting allies as enemies. Even the best Handler needs safe harbour and a friendly shoulder.'

'And was that you?' Uriah asked. 'Were you her friendly shoulder?'

Derrik laughed before sighing. 'Her head rested on another's shoulder, though I certainly would have been there for the asking.'

'Who then?' Uriah asked.

'Nobody you know. Died before your time,' Derrik said, fixing Uriah with a look.

Uriah caught the gaze and understood immediately. 'Percal killed her lover.'

'No murders to speak of in House Delaque,' Derrik said.

'Only accidents,' his assistant responded, nodding her head.

'But we all knew,' Derrik said, 'especially Bettyna.'

'What happened?' Uriah asked.

'She fled. Once she realised the extent of Percal's deceptions, she just ran.'

'Just like that?' Uriah asked. 'She quit being a Handler and vanished?'

'Nobody simply stops being a Handler, especially anyone serving under Percal,' Derrik said. 'She escaped, with help from allies, but Percal wouldn't leave it alone. He tried to find her, like some petulant child looking for his favourite toy.'

'For how long?' the assistant asked.

'Months. Eventually Bettyna realised she was no longer safe here. Rumour was she fled to another hive.'

'Are there such things?' the assistant asked, her eyes wide in amazement.

'Nobody knows for sure. I like to think there are,' Derrik said with a chuckle.

'Where is she now?' Uriah asked.

'I wish I knew,' Derrik said with a sad smile. 'I miss her kind face. I lost track of her after she left, but I'd like to think she's doing well.'

Uriah nodded and remained quiet for a moment. Partly to digest what he'd just heard, but partly in respect for Derrik and his memory. Finally, he spoke. 'What of the man who was executed?'

'Nobody missed him,' Derrik said, remembering. 'He was a bastard. Elias, I think was his name. Worshipped the ground Percal stood on and followed in his steps with ruthless ambition. Now there was somebody truly hated.'

'How long after Bettyna was Elias?' Uriah asked.

'A few years. Bettyna was Percal's first or second prize Handler before his skills in manipulation grew. I do remember a quick succession of Handlers following Bettyna, but they either proved inferior by Percal's standards or died on assignments. Elias survived longer than any of them.'

'What happened to him?' Uriah asked.

'Caught stealing secrets from us and selling them to the other Houses. Slow and messy execution. We like being the betrayers, never the betrayed,' Derrik said with a twinkle in his eye.

'A traitor under Percal's nose? And his reputation didn't suffer for it?'

'It was Percal who caught him and presided over his execution. But I will give Elias his due. He was stoic during his ordeal.'

'So,' Uriah said, stringing the pieces together, 'after Elias, Percal trained more Handlers, but none really survived until I came along.'

'Like I mentioned,' Derrik said, 'arrogant.'

'You tell me, then,' Uriah said. 'Am I equal to Bettyna and Elias? Or am I some distant third.'

'Bettyna: you two would have challenged each other. I think you would have liked her, though. But you're better than Elias,' Derrik said. 'And better than Kaden.'

'Thank you,' Uriah said. 'I'm sorry people didn't think they could trust me earlier.'

'After Bettyna, we tried ignoring the affairs of the Handlers. It was not our place and frankly it's hard knowing which of Percal's protégés to trust. You all happen to fall under someone's long shadow.'

'And now?' Uriah asked.

'I've always liked you, Uriah,' Derrik said. 'I may not have revealed certain truths to you, but I did treat you better than most. And you always responded in kind.'

'Not better than all, though,' Uriah said, laughing.

'Ah, Bettyna – nobody can ever replace her in my heart.'

'Maybe not,' Uriah said, standing, 'but I hope to hold similar respect in your eyes. Thank you, Derrik.'

'Good luck hunting Rival,' Derrik responded. 'I can't withhold information from Kaden for long, but I'll certainly give you a head start.'

Uriah nodded to the assistant before taking his leave.

* * *

THE ANACHROLIS DISTRICT was an enormous pit, literally. The circular chamber rose over forty storeys high, with the hab blocks and kiosks along the interior shaft overlooking a kilometre-wide courtyard. The street was a wide ledge that corkscrewed its way down to the bottom. No stairs to take, just industrial elevators large enough to accommodate vehicles and the long, winding road.

Stores and food vendors were crammed into shallow niches no more than a couple of metres deep; they catered to the press of human traffic on the street. Unlike Jaffa Hur's junk-pile camp, this Goliath territory was open for commerce.

'Ever been here?' Uriah asked.

'If I remember correctly,' Voice said, 'you owe me the questions.'

'I wasn't pressing you for information,' Uriah said, leaning against the balcony and staring down the maw of the forty-storey pit. 'What I want to know is do I have to describe this place to you?'

'No,' Voice said. 'Some of my favourite cooks are there.'

'Ah, really. Which ones?'

'Try again,' Voice said, laughing. 'That's one question I won't answer.'

'Fair enough,' Uriah replied. 'Did you find the information I need?'

'Yes, I did,' Voice said. 'Rival makes his home there. But the Black Rats don't control the territory with an iron fist.'

'Rare for Goliaths. How come?'

'Because they make more money this way. Avoids scaring away the visitors because of gang skirmishes.'

'Rival sounds like a reasonable man.'

'Perhaps,' Voice said. 'At least until you ask for the implant.'

'True,' Uriah said with a sigh. 'So where am I going? Other than the fifth level.'

'Look for the burnt-out temple – to something called the Adeptus... something or other. I can't pronounce it. The Goliaths make their home there.'

'Any idea of their numbers?'

'Many,' Voice said.

'Wonderfully helpful. Thank you.'

Uriah shouldered his way through the crowd. Everyone here came for supplies and the food, so the mass of people moved at a sluggish clip as they perused the wares and edibles displayed on tables and rugs.

After half an hour of fighting the crowds and navigating only four storeys down, Uriah headed for the elevators. The lines were certain to be long, but not the hours it would take him to walk to the fifth level some thirty storeys down.

As Uriah approached the long line to the bank of industrial elevators, someone behind him cursed.

'Watch where you're going!' a woman said.

Uriah turned. Three Orlock gangers were pushing through the crowd, their eyes locked on him.

Soulsplitters Uriah realised.

Uriah pressed harder into the back of the crowd, pushing his way past people and drawing his share of insults. The three Orlocks kept pace.

'Trouble,' Uriah said.

'Already?' Voice asked. 'Incredible.'

'No, Soulsplitters are here.'

'What're you going to do?' Voice asked.

'Find help,' Uriah replied.

Uriah couldn't hear Voice's response over the insults shouted at him by passers-by. Instead, he directed himself straight to the four Black Rat Goliaths standing near the elevators. The three Orlocks continued their chase, oblivious to the other gangers.

'Orlocks!' Uriah said upon reaching the Goliaths. He pointed to the three advancing men who showed no indication of slowing. Before he could move on, a safe distance from the anticipated firefight, one of the Orlocks shouted:

'It's him! Grab him!'

To Uriah's horror, a flash of recognition crossed the Goliaths' eyes, and four pairs of meaty hands grabbed him. He tried to spin away, but their grip remained true.

The thought floating in Uriah's head was one of simple shock. *They're working together.* Then the rain of fists and feet fell, pummelling him in the face and in the stomach; the four Goliaths and three Orlocks unleashed their fury against him.

After a moment, everything went numb under the painful haze of blows.

Then darkness swallowed Uriah whole.

THE WORLD TASTED of iron, a bitter taste to be sure. His tongue filled his mouth like a fat worm, and there was a gap where one of his molars had sat. Uriah slowly awoke to the world, one filled with a slow, growing awareness of pain.

Something on Uriah's forehead itched and he reached up to scratch it. His arm jolted short of it, however. Someone had shackled his wrists.

'He's awake,' someone said.

Uriah tried to open his eyes, but only one opened fully. The other hurt; he suspected it was swollen almost shut. With his good eye Uriah looked around. He was sitting on the floor, propped up against the wall. His wrists were shackled together and connected to chains bolted to the floor.

The chamber itself was a side-chapel with fire-blackened walls, columns set at intervals and a vaulted ceiling. An arched doorway led into the darkness of the burnt-out temple. Looming over Uriah were a handful of Black Rat Goliaths and Soulsplitter Orlocks. Two stood out in particular. The first was Rival himself, a Goliath ganger shorter than his confederates, but just as well muscled. He stared at Uriah, a mix of derision and intelligent appraisal in his one-eyed gaze. The other eye was covered with an eye patch. The implant was missing.

The second man was Slag.

'The boy don't look like much,' Rival said.

'That's his cunning,' Slag said. 'And your death if you're not careful.'

Uriah's head lolled to the side as the weight of the pain came crashing back in. He was losing consciousness again, unable to muster the strength to keep his head up. In the growing dim, Uriah caught the last of the conversation.

'Gonna kill him?' Rival asked.

'When he's healthy enough.' Slag handed something to Rival. 'I'm going after Corsikan. Get whoever was on the end of his ear piece.'

Somewhere, deep in the back of his cranium where the darkness had yet to flood in, Uriah realised they were holding the receiver that had been in his ear.

Voice, Uriah realised. *They're going after Voice.*

Uriah tried to activate his microphone, but the burn in his throat told him that too was gone.

ONE BY ONE, the threads of shadow snapped, slowly unfettering Uriah from unconsciousness. He drifted back to the surface of awareness, the growing pain and ache in his body serving as his anchor. One eye opened, the other feeling like it'd been welded shut.

'Still don't look like much,' Rival said. He was squatting in front of Uriah, studying him. In his hand was a nickel-plated jolt rod.

'That's funny,' Uriah said, feeling his words drag across his tongue, 'considering you're rather short for a Goliath.'

Rival shrugged. 'Not telling me nothing I don't already know.'

'What are you doing with Slag?' Uriah asked.

'Slag and me came to an arrangement for the implant and for help catching you. If you couldn't tell, I'm providing for my end of the bargain.'

'Slag negotiated?' Uriah asked, the thought amusing enough to draw a chuckle from him. 'I can actually imagine you simians grunting at one another.'

'You got caught because you underestimated us once. Don't think you want to keep doing that by opening your yap.'

'You got lucky,' Uriah said. 'Filling a room with bullets to kill someone isn't skill, it's called luck. Or clumsiness – not sure which.'

'I'll take either, just the same,' Rival said. 'And don't think I don't know what you're doing. You're smart, I'll give you that. Trying to goad me on like that. Trying to get me to drop my guard around you. You're pretty cagey for a small guy.'

'I could say the same about you,' Uriah said, smiling.

'Ain't gonna get to me through vanity, either,' Rival said.

'All right,' Uriah said, growing more aware of his surroundings. 'How about I match Slag's offer for the implant and for freeing me – plus something extra. Like another eye.'

'Ain't happening,' Rival said. 'I ain't much fond of Delaque. And Slag's more suited to my temperament. Besides, the Soulsplitters promised me a better eye for the one I gave them.'

'Slag'll get you killed,' Uriah said.

'And you'll stab me in the back. I know how you Delaque work. I'm in better company with the Orlocks. Better fit. They understand business.'

'Your choice, but the Orlocks are the ones you have to watch out for.'

'No,' Rival said. 'You're the one who's got to watch out for them. Slag wants to torture you something fierce.'

'Speaking of ugly, where is he?'

'Don't you worry about that,' Rival said, slapping the rod in his open palm. 'Slag asked me to see to your recovery, and what I find gets a man kicking is some juice.' With that, Rival poked Uriah in the ribs, hard, unleashing a jolt of electricity.

Uriah's muscles seized up and his arms snapped against his chains. The electricity contracted all the muscles in his body; he went rigid, like a corpse and couldn't concentrate past the pain. Spattered images of Percal torturing him, teaching him to act despite the pain, flooded back into his memory. But in the deepest recesses of his brain, Uriah realised this was not the time to display this particular skill. Let Rival have his fun, despite the agony caused by the electricity.

Seconds passed with the agonizing crawl of hours, until finally, Uriah collapsed back to the floor, the pain suddenly gone.

'How's that feel?' Rival asked, his face split into a grin.

'A little more to the, unh, left next time,' Uriah managed to say.

Rival's grin evaporated instantly, and he jammed the rod into Uriah's ribs much harder.

Uriah went rigid again, his muscles steel-hard, his teeth grinding under the pressure.

* * *

URIAH HIT THE floor hard after the Black Rat and Soul-splitter guards tossed him into the cage. Landing on the stone floor was pain enough to shove away the cloying shadows threatening to overwhelm his perceptions. Right now, he was playing dead – waiting for the right opportunity to escape. He couldn't risk falling unconscious and awakening with Slag's fingers sliding around his throat.

It was a struggle. Uriah hurt so much, he was on the verge of collapse. His muscles screamed and his joints ached. His body felt like a single bruised nerve, and his mind wanted to retreat from its constant wail of pain. He was a stitching needle, coursing through the fabric that separated him from exhausted unconsciousness. It was in this moment that Uriah was grateful for Percal's training, for stretching his endurance to the breaking point and teaching him to surpass his own limitations. Then, of course, another part of him cursed Percal for putting him into this predicament in the first place.

No, Uriah decided, better to blame Percal. Hate was a stronger emotion to keep him awake.

'When's he getting back?' one of the guards asked as they walked away.

'You impatient or something?' guard two asked, his voice distant. 'Slag's still looking for Corsikan. Coward went into hiding when he heard there was a bounty on the implant.'

'Figures,' the first guard replied before their conversation was lost to the corridors of the temple.

For that tidbit, Uriah was grateful. If Corsikan was hiding, Uriah still had a chance of finding the last implant and wrapping up this endeavour. Unfortunately, one small matter took precedence over all others and that was rescuing Voice. Uriah had precious little time to lose, and even less strength to spare. He pushed himself up from the ground and sat on the stone floor. Gravity conspired against him, threatening to pull him back to the ground where cool unconsciousness waited, but Uriah fought the sway. He needed to collect his strength. He needed to collect himself.

CHAPTER: TEN

Fight the inevitable with all your strength, but when war comes upon you, do not hesitate. Use every ounce of cunning and every shred of your cold heart to win the day and strike fear into your enemy.

– Delaque Operational Commandments
from the *Book of Lies*.

URIAH SAT ON the stone floor, his legs crossed, his eyes closed. His strength was still dim and his bones felt splintered under the weight of his heavy muscles, but he was feeling a little stronger. He focused on that energy, that small kernel of strength growing in the barren wastes of his chest. With Voice's life on the line, whatever meagre reservoir he could muster would have to do.

Thoughts drifting, Uriah recounted the events of the last few days. Everything was moving so quickly, he'd had little chance to examine and consider what had happened. Without Voice or Morgane to provide feedback, Uriah spoke to himself, his lips moving but his tongue silent.

Soren is dead, Uriah thought, his implants stolen and sold to Cantrall. But why? Soren's death couldn't have been mere coincidence. He was to rendezvous with

House Delaque agents to sell them new Van Saar implants. And he was negotiating with the Orlocks as well.

Uriah paused to wipe the sweat from his brow. There was too much at stake and nothing made sense. If Soren was murdered for his implants, then why not simply steal the implants. Why sell them to Cantrall? Perhaps he was murdered by a free agent who knew enough about the implants to sell them? It wasn't uncommon for greed to spoil the deal. The Orlocks might have hired someone to find Soren, only for the killer to steal the implants for himself.

Still, why did the Van Saar refuse to purchase the implant back from Rot-Tongue? Was it older technology, like Morgane's friend claimed?

That brought up the possibility that Soren was selling slightly older tech to the Delaque and Orlocks, and promoting it as new. I liked Soren, but he was a fool for pitting two Houses against one another. Still, I wouldn't put it past him to try to dupe both Houses into buying inferior technology by Van Saar standards. Perhaps his murderer realised the technology was inferior and only worthy of a bio-surgeon's interests.

Then, there was that entire incident with Percal and his strange behaviour. Is Percal testing me, Uriah wondered, or have I fallen from his grace? If I have then why?

Uriah sighed and was about to continue his reflections when he heard a whirr. A soft purr of noise brought his attention into focus. He listened carefully but kept his eyes closed. The whirr drifted closer, to somewhere outside the metal bars of his cage.

'You know,' a man said, the voice mechanical and raspy, 'you move your lips when you think.'

Uriah's eyes flew open when he realised it was Kaden's voice. Instead of Kaden, however, Uriah stared at a probe built from a real human skull. A camera-lens glittered from inside one eye-socket, a speaker grille covered the mouth and bundles of wires hung from heavy jacks lining both sides of the pari-etal bone.

Uriah recognized the skull-probe as the one from Rot-Tongue's assassination – the one in Kaden's pos-session.

'Wish I could read lips,' Kaden said. The skull bobbed.

'Lamenting your inadequacies must be a full-time job for you,' Uriah said.

'You're a funny bird, being in a cage and all. Sing for me. Tell me how I beat you good.'

'The game's far from won.'

'I've got two implants,' Kaden said.

'You missed four.'

'That's what Percal keeps yapping on about.'

'That's a mistake,' Uriah said. 'Percal would be upset if he knew how liberal you were being with his name.'

'Percal's an idiot,' Kaden said. 'Playing the game like it's the only thing that matters.'

'And you don't?' Uriah asked, almost laughing. 'You revealed my location and identity to the enemy. You broke into my hab to steal documents. You betrayed a fellow Handler.'

'Hey!' Kaden said. 'I'm just playing the game. If I wanted you dead, you wouldn't be here. I would have done you in a long time ago. At Cantrall's I could've fixed you. At Rot-Tongue's I had you dead to rights.'

'But instead,' Uriah said, 'you're willing to help other people kill me rather than sully your own hands.'

Kaden laughed. 'Don't take it like that. I was pro-viding you with a challenge. I've got to admit it gets

boring running the same scams on the same idiots –
knowing they'll never learn better.'

Uriah shook his head. 'Don't pretend that was you.
Don't feign such creativity. Percal's been the one to
test me. You're only following orders like a good
pup.'

'Hey!' Kaden said, almost shouting through the
speaker grill, 'Percal told me to test you but I came up
with those ideas myself.'

'Percal let you think that,' Uriah said. 'He's good at
directing the course. He manipulated you.'

'Nobody manipulated me,' Kaden replied. 'Breaking
into your place, that was me. Getting Rot-Tongue to
rough you up – that was me too.'

'And telling Slag to find me at Corval's?'

That comment drew silence from the skull-probe. It
caught Uriah off-guard.

'Your silence is damning,' Uriah said.

'Who the hell is Corval?' Kaden asked.

'The woman in Cantrall's implant recordings. The
Cybilline Sisterhood Escher,' Uriah said. 'Are you saying you had nothing to do with that?'

'Corval,' Kaden said. 'She's why there's this vendetta
war between the Orlocks and Escher. You saying you
did her in?'

'You had no hand in that?'

'Hell no!' Kaden replied. 'Like I said, I'm not about
to kill you. Just remedy you with a dose of humilia-
tion.'

'Then what about that bit at Rot-Tongue's? He was
going to kill me.'

'Like hell,' Kaden said. 'I had Rot-Tongue and his
boys covered. I just wanted you to sweat.'

Uriah was quiet. *If he's telling the truth* he thought,
*then that means someone else tipped Slag as to my
location with Corval.*

'You gave Percal the eye's recordings, what Cantrall saw, correct?' Uriah asked.

'What about it?' Kaden asked.

Uriah sighed and pressed his head against the back of the bars, suddenly realising that Percal had betrayed him.

'Hey! What about it?' Kaden asked.

'Nothing,' Uriah said. 'It's just that you picked a dancing partner who dances better than you.'

'Meaning?'

'You're in over your head. I'm afraid I might be too. We're being played, Kaden.'

'Like hell!'

'I'm afraid so. Percal is using your dislike of me to keep you distracted from the truth. And he's using you to keep me distracted.'

'He says he's testing you,' Kaden said. 'Seeing if you've got claim to being his protégé. Personally, I think he's lost faith in you. Says you're sounding more and more like a Van Saar. Getting too comfortable with their way of thinking.'

'Percal thinks I've turned against the Handlers?'

'Looks like, and you done nothing to convince anyone otherwise.'

'I'd never betray the House!'

'Then why were you acting all friendly with Soren? Did you turn him? Or did he turn you? And why are you talking to devices now, and using Van Saar tech? And don't claim otherwise. I've seen your place.'

'I obtained those devices when I was undercover with the Van Saar!' Uriah said, trying to control his anger. 'An assignment Percal sent me on! I befriended Soren, again at Percal's behest! I'm chasing after Soren because Percal wants Van Saar tech. And now that I'm doing my job well, I'm called into question for it? You tell me something, Kaden; how am I supposed to steal Van Saar secrets without befriending them or learning to speak the way they speak.'

And then the thought struck Uriah. It fell with the clarity of a blow to the back of the head. Has Percal sent me on these assignments to set me up? Has this been one long play over the years to move his chess pieces into position? Has Percal been setting me up to appear a traitor? Choosing assignments specifically to account for my supposed guilt? Unfortunately, while Uriah reeled from the thought, he knew he couldn't ponder the matter.

'Frankly, Uriah,' Kaden said, 'I don't rightly care. Percal's lost faith in you. But me – he knows I can deliver the goods.'

'He knows he can manipulate you,' Uriah said.

'Now you see, you keep singing that tune. But the fact is I think your time has come and gone. And I think you know it too.'

'Really? Prove it, then. Free me from here and we'll confront Percal. No games. No pretence. Get everything out there on the table.'

'Now, see,' Kaden said, 'I got me a small problem with that. I like you where you are just fine.'

'They're going to kill me,' Uriah said. 'I thought you didn't wish me any real harm.'

'They ain't up to killing you yet. Not until Slag comes back, from what I hear, and he's too busy trying to find that last implant. So am I.'

'I know who has the last implant,' Uriah said. 'Release me and I'll–'

'Don't bother,' Kaden said. 'I overheard them talking. I know who's got that last implant and I know he's hidin'. And frankly, I aim to get it without you interferin'.' The skull-probe began floating away.

'Kaden!' Uriah said, watching it leave.

'Don't worry. I'll be back to fetch you when I'm done. Enjoy the rest.' And with that, the skull-probe floated out of the small window of the chamber.

Uriah shook his head. Idiot, he thought. Percal's playing with our lives and he's too stubborn to realise we may share the same fate. Still, if Kaden had accomplished one thing, it was in stimulating Uriah's strength and giving him focus. He felt stronger.

It was time for him to escape.

URIAH SPENT A few moments searching for the right sized stone. It was lying less than half a metre outside his cage, forcing Uriah to reach through the bars with his boot before scooping up the stone.

The rock was a remnant of the wall, with sharp edges lining the corners. Uriah spent a few minutes further sharpening the stone against the rusty bars, until it was sharp enough to draw blood. He pressed it against the lump behind his right ear and pushed hard. The pain was intense and Uriah felt a trickle of blood flowing down his neck. Thankfully, there wasn't much of it. Uriah completed the inch-long incision and cupped his hand over the wound.

Despite the sharp pain that shot through his neck, Uriah gritted his teeth and jabbed the injury; he found the plastic edge of the double-chambered ampoule beneath the fold of flesh. The agony flared, but he pulled the ampoule free of the skin pouch; he then spent a moment breathing hard while keeping his hand pressed against his neck. When the bleeding stopped completely, Uriah gently cracked open the ampoule's seal and removed the metal splinters hidden inside.

Before Uriah could react, someone fired a shot, followed by another. It was enough to startle him; he almost dropped the ampoule.

The gunfire continued, but it was coming from out-side. Shouts followed the gunfire, as did crowds of people screaming. It was a gun battle.

With little time to spare, Uriah withdrew the blue splinter from its sheath and gripped its disc-like head between his forefinger and thumb. He then reached through the bars closest to the cage door and felt around for the lock. When he finally found it, after some fumbling, he jammed the splinter into the door's lock and pressed the disc head as hard as he could. He let go of the splinter when he felt the flash of heat from it. A second later, the splinter consumed itself with a tiny pop, melting the lock in a quick chemical flash. The interior of the lock dissolved and the door unlocked.

Uriah shoved his way through the door, aware now that the gunfire was increasing in volume. More shoot-ers were joining the fight.

What the hell is going on out there? Uriah won-dered. He raced to the wall of the chamber, adjacent to the door, and listened. The gunfire continued, growing in pitch and fury. Uriah felt naked without any firearms, but he wasn't defenceless; at least not entirely. He withdrew the red splinter from the ampoule and kept that between his fingers. The gun-fire outside grew worse.

Both Slag's and Rival's men, were shouting to one another as they raced to the entrance. The temple itself was under barrage by heavy weapons that sent shud-ders through the stone walls; dust trickled down and coated the air itself.

Uriah slipped out of the chamber and into the shad-ows of the corridor. Ahead, the passageway opened up into the main chapel of the temple. The chapel served as the heart of the temple. From its cross-shaped floor, smaller passages radiated outward, while the entrance lay at the foot of the nave. Uriah, however, was further along the length of one wall, just below the corner of the transept.

Columns, both broken and untouched, lined the length of the nave and transept in tight formation and spread the height of the tall arched ceiling. Once out of the corridor, Uriah kept his back flush against the temple wall where the columns hid him in darkness. He allowed himself a glimpse towards the entrance, where Black Rats and Soulsplitters held the line. At their feet lay numerous bodies, including those of well-built Escher who'd managed to charge the line.

The Escher are attacking, Uriah thought before a chuckle escaped his lips. That's what you earn from supping with Orlocks, Rival.

More men raced to the entrance while a couple of those wounded were forced from their position. All were preoccupied with holding the double doors, which the various Escher gangers hammered with heavy bolt weapons that tore at the masonry and slowly widened the entryway.

Uriah continued his way along the wall, finally reaching the corner where the transepts split from either side of the chapel's nave. He waited, trying to determine the best escape. Unfortunately, if there were any exits to be had, only Rival's men would know about them.

The battle continued with grenade explosions rattling the temple interior and sending more dust raining down on everyone's heads. Uriah suppressed his coughs and watched carefully while a large Black Rat Goliath appeared from a passageway adjacent to the empty transept chapel. He gathered four men racing to the entrance and motioned for them to follow.

'...from behind...' Uriah heard the man say.

My escape, Uriah thought. They're going to come up behind the Escher. Uriah waited for the men to vanish

into the corridor before he darted across the transept
and followed after them.

THE CORRIDOR TWISTED and turned like a fire-blackened
vein. It opened in chambers and intersected more tunnels as it wound its way through. The gangers carried
bright-sticks, and Uriah followed the distant glow
reflecting off the walls.

As Uriah approached one corner, he suddenly realised
that the reflected lights were growing in intensity. Someone was approaching. Uriah doubled back, barely
managing to duck into a side corridor when someone
turned the corner. Breath held, Uriah waited for the
ganger to pass. He was surprised when Rival marched
past, intent on reaching the main chapel.

Uriah's indecision lasted the briefest of seconds. Rival
was alone; he wouldn't get another chance. *Then again*,
Uriah wondered to himself, *was it worth going after Rival
at this time?*

Part of Uriah thirsted for revenge, but that was not the
part that drove him. Rival was an enemy who knew his
identity, and Uriah couldn't afford having another Slag
in his life.

Splinter in hand, Uriah darted out of the corridor and
padded silently after Rival. It was difficult, however.
Rival walked with purpose, his legs in quick motion.
Uriah had no choice but to rush up behind him; he was
not as silent as he would have wished.

Rival turned just as Uriah slammed into him. Both
men struck the wall hard, but Rival was obviously better trained in combat and in better health than his foe.
Rival swung and popped Uriah hard in the jaw. Uriah's
world sparkled under the hard blow before dimming at
the edges. His grip on Rival's vest slackened. Rival
pressed the matter and grabbed Uriah by the neck in a
one-handed chokehold. He slammed him into wall

repeatedly until Uriah could no longer stand. Uriah dropped to the floor, breathing hard; starbursts of white light cluttered his vision; Rival stood over him.

'I don't care what Slag says,' Rival said, breathing hard. He pulled a bolt pistol from his waistband. 'I don't like houseguests and you overstayed your welcome.'

'Thanks,' Uriah said, out of breath himself. 'I needed a pistol. In fact, is that mine?'

'That it is,' Rival said, studying the weapon. 'Not that you need it now. I just like the poetry of it – killing you with your own weapon.'

'That is poetic. You sure you can aim properly with one eye?' Uriah asked, pointing to Rival's eye patch.

'Let's find out,' Rival said. He pointed the pistol at Uriah.

'Your aim seems good,' Uriah said, dusting himself off and appearing calm. 'Too bad you died about ten seconds ago.'

Rival threw Uriah a questioning look before shaking his head. He cocked the pistol and was about to pull the trigger when tremors overtook his body. Rival's good eye widened as he realised Uriah had done something to him. Uriah used the moment to his advantage and kicked Rival in the knees. The ganger went down, howling in pain as his kneecap shattered at the end of Uriah's boot.

The tremors were now crippling, and Rival shook uncontrollably on the ground. His howl turned to grunts as Uriah clamped his hand over Rival's mouth; the ganger was too weak to fight back. Uriah took the gun from Rival; after ensuring nobody was coming to the gang leader's rescue, and stared him straight in the eye.

'I figure every man has a right to know what killed him.' With that, Uriah removed the small splinter that he'd rammed into Rival's bicep when he tackled him.

He showed it to the gang leader as the Goliath's tremors slowed and finally stopped. Rival lay absolutely still, a prisoner in his own body.

'Nasty little poison, this,' Uriah said. 'Kills all muscle control in your body. Your outside flesh is essentially dead, your organs untouched. You're living inside a corpse's shell. Soon, your lungs will stop breathing, leaving all but your brain untouched. You'll suffocate to death, aware of it all.'

Rival didn't react, his face an emotionless mask.

'But unlike you,' Uriah whispered, noting the colour leaving Rival's face, his one eye filled with horrible awareness, 'I'm not a cruel man.' Uriah raised the pistol to Rival's forehead and fired one shot into his brain.

The shot echoed off the wall before melting into the sounds of nearby gunfire. Uriah realised the fight was drawing closer. The Escher had penetrated the temple and the battle was spreading everywhere.

After closing Rival's one good eye, Uriah took two ammo clips from him. He had just managed to stand and gain his bearings when gangers – Orlocks and Goliaths – entered the corridor from the temple area. Uriah hesitated, but the gangers were preoccupied with exchanging gunfire with their pursuers. The Escher were pushing back the male gangers.

Uriah turned and ran down the corridor, away from the fight.

'Hey!' someone behind him shouted.

Uriah ignored the voice, but he hunched over just in case. He was around the corner when the first shot rang out. It didn't slow him down in the slightest. Uriah followed the corridor, praying it wouldn't branch off before it reached the exit. Shots continued to ring out behind him, always too late, fortunately Uriah was tired of being shot at. The good news was that while he hadn't turned around to see who was shooting at him, it sounded like a single pursuer who'd broken away from the pack.

After rounding one turn, Uriah spun around and aimed down the corridor, using the passageway's corner as cover. A single Goliath ganger came around the bend in hot pursuit, not expecting to run headlong into his quarry. Uriah fired a single shot, right into the meat of the man's thigh. He went down, grunting in pain; his heavy bolter clattered to the floor, several feet from him. The Goliath crawled forward to grab his weapon, but Uriah was already on top of it with his pistol aimed at the ganger's head.

'Do you want to die?' Uriah asked.

The wide-eyed ganger shook his head; his long black ponytail flopped around like a dying snake. Uriah kicked away the heavy bolter, suddenly aware that the gunfire was drawing closer again.

'Rival stole some of my equipment. What did he do with it?'

The ganger seemed confused by the question. He shrugged. Uriah responded by drawing closer to the man, his pistol barrel centimetres from his face. The ganger flinched.

'I told Rival I wasn't a cruel man,' Uriah said. 'Don't make a liar of me.'

'I'm sorry, I don't know where it is,' the ganger said.

'Did Rival follow Slag's instructions?' Uriah asked. 'Did he send men out after my friend?'

'I – I think so,' the ganger said. 'Before the attack Rival sent a bunch of guys to capture someone.'

'Damn it,' Uriah said, hissing.

'Please don't kill me,' the ganger pleaded. 'I got nothing to do with your friend.'

The gunfight sounded right around the corner.

'I'm not going to kill you,' Uriah said. 'I'm sure the Escher will see to that if you remain.'

Uriah turned and ran back down the corridor. No gunshots followed him, not that he expected any. Instead, he followed the twisting corridor until it reached a set of stone stairs that rose up to meet a large door one storey above. He took the stairs and, after a few seconds examining the featureless door, pressed his shoulder against one corner. It swivelled open and Uriah walked into hell.

THE FIGHT CONTINUED outside, with the Black Rats and Soulsplitters trying desperately to escape. The Escher pressed their attack inside and outside the temple. Inside, the fight was done. Outside, was pure pandemonium.

The thick crowds surged away from the fight, either seeking shelter in stores, or escaping along the corkscrew path. In their wake, bodies lay everywhere, some the victims of indiscriminate fire and explosions, others crushed against walls or trampled underfoot. While the immediate level was relatively free of innocents, those on the two storeys above and below the temple still hoped to escape. The mob of people collapsed into denser clusters of desperate people trying to move, but there was only so much pushing to be done before folks pushed back. Fights broke out between the escapees and those who didn't understand the situation.

As Uriah surveyed the chaos, a steady trickle of bodies fell from the upper tiers – unfortunates forced over the railing by the mob displacing the crowd. By the end of the fight, Uriah wouldn't have been surprised to hear that a few hundred had fallen to their deaths. Still, this was not the time to mourn their plight. A wall of people blocked either end of the corkscrew path while a firefight still raged in the area; Uriah was trapped with no time to lose.

There must be another way out, Uriah thought, darting from alcove to alcove; he was still in the alley just off the main strip. Over the side? Uriah wondered. He was only five levels up, which meant the drop was certainly easier than the climb. Unfortunately, the strip of street between the alley and the railing was heavily contested. A pack of Orlocks and Goliaths were using the lip of the alley for cover while they exchanged gunfire with the Escher. They hadn't turned around to notice Uriah, fortunately, but neither could he race past them without earning several easy shots to his back.

The Escher, Uriah realised. They had been coming up behind him earlier. Uriah glanced around the alley, desperate for a hiding place. The building extended from floor to ceiling, so there was no scampering to the rooftop. The doors in the alley were likewise shut and well-bolted. Uriah ran back the way he had come, racing past the hidden door into the temple. Still, there was little cover to be had. Even the lack of trash surprised him.

Trash, Uriah realised. Where's the build-up of trash? Then he saw it; at the far end of the alley was a trash chute and Uriah's hopes for escape.

The secret door to the temple swivelled open behind Uriah. He barely heard it and glanced back in time to see an Escher poking her head outside; she was looking away from him, down the alley in the opposite direction. Uriah ducked into another alcove, hoping she wouldn't turn around in time. He pressed himself face first into the corner of the door, trying to blend into the alcove's shadow.

Uriah heard nothing at first – then movement behind his door. In a truly absurd moment, he heard a voice whisper from beyond the door: 'Who's there?'

Uriah said nothing; he didn't want to attract attention to his position. He hoped the female gangers had noticed the gun battle at the lip of the alley, but he wasn't even sure the Escher weren't heading his way already. He dared not move in either case.

'I know someone's out there,' the voice beyond the door hissed. 'Go away! Or I'll blast you through the door!'

'Shut up!' Uriah said in a low voice. 'There are Escher outside!'

'I know!' the voice said, snapping back. 'You'll bring them to me. Go away or I'll shoot!'

'You shoot,' Uriah whispered through the door, 'and they'll come for certain.'

There was a momentary silence from the other side. Uriah was ready to breathe again when he saw the movement of shadows through the crack between the door and the doorframe. His senses screamed for him to escape; he quickly backed away from the door and nearly fell from the alcove itself when a long, thin blade pushed through the door's crack.

They're trying to stab me! Uriah realised indignantly before peering down the passageway again.

A small group of Escher had snuck into the alley, and were now taking up sniping points behind the Orlocks and Goliaths.

They'll be cut to ribbons, Uriah realised. Worse yet they won't last long enough for me to make my escape unnoticed. He needed them engaged.

Uriah waited until the Escher moved into their final firing position; they raised their weapons for the kill.

'Look out!' Uriah screamed from the alcove and fired a shot over the gangers' heads.

The Escher spun around, surprised, momentarily forgetting their ambush. The Soulsplitters and Black Rats did the same and suddenly realised they'd been flanked. The male gangers spun around with their guns facing their female counterparts. The female gangers remembered their real adversaries and turned to meet their original targets. They all opened fire at the same time. The alley lit up with muzzle flashes and bullet arcs.

Taking a deep breath, Uriah jammed the pistol into his waistband and ran into the alley with bullets screaming past him. He was in the thick of it, no doubt, and felt the heat of several rounds pass close enough to burn his skin or clothing. He focused on the trash chute, desperate to reach it in time. One bullet nicked his shoulder, another his arm. Nobody was aiming for him specifically. It was the nature of wild fire.

Uriah reached the mouth of the large trash chute and paused long enough to pull the door down. Three shots struck the wall next to him; he leapt in, legs first. The world slipped out from beneath his feet, and his stomach lurched from the sudden plunge. He shot out his arms to the opposite walls of the chute, hoping to slow his plummet. His palms skipped over the metal surface, stuttering on the dry portions and slipping on grimy coatings of mould.

It all happened so quickly. He fell at blinding speeds before finally crashing into a pile of refuse. Before Uriah could recover, he tumbled down the two-storey filth-slope of trash, striking hard objects along the way and cutting his arm against jagged metal. The smell was horrible and overwhelming. It dug deep into the back of his nostrils and it coated him in its fetid, decaying stench.

Uriah finally came to rest at the bottom of the slope. The air was thick with flies and the entire floor was dark. He was on the kilometre-wide composting floor, the decomposing hell that lay just beneath the pit of the Anachrolis District. Here, the waste and debris pyramids would be left to decompose for several months before gatherers finally collected the vile waste as fertilizer for the fungus farms.

Uriah retched at the smell and tried desperately to cover his nose and mouth, but the filth was soaking into his clothing. He felt light-headed and nauseous; methane and carbon monoxide build-up he realised; he stumbled across the solid lake of trash to reach one of the exit hatches.

Fortunately, he was close to the wall and a set of stairs leading to an airlock. He stumbled up the stairs, his vision growing blurry and his head pounding. He reached the hatch and mustered the strength to spin the door wheel. It popped open, and Uriah stumbled through before shutting it behind him. He fell to the grated floor, breathing in huge gasps of oily air. It tasted foul and bitter, but he could still breathe it in.

'Oi! You ain't supposed ta be 'ere!' a man shouted. He was a large, old man covered in dirt, his overalls black from it.

'Water!' Uriah groaned on the floor, clutching his wounds. 'For – for the love of the Machine God, throw – throw water on me!'

'Aye, ya are smellin' ripe there!' the man said, laughing. 'How much d'ya think dat water's worth ta ya?'

'I don't know,' Uriah said, pulling the pistol from his waistband. 'How much does one of these bullets cost?' he asked.

'Sheesh,' the old man replied. 'Ya got no sense o' fair bargainin'.'

'Not right now, no,' Uriah replied, still suffering under his own stench. 'I tell you what. Get me water and show me the way back to the surface, and I'll make it worth your while.'

'Throw in somethin' extra and I'll tend ta dose wound's a yours 'fore they infect.' the man replied.

'Deal,' Uriah said, slowly recovering.

A moment later, a hard jet of hose-water hit Uriah and slowly blasted the stink off him.

CHAPTER: ELEVEN

*If it comes down to your life or that of an asset's, always
save yourself. No war was ever won because the general
sacrificed his life to save those of his soldiers.*

– Delaque Operational Commandments
from the *Book of Lies*.

THE OLD MAN had done a decent job on Uriah's wounds.
The stitch-work was good enough to bind them closed,
and the antibiotic salve was scrubbing his injuries clean
with eye-watering efficiency. Uriah felt like he was on
his second-wind, though he wasn't sure how long that
would last. His body was badly hurt, and he was certain
it couldn't withstand much more punishment before he
collapsed.

Uriah rode his cycle hard, kicking the green monster
into a long sprint. The wind racing past him did much
to dry his clothes, but it also set a small chill in his
bones. Uriah was going to need a full range of Van Saar
remedies to stave off the certain pneumonia.

For now he had no other concern than saving his ally,
Voice.

He prayed he wasn't too late.

Uriah raced his heavy bike through container alleys, a
green bandit screaming through the grid of streets.

Faded lot numbers streaked past him, but he'd been here often enough to remember the way to Voice's lair.

Cutting through one alley, then another, Uriah was nearing the home stretch; his heart sank when he saw smoke billowing into the dark sky. The black column rose from the vicinity of Voice's container. Uriah drove his wrist forward, gunning the throttle while he popped the clutch. His tires screeched and he wanted to scream alongside them.

Uriah nearly bounced off a container as he pulled the bike out from a tight turn. Voice's smoking residence was directly ahead; he counted three damaged and smoking bikes lying on the ground out front. Five blackened bodies also lay on the ground, the corpses still smouldering and lit with tiny embers. Uriah pulled alongside the container, pistol in hand, and studied the damage. The walls and roof were shredded, flowers of twisted metal blossomed outward like petals around an exit wound. Smoke poured skyward in heavy braids.

It took Uriah a moment to understand the carnage. An explosion from inside had ripped the container apart. By the damage to the bikes, they weren't expecting the explosion either. It was a booby trap set by Voice. Uriah quickly studied the interior of the container; it was empty except for the destroyed remnants of small equipment.

'A decoy,' Uriah muttered to himself. Voice was using the container as a relay station and drop-off point for her clients. 'Where are you?' Uriah said to himself. Voice had to be nearby to pick up money and the items dropped off. Possibly some place overlooking this one. Uriah scanned the area, looking for some telltale sign of Voice's presence. That's when he heard something over the rumble of his bike's engines. He killed the motor, the sounds of crackling fire from the giant storage container his only companions.

Gunshots rang out nearby and scattered in echoes through the alleys. The direction of the sound was hard to pin down, but the muzzle flashes were beacons to his eyes. Uriah kicked the bike into a hard, throaty roar and shredded street as he took off. He accelerated down Underhive streets, popping the brakes and swerving hard at the last second to take the corners.

More gunshots, this time muzzle flashes dancing off the containers in the next alley. Uriah banked his cycle hard, turning in to the intersection and almost losing control. Up ahead, three bikes threaded the alleyways. Two of the heavy black bikes were Soulsplitters by the double-headed axe adorning the flags that fluttered behind them. The third yellow bike was smaller and more nimble, but definitely a bite-size morsel for the two Orlocks. A well-built woman in a green tank-top, with a bald head save for a long ponytail rode the yellow chopper.

'Voice,' Uriah muttered.

Uriah gunned the throttle and gave chase after the train of bikes. Voice was surviving only by wit and manoeuverability. She took tight turns, dodging and weaving around objects in the hopes of losing her pursuers. No such luck. The two heavier bikes, while slower, dug well into the turns and never missed a beat.

This was a chase of pure speed. The drivers didn't dare pull their weapons and fire on one another; at least not without risking a wipe-out. Instead, they focused on keeping the throttle open and the wind screaming in their ears. Uriah banked and turned with the three bikes. Although he was a distant fourth, he was drawing closer to the chase. Unfortunately, the Orlocks were also drawing closer to Voice.

Uriah approached the rearmost Soulsplitter bike and gunned his engine. The Orlock driver must have heard or sensed movement to his side, because he veered away from Uriah's bike as it pulled parallel to the ganger.

The goggle-wearing Orlock glanced at Uriah twice before his eyes widened; he recognized the Delaque handler. Uriah accommodated him by waving back. The Orlock was caught off guard, enough for Uriah to swerve into the ganger. It was deliberate and timed. Uriah never intended to hit the other bike.

The Soulsplitter swung away again right into the open door of a container. The door slammed shut from the impact, but the Orlock lost control of the bike and hit the ground hard. The rider tumbled along the road, breaking bones and grinding away flesh on his mad slide. His bike hurtled into another container, exploding on impact.

'One down,' Uriah muttered.

The lead bike ganger saw his compatriot go down in flames. Voice did as well. She did a double-glance when she saw Uriah, but neither her nor the last ganger slowed their chase. Uriah accelerated once more.

Judging by her driving, Voice was trying to keep the Orlock from overtaking her while still keeping Uriah within sight. Uriah waited for her to turn again before signalling her to drive straight ahead. She complied.

Voice drove straight through the grid of streets. She was pulling ahead of the Orlock ganger who, in turn, could now shoot at her. Fortunately, that's what Uriah had hoped. He too was drawing a bead on the Orlock.

Voice continued driving straight, though she weaved to avoid the gunfire. The Soulsplitter peppered the road ahead with a fast-repeating bolter that sprayed out a trail of shots. Uriah took aim; his shot had to count or the Orlock would realise he was the hunted.

The Soulsplitter zipped into Uriah's line of sight. Uriah fired as the ganger ripped loose another barrage and struck the Orlock dead centre of the spine; the ganger was equally lucky, striking Voice's bike and leg.

Uriah watched in horror as both riders lost control of their bikes and struck the ground. Voice fell and tumbled forward, her arms wrapped around her unprotected head. Uriah could do nothing but watch as Voice slowed to a halt, her body battered and bleeding, chunks of skin left behind on the road. The Orlock too had come to a halt, his bike a smoking ruin and straddling his still body.

Uriah was off his bike before it had even slowed to a halt. It crashed to the ground as he raced to Voice's side.

Voice was in a bad way, her arms torn and eaten by the road and her leg broken badly enough to see bone. She was barely conscious. Uriah tore off his shirt and jacket, ripping what he could into strips to stop the bleeding.

'Jester,' Voice mumbled in half-groans. 'You're hurt.'

'I'm fine,' he said. 'Hang on. Don't quit on me.'

Voice said nothing, instead her head lolled from one side to the other.

After binding the open wounds and scrapes as best he could, Uriah studied the area around him. He spotted several shafts of iron lying between nearby containers. He retrieved them and set about making a splint. The tricky part was going to be resetting her broken leg. Unfortunately, if he wanted to move her, he had little choice.

'This is going to hurt,' he said before jerking the bone and leg back into place. Voice howled in pain, an anguished cry that bounced off the canyon walls. Uriah winced, but Voice promptly fell unconscious. Uriah worked on the splint and watched the makeshift bindings become soaked in blood. He didn't have much time to save her.

* * *

WITH VOICE TIED around his waist, her arms over his shoulders and her hands bound tight, Uriah navigated the Underhive's streets. It was difficult steering, but he managed.

'Voice. Voice!' Uriah shouted. 'Stay awake. Talk to me.'

Voice mumbled something in his ear – something lost to the wind.

'I can't hear you. Louder!'

'Where are you taking me?'

'To a healer,' he said. 'She operates in the Underhive. It isn't much further. Stay with me.'

'Not going anywhere,' she mumbled before Uriah felt her head droop against his shoulders.

Uriah nudged his shoulder, forcing her head back up. He needed her to focus on something, anything. His undershirt was growing wet with her blood. 'Stay with me, Voice. I – I still owe you a question!' he said.

'Four,' Voice muttered.

'What?'

'Owe me four questions,' she replied.

Uriah laughed. 'Good girl,' he said. 'Keep it up. What's your question?'

Voice was silent, her head dropping to Uriah's shoulder.

'Voice!'

She was startled, her head lifting from his shoulders.

'You scared me,' he said. 'What's your question?'

'Name,' Voice finally said. 'What's your real name?'

Uriah hesitated. He'd only revealed his full identity to one person outside House Delaque, and that was Morgane. Even Soren never knew his real name. Then again, that was a lesson taught to him by Percal: *Never trust.*

Voice was going limp again.

'All right!' Uriah shouted, trying to grab her attention. 'Storm. My name's Uriah Storm.'

Voice laughed. It was weak, but it had spirit. 'Should have stuck with Jester,' she mumbled.

Uriah laughed alongside her until she went limp again.

WITHIN MINUTES OF arriving with Uriah, Voice was strapped into a gurney with a coagulant accelerant piped into her arm. The nurse was wheeling her into the bowels of Mother's Den for emergency work while Uriah and Mother ran alongside the gurney.

'Look at you, the mother hen,' Mother said.

Uriah stared into the blue eyes of the pale and plump old woman. 'Save her Mother,' he said.

'I saved you plenty of times, m'boy,' Mother said, pushing open Voice's eyelids. She nodded. 'She needs care now,' Mother told the nurse. The nurse, her skin dark like obsidian, nodded.

'An Orlock gang is after her,' Uriah said.

Mother pulled aside her blood-splattered grey smock; a mean-looking bolter was tucked into the waistband of her pants. 'Let them come,' she said. 'Been dealing with their kind since long before someone was wiping your ass.'

Uriah nodded. He knew Mother was tougher than most, himself included.

'How are those legs of yours?' Mother asked.

'I'm running, aren't I,' Uriah said with a tired smile. 'But,' he added when he saw her face redden, 'if it weren't for you, I wouldn't be walking. You have my eternal gratitude.'

'That's better,' she said, 'now run along so I can tend to this lass.'

Uriah was about to stop and let them continue down the sloping hallway when Voice reached out and grabbed his arm.

'Uri – Jester,' Voice said, correcting herself.

'It's okay,' Uriah responded. 'You're in the best care possible.'

'No,' Voice whispered. 'The implant. I found out. I found out.'

Uriah drew in closer. Voice whispered in his ears.

And the pieces fell into place with a crescendo of hammer strokes...

'You CERTAIN?' MORGANE asked.

Uriah nodded and winced at the needle being pushed into his neck. 'Ow!' he said.

'Stop squirming,' Morgane said, 'this should accelerate the healing process.' She tended to the wound behind Uriah's neck, sealing it up after having inserted a new packet. 'Did the ampoules help?'

'Saved my life,' Uriah replied. 'Used the fuse pick to burn open a lock and used the poison needle to kill a frightening man.'

'Well, I've given you the same packet,' Morgane replied, 'though I can't promise that the tissue over the pouch won't scar over. It'll be harder to open the next time. Are you certain you don't want another pouch implanted behind the other ear? I can arrange for the same surgeon.'

'Positive,' Uriah said, gripping the table's side. The table was littered with bloodied bandages; this was not the ideal place to be handling this, but they had little choice; another clandestine rendezvous with Morgane, in another inn of questionable repute. 'Inserting the pouch is painful enough. I don't need more of those things in my body.'

'Done,' Morgane said, patting the wound and dissolving the crusted blood with a salve.

Uriah sighed in relief and almost melted into the chair. In every portion of his body, his muscles ached and protested. Everywhere they could, his joints ached in dull pain. Even his bones throbbed and felt ready to splinter under the weight of his body. Morgane slipped her arm under his armpit and helped Uriah to the bed. He collapsed on the sheets his head spinning from fatigue.

'How's your friend?' Morgane asked.

'Voice,' Uriah mumbled, eyes heavy enough to close. 'Mother stabilised her. She'll live. Hurt, but alive.'

'That's good,' Morgane said. She stroked Uriah's hair, which plunged him deeper into sleep.

'Don't,' Uriah muttered.

'Doesn't it feel nice?' Morgane whispered in his ear.

'Making me sleepy,' Uriah muttered. 'Have to find Corsikan.'

'Corsikan has gone into hiding,' Morgane said. 'The Orlocks are no longer concealing their agenda. They've put out a hefty bounty on the ganger. No one's claimed it yet.'

'I know,' Uriah said. 'Have to find him first.' He tried to get up, but collapsed back into the bed. 'I can't – I can't get up. So tired.'

'I know, love,' Morgane said, kissing him on the forehead. 'The injection I gave you included a hyper-sedative–'

'You drugged me?' Uriah asked, his head swimming.

'Yes, you stubborn mule, I drugged you. It's a Van Saar sedative designed to simulate a full eight hours sleep over the span of an hour. The dreams are fast and pitched, but you will feel rested for the while.'

'But Corsikan,' Uriah said, his fingers slipping from their grip on consciousness.

'Corsikan is in hiding, but I know how you can find him. Now sleep. I'll be here to watch over you. If you trust me, you'll let go.'

Uriah felt himself nod, his neck sluggish. He let go and plunged into a deeper darkness than any sleep he'd ever known.

THE ORLOCK RESEARCH outpost of Stainstrip owed more to machine shops than the relatively sterile facilities of the Van Saar. Oily chains hung from the sleds mounted on ceiling tracks, metal fillings littered the floor and a variety of instruments were crammed against the laboratory's walls. Band saws, mounted chain-blades, drill pistons, compressed tanks of actuator fluid and all kinds of heavy industrial equipment. Where the Van Saar used finesse, the Orlock's Tech-Trust was more about rivets than screws, skin bolts than bone pins, iron than chrome-plated alloys, machetes than scalpels.

In short, Stainstrip exemplified the nature of Orlocks and their heavy-handed approach to technology.

'Well?' the chief Tech-Trust ganger asked, looking over the shoulder of his subordinate.

The subordinate, a beefy man with black hair set in a crew cut, stopped staring into the mounted magnifying lens and swivelled it away. He looked back at the white-haired Tech-Trust chief with a sneer.

'Stop that, will you,' the subordinate responded. 'Hate you looking over my shoulder while I work.'

'You'll adapt,' the Tech-Trust chief responded absently. He was still looking over his subordinate's shoulder, studying the implant.

The subordinate shook his head and went back to studying the leg implant through the magnifier. 'I can handle this,' he muttered.

'Then perhaps you'd like to explain that to Slag.'

'Slag?' the subordinate said, straightening up. 'This comes from Slag?'

'Indeed,' the older man replied. 'Now, would you like to continue?'

The subordinate swallowed hard and returned back to studying the implant. He proceeded far more cautiously this time.

'I've cracked the housing,' the subordinate said.

'Good. Take your time. No mistakes.'

The two men worked in silence, slowly removing the articulated exo-plating on the implant, peeling away the exterior until they'd opened the core. The ganger chief handed the stripped exo-plating to a messenger who'd just arrived, a young man with blond hair.

'Take this to the Iron Ferriers,' the old man said. 'See if they can't fathom its metals.'

The messenger departed as the subordinate snapped his fingers at the Tech-Trust chief.

'Hang on,' the subordinate said. 'What have we here?' He was studying the internal mechanisms of the implant.

The old man leaned in to look at the device. 'What is it?' he asked.

'The devices within the implant. I'm – I'm not sure I understand their function.'

'Hm. We'll salvage what we can but–' the Tech-Trust chief paused, looking through the magnifier. 'Wait. What's that? I've never seen that before in an implant.'

Both men leaned in, taking a closer look at the small chip soldered into the wall of the implant.

'It's not connected to anything,' the subordinate said.

'Pry it loose,' the older man said.

The subordinate extracted a set of fine tweezers from the table and gently fitted the prongs around the chip. Carefully, he pulled the chip from its unusual socket…

THE MESSENGER RACED through the halls of Stainstrip, on his way to finding the metal-smiths of the Orlocks, the Iron Ferriers. Suddenly, thunder shook the walls of Stainstrip, knocking the Orlocks off their feet. The messenger fell as well, the exo-plates spilling to the floor.

It took everyone a moment to realise the thunder was an explosion in the machine labs. As the messenger turned to look back down the corridor he'd just left, he saw the plasma fire flood across the ceiling. It was fluid and angry. It scorched all in its path, turning walls instantly black and setting ablaze those caught beneath it. The screams were instant, though the messenger couldn't discern his own screams from the roar of the inferno or those of its victims. He cradled his head between his arms, a reflex at the dying moment.

But the heat died upon reaching him. Death did not come. The messenger peered between his own arms. The fire had died out, with him on the threshold of grace. All that was left of the corridor and the sections beyond it was a blackened pit filled with sparks from exposed wires. The messenger felt like he was staring down someone's charred and charcoal throat. The machine labs beyond had been engulfed in the explosion.

URIAH LAIRED IN the deepest darkest ocean, foetal and floating; dreams passed over him, mercurial and comfortingly muted. Suddenly, a single thought emerged, the first to find root in his thoughts in what felt to be an eternity.

Corsikan.

Uriah felt propelled upward and rushed up to the lit surface.

He broke through the waters and found himself sitting up in bed. He was awake in a moment of instant clarity. Morgane sat on a chair next to the bed, reading something from a display pad. His bolter pistol lay on her armrest. She smiled at him.

Uriah felt rested, his body aching from some long sleep but definitely lessened of its burden. His spine felt coiled and he accommodated it with a stretch and a yawn that travelled the length of his body.

'Hello, love,' Morgane said. 'Do you forgive me?'

'How long was I unconscious?' Uriah asked, swinging his legs over the edge of the bed.

'An hour and a half,' she said. 'You were more tired than I anticipated.'

'An hour and a half,' Uriah repeated, marvelling at the infusion of energy. 'I feel incredible.'

'Be careful, love,' Morgane said. She stood from the chair and brought the pistol to him. 'The infusion is temporary. The drug I administered is masking your body's pain. When it wears off, and it will, then everything you felt before will be revisited. You'll need real rest, then. I just – I couldn't bear to see you so exhausted, so hurt.'

Uriah nodded. He took the pistol and kissed Morgane on the cheek. 'All is forgiven, then. How long do I have?'

'A day,' Morgane replied.

'Then I'll make the most of it,' he said. He dressed himself, buttoning the fresh black shirt and jacket Morgane had purchased for him on her way over. 'Now, you mentioned finding Corsikan?'

'Yes,' Morgane replied. 'Corsikan is in hiding, correct? And the Orlocks won't stop hunting him for as long as he…?' Morgane asked, trailing off.

'For as long as he has the implant,' Uriah concluded. 'Oh, why didn't I see that? Corsikan's a hunted man so long as he wears the implant. All he has to do is find someone to remove the implant and hand that over to the Soulsplitters. And he's safe again.'

'So?' Morgane said. 'Where are you going to start?'

'We're creatures of habit,' Uriah said. 'So Corsikan will likely approach a bio-surgeon he already knows, someone from his patch.'

'Sounds like a plan,' Morgane said with a smile.

'I wish it were that easy,' Uriah said. 'If you've thought of this, then so has Slag. This is still a race, my love, and the fight for the prize is greater than ever.'

'Even with what Voice told you? I believe she's right.'

'As do I,' Uriah said. 'Which is precisely why I have to find the implant first.'

'Is there anything I can do to help?' Morgane asked.

'No, sadly,' Uriah said. 'I have to see this thing through. But I'm better prepared for Voice's information and I'm better armed for your help. I'll see you when this is said and done.'

'That you will,' Morgane said, kissing Uriah on the lips. 'Be careful, love.'

'Thank you,' Uriah said, 'despite my stubbornness.'

'DON'T TELL ME – another pistol lost,' Weapon's Master Coryin said when he saw Uriah walking towards him. The noise on the firing range was loud.

'No,' Uriah said. He pulled Coryin along with a tug at his elbow and whispered, 'You're rated to defuse and arm explosives, are you not?'

'I am,' Coryin said, squinting.

'Good,' Uriah said, 'then I need your help with a matter. I need a piece of equipment off the record.'

Coryin sighed. 'All right, Uriah. What is it you need?'

DERRIK SEEMED SURPRISED to see Uriah walking through the door. 'What spat you up?' Derrik asked, spying Uriah's new injuries and bruises.

'Are your walls deaf?' Uriah asked.

'As deaf as a nine-hundred year old mother hen,' Derrik said. 'Close the door.'

Uriah did before leaning against Derrik's desk. 'I need help finding someone,' Uriah said.

Derrik nodded and looked at his assistant. She walked over and deposited a folder on his desk. She smiled at Uriah before returning to her seat.

'Perchance,' Derrik asked, handing the folder to Uriah. 'Is it someone named Corsikan?'

Uriah's eyes went wide. 'How did you know?' He immediately flipped through the pages, studying the documents within.

'Kaden came in a few hours ago requesting any information we had on Corsikan. I kept it aside in case it related to your current predicament. This is the *complete* file.'

Uriah glanced up to study Derrik's face. 'The complete file? You saying Kaden was not given all the information?'

'Some documents might have slipped loose,' Derrik said.

'I'm clumsy that way,' Derrik's assistant replied with a grin.

'I could kiss you both, twice over,' Uriah said, laughing.

'I'd prefer you didn't,' Derrik replied.

His assistant said nothing, but her smile stretched across her cherry-red face.

'I assume he's one of the optographs you gave me to study?' Derrik asked.

Uriah nodded. 'Yes, the last man to take an implant, I believe.'

'We had plenty of intelligence on him, but we never had any optographs before. Sorry we missed him.'

'No worries. I do have one last question to ask you, though,' Uriah said.

'Ask away,' Derrik replied.

'I asked you about Elias, Percal's protégé who was executed?'

'I remember. What of him?'

'Is it possible he wasn't the traitor others believed him to be?'

'What do you mean?' Derrik asked.

'I think you know exactly what I mean,' Uriah said smiling. 'Is it possible Elias wasn't operating alone?'

'Ah,' Derrik said. He leaned back and rested his hands behind his head. 'Now there's a question whose answer might be equally deadly.'

'I know,' Uriah said, 'which is why I'm asking it.'

'All right,' Derrik said. 'I don't think he was alone, but you better not make any such accusations publicly, not without protecting yourself.'

'Don't worry,' Uriah said. 'I'm working on that part right now…'

CHAPTER: TWELVE

Turn everything you have into a weapon and you'll never be defenceless.

> – Delaque Operational Commandments
> from the *Book of Lies*.

ALONE URIAH THOUGHT to himself. *Without Voice's companionship and guidance, I am alone in this.* The thought bothered Uriah; Percal had taught him to be self-reliant, and for years he was. Then he met Morgane and slowly, she managed to slip past his defences. He wanted her too. He was tired of being alone, though he never vocalised that particular sentiment.

It was always something there, in the back of my thoughts, but refusing to speak aloud.

Then came Voice. Uriah needed Voice's help with an assignment, and she came highly recommended. Her skills with the Machine Spirit were extraordinary, nothing short of something he'd expect from a gifted Van Saar tech. Even if Voice never believed in the Machine Spirit, she still managed her way around it.

Uriah continued using Voice in different assignments, but the truth was, he didn't need to, not truly. He liked the company. He enjoyed the presence of another person's voice in a job that demanded his solitary involvement. It didn't occur to Uriah until now, but:

He needed Voice. He didn't want to die alone, with nobody knowing his fate or his last words.

Voice was welcome company on his assignments. She reminded him that he was still human when it was so very easy to become inhuman. And that's where Percal had failed. By forcing isolation and distrust upon him, Percal drove Uriah to seek out the very opposite.

Percal's good at what he does Uriah thought to himself, good enough to control reactions and even outlook. Eventually, however, he loses control. He cannot maintain that hold because there comes a time when control slips. And when it slips, everything that it held back pours out in a flood. And therein lay Percal's failures and weaknesses.

Percal had misjudged Uriah, and he betrayed him; it now appeared that Percal was manipulating Uriah into a position where his loyalties could easily be called into question. For what reason, Uriah only suspected at this moment, but the betrayal was there. Now Uriah needed to confirm what Voice had discovered about Jaffa Hur's heart accelerant to tie up the loose ends. With the implant destroyed during Voice's flight from the Soulsplitters, however, Uriah's only hope of corroborating Voice's findings was to find Corsikan and retrieve the last implant – a lung scrubber that neutralised harmful gases and airborne poisons.

Time to end this. Uriah thought.

Uriah exited the tram at a tower station. Immediately, two thick-necked district Enforcers in black carapace body-suits stopped him from taking the stairs to the bottom level.

'Restricted district,' one of them said.

'Appointment,' Uriah replied. 'With Hauser Demlok. He's a–'

'We know who he is,' the other Enforcer said. 'What's your business?'

Uriah smiled and looked one way, and then another. He offered the two men his profile, showing them the bruised skin and recent wounds.

The two Enforcers looked at each other before the first one motioned Uriah past with a flick of his head.

Uriah headed down the tram tower's stairs and into the well-lit streets of Shina District, Corsikan's turf. The buildings were unusually decorative for this part of the Hive, with small balconies running across their fronts, arched ceilings stretching above the streets, and vendors selling wares from the baskets on their bicycles.

Shina District operated under the aegis of one corporate entity with multiple House partnerships. The local business was water reclamation and filtration for the rich inhabiting the Spire a mile above, and the Enforcers were a strong presence. The district was supposed to be neutral territory, above the House turf wars because of its importance to the Spire; while the local gangs kept matters civilised, the Enforcers overlooked their activities.

The area seemed calm, a definite change from the chaos of Rival's temple or Corval's building. Uriah knew that would change soon. The information Derrik withheld from Kaden included the names of several acquaintances including a bio-surgeon named Hauser. It wouldn't take Kaden or Slag long to uncover that bit of intelligence, if they realised that Corsikan was trying to remove his implant.

And currently, Uriah had no reason to believe that Slag and Kaden wouldn't reach that conclusion.

Uriah stopped on the edge of the street and reviewed what he knew. Corsikan, unlike the other gangers Uriah had faced, wasn't violent. It didn't mean he wasn't capable of it, but the data on him indicated he served as an arranger. Be it sex, drugs or hard-to-obtain items, Corsikan and his gang, the Shina Boys, procured and sold them. Unlike the Goliaths and Orlocks, the Shina Boys rarely engaged in gunplay, though as independent operators they were likely to be well-armed to protect their investments. They'd remained safe thus far, however, because of the strong Enforcer presence in Shina.

Uriah realised this wasn't going to be easy, especially now that Corsikan knew he was being hunted. The situation rested on too many conditionals – would Corsikan remove the implant? Would he come to Hauser for the job? Or were Derrik's files incomplete and Corsikan knew someone who could help him? Perhaps Corsikan had already removed the implant and was long gone. The fact was, Uriah didn't know, but from what Uriah read of the ganger's files, Corsikan was a practical man and likelier to pursue a practical solution.

Uriah felt he was on the right track.

The habitation complex on the road opposite Uriah was surprisingly extravagant if only in one respect – that of space. Four hab block buildings, ten storeys apiece in a district whose cavernous ceiling measured twenty, each sat at one corner of a three storey annexe. The habitation buildings were made of ferro-iron and concrete, while the annexe was covered by a half-cylindrical skylight made of stained glass under a ferro-iron lattice. Outside the annexe's double doors, three gigantic fountains sent streams of water high into the air; it was an extravagant display, showing off Shina District's prominence and wealth. Giggling children swept their hands and feet through the blue pools of water.

Uriah surveyed the area and immediately spotted a ganger waiting outside the complex's main door. He looked normal enough and most people might have mistaken him for a concerned parent. Only Uriah saw the unmistakable bulge of a weapon hidden under his coat or the killer's stare he used to assess anyone approaching the building. He didn't appear to be Orlock. He dressed normally and looked relatively clean-cut, much like Corsikan himself. He was definitely a Shina Boy.

That's a good sign, Uriah thought. It means Corsikan might be here as well.

Considering the matter for a moment, Uriah hunched his shoulders and introduced a shuffle into his step; he kept his eyes downcast and walked up to the front double ferro-iron doors of the annexe. The sentry glanced at him once, then promptly ignored him as innocuous. Cool, filtered air struck Uriah as he pushed through the doors and into the central annexe.

The annexe rose three storeys in height to meet the ribbed stained-glass ceiling; there was a strange mural depicting Hive Primus itself with a bucolic landscape surrounding the city. Uriah chuckled to himself; the city exterior was Hell re-imagined on an industrial scale.

The annexe's interior was open, with long tracts of gardens. Carved sculptures of noblemen served as columns that supported the second-storey ledge running the circumference of the annexe. Open stalls ran the length of the second-storey ledge. It was a tranquil place and one of the few obvious gems to be found below Hive Primus's Spire.

Uriah recognized the principle at work here. The conglomerate that ran the water purification plant likely provided this market space. It allowed the spouses of workers to manage their patch of the communal field, either harvesting food and animals for themselves, or selling their goods in the shops on the second floor. The practice kept the workers happy, but importantly, made them and their families more dependent on the conglomerate's good graces.

Uriah studied the market for a moment, impressed by the operations and briefly entertaining the notion of bribing a conglomerate foreman for a hab here. The scene was certainly pastoral, and it would be nice to find a safe haven for Morgane and himself. Unfortunately, despite the airs here, habs were reserved for high-ranking conglomerate members. All the other workers slept in dormitories.

With a sigh, Uriah tore his eyes from the scenery and shuffled his way toward the north-west building's interior entry. Hauser's operation occupied the entire fourth floor of the building, at the back of the annexe, as part of a legitimate practice. His prominence in this habitation block told Uriah that Hauser's family was well-connected with the Spire or the conglomerate running Shina district. Unlike street surgeons who cobbled together scraps for their clientele in back alleys and abandoned basements, legitimate surgeons were in great demand by wealthy clientele living in or near the Spire. They procured higher-end implants and surgical tools than their street counterparts – who were part mechanic, part butcher – and their choice in living space was a reflection of that.

Uriah headed for the north-west building.

Standing next to the bank of elevators leading to the upper floors were two more men who looked average, but carried themselves with a killer's bearing. Uriah shuffled by them as well, unmolested. He entered the elevator and closed the doors.

No sooner had the doors closed when Uriah immediately pried the punch-code panel open with a knife. With a prayer to the Machine Spirit, Uriah stripped and then crossed two of the wires leading from the panel, sending a shower of sparks to the floor. The elevator was secure, meaning only residents and their invited guests could reach the upper storeys. Uriah was trying to bypass that security measure and prayed the two men standing guard outside the elevators wouldn't notice that this one had yet to move. After a second of short-circuiting the wires, the elevator buttons lit. With a sigh of relief, Uriah punched the sixth floor – two above the one he needed – and sealed up the panel. With so many men on lookout, the floors above were probably clear.

Uriah disembarked on the sixth floor. He was standing in a wide corridor that led straight to iron double-doors and dormitories beyond. To his right were doors leading to the stairwell. To his left, doors to a communal shower block. Uriah entered the block and was immediately grateful to see that windows lined one wall. Someone was taking a shower in one of the stalls to his left.

Uriah pulled out a small pouch as he walked to the window. He'd prepared well tonight, restocking his inventory of toys with anything and everything he could procure off the books. The windows faced the annexe and the adjoining south-west building, but Uriah had little choice at the moment. He'd have to risk exposure to have his answers. Uriah attached two small suction cups to the glass and, with a glass-cutter, sliced out a pane from the window. He gently pulled on the suction cups' grips and yanked the glass free. After retrieving the suction cups, Uriah was on the metre-wide ledge, praying nobody outside would see him.

Reasoning that each floor was relatively similar in lay-out, Uriah lowered himself over the ledge to the fifth floor and stared through the windows of the next shower block. A man was washing his face with a rag, but had yet to notice him. Uriah carefully scaled over the ledge of the fifth floor, down to the fourth. The block there was empty.

Uriah walked along the ledge, staring through each window to gauge the lay of the land. The first windows after the bathroom were those overlooking reception. A quick peek and Uriah spotted four heavily armed men sitting around. Their backs were turned so Uriah simply snuck past.

The next four windows belonged to private rooms for recovering patients. All of them were empty.

Hardly surprising considering the current client, Uriah thought. Hauser had probably had to clear his patient roster before admitting Corsikan.

Uriah continued, rounding the building corner. No windows along the way this time. They'd been plascreted over.

Surgical bays, Uriah concluded. He ran across the ledge to the next corner and found the next set of windows. This time, it was a supply room, the window overlooking the stained-glass roof of the annexe.

As good as place as any, Uriah thought. He kept this entry point in mind while he examined the next window. It was Hauser's office, with a gigantic metal desk and volumes of vellum bound books lining the shelves. The room was empty.

Uriah returned to the supply room window and cut the pane out with the suction cups and glass cutter. He slipped inside the rectangular room with its white walls, careful not to disturb the metal racks filled with medical supplies and sheets. Uriah crept up to the door and listened. The voices on the other side sounded like more men.

'…much you think we'll get?' one man asked.

'Not certain. We'll see,' someone answered.

'When they finishing in there?' the first man asked.

'Do I look like a damn bio-surgeon?' the second man answered.

The voices drifted off, their footsteps trailing away. A moment later, everything was silent again. Uriah pulled a retractable wand with a small circular mirror attached to its tip from his belt. He extended the wand to its full length and slipped the mirrored portion beneath the door frame. The hallway outside appeared empty. After collapsing the wand and sheathing it, Uriah opened the door carefully.

To Uriah's left, the hallway continued to Hauser's office before turning the corner towards reception. To his right, the hallways led to double swing doors. The sign read 'No Entry.'

The surgery bays Uriah thought.

Uriah slinked to the double doors and pushed them aside to peer inside. He entered. It was an ante-room separating the operating theatre from the rest of the clinic. To the side was a door marked 'Private,' probably where the doctor prepares himself, Uriah thought. Directly ahead was another double door leading to the surgery bay. This time there were two small porthole windows offering a view inside, into the operating theatre. Uriah chanced a look.

Hauser was a tall, skinny man with a widow's peak. On the operating slab in front of him rested the body of Corsikan, his chest cracked open and kept apart by a bloodied chest spreader. Overlooking the process were two more well-groomed men, both of them armed. One was smoking.

That's when the incongruities caught Uriah's attention.

Neither Hauser nor the two men wore masks.

None of the equipment meant to keep Corsikan alive were turned on.

Corsikan himself was bare-faced – no respirator to keep him breathing. In fact, no intravenous tubes to feed him blood or pulmonary wires to keep his heart beating. Corsikan was dead. And Hauser was cutting away the implant with little heed to the surrounding tissue. That's when Uriah heard someone in the hallway behind him yell:

'The Soulsplitters are here for the implant.'

Realisation collided with Uriah enough to sicken him. Corsikan's men had betrayed him for the reward. Now the Orlocks were here, probably with Slag in the lead. And again, Uriah was facing two groups alone.

Not this time Uriah thought to himself with a snarl. He charged into the surgery bay with his bolt pistol pulled. Hauser looked up in shock. The two gangers briefly considered pulling their weapons, but stopped when Uriah pointed his pistol at their faces.

'What is this?' the black-haired ganger snarled.

Uriah smiled. I'm not facing two more groups of enemies, he thought to himself. 'Compliments of House Orlock and the Soulsplitters,' Uriah said. 'We've decided we aren't paying for the implant. Now, Doctor Hauser. Hand over the device, please, before you find yourself with a third eye.'

That did it. Both men appeared livid, and Hauser confused.

'We had a deal, Orlock,' the brown-haired ganger with the pony-tail said, his fists clenched to his side.

'Oh, you're naïve,' Uriah said, laughing, 'how quaint.'

'Orlocks are here!' someone said, shouting in the hallway behind Uriah.

'Kill them!' the black-haired ganger shouted, dropping to the floor behind the surgical slab. A mortified Hauser followed him down. The brown-haired ganger pulled his Las pistol, but Uriah dropped him with a head shot that echoed off the walls.

Uriah dropped to the floor and spun around in time to shoot another ganger coming through the bay's doors.

'It's a double-cross!' someone in the hallway shouted. 'Kill the Orlocks!'

Uriah pushed backwards, hiding behind the waist-high toolbox on wheels. Two Las shots ripped by

Uriah's cover, carbon-scorching the edges. Another shot struck the toolbox. Uriah felt the metal behind his back heat up.

Somewhere outside, more shots rang and echoed. The firefight had begun in earnest, the Orlocks fighting it out with Corsikan's men. Uriah pushed against the toolbox, engaging the wheels and steering it towards the operating slab. Another ganger burst through the double doors and met a swift end when Uriah shot him.

More las-bolts struck the toolbox, and Uriah felt the box spike in temperature again.

The next couple of shots are going to burn through the metal, Uriah realised, but he was close enough to the operating slab where Coriskan lay silent. Uriah leapt from cover and jumped over the slab. The black-haired ganger sailed into view below him, a look of astonishment frozen on his face. Uriah spun in mid air and shot the ganger mid-chest before striking the ground with his shoulder.

At least I'm safe behind cover, Uriah thought. With that, he brought his pistol to bear on Hauser.

'Don't shoot, don't shoot!' Hauser squealed, holding his hands in front of his face.

'The implant, where is it?' Uriah asked.

'Still attached to the patient's lungs.'

'Wait,' Uriah said. 'Can you still call him a patient after you've murdered him?'

'Please, they said they'd kill me if I didn't cooperate.'

Uriah shook his head and pressed the pistol's barrel against Hauser's forehead. 'You're lying to me and I'm likelier to kill liars than spare them.'

'No, no!' Hauser screamed. 'I'm – I'm an important man here. You don't know who you're dealing with.'

'A talking corpse?' Uriah ventured. 'Likely to be a silent corpse in a moment.'

Uriah heard movement near the doors. He peeked around a corner of the operating slab and caught a ganger trying to sneak in low to the ground.

'Hello,' Uriah said to grab the man's attention before shooting him dead.

Meanwhile, the fighting outside was drawing closer. Corsikan's men were definitely outgunned.

Uriah retrained the gun on Hauser, who was too frightened to move.

'Now,' Uriah asked. 'Where were we? Something about shooting you, was it?'

'No, you want the implant!' Hauser said.

'Ah yes, the implant,' Uriah said. 'Where is it again?'

'Still attached to the lungs.'

'Well?' Uriah asked. 'Shouldn't you be removing it?'

'But... but... there's a gunfight outside. What if someone shoots me?'

Uriah sighed. He reached up, grabbed Corsikan's hairy forearm; with a tug, he pulled the corpse down next to them. Corsikan dropped to the floor with a heavy thud, his body twisted, his neck at an uncomfortable angle.

'Now,' Uriah repeated. 'The implant.'

Hauser nodded. He began reaching up for the instruments on the slab above his head when Uriah shoved the pistol against his nostril.

'Careful there,' Uriah said. 'I'm not a surgeon by trade, but I'm wonderful at alterations.'

Hauser nodded, more vigorously this time. He slowly reached for the instruments and pulled down a scalpel. With it in his hand, he peered into Corsikan's chest cavity and prodded the greying organs. Hauser cut into the lungs to continue removing the rust-coloured spherical device with intake wings clamped on both lungs.

Uriah shifted his attention between the door and the surgeon. Stray shots and las-bolts blasted through the door. The fight, by all accounts was in full pitch, with the Soulsplitters in greater numbers, but with Corsikan's treacherous crew holding the choke points.

'Hurry up, man!' Uriah said.

'Why bother,' Hauser said, his hands shaking. 'I'm a dead man either way.'

Uriah smiled. 'Come now. Pessimism is a sour quality in a physician. Who wants their physician spouting doom and gloom during their prognosis?'

'I'm a surgeon.'

'Yes, and a slow one at that. Are you done?'

'Yes,' Hauser said. In his hands was the bloodied piece of technology with lung matter stuck to it.

'You couldn't clean it?' Uriah asked with a devilish twinkle in his eye.

Hauser stared at Uriah, unsure if he was being serious or not. Uriah just shook his head and yanked the implant from his hands.

'This will do,' Uriah said. 'Now. Throw the scalpel away.'

Hauser complied. 'Are you going to kill me?' he asked quietly.

'I'm afraid not,' Uriah replied before striking him across the temple with the butt of his gun. Hauser fell to the floor, unconscious. 'I suspect I'll need all my ammunition for the battle to come.'

Uriah wiped his hands on Hauser's white smock and examined the implant. After fiddling with one of his pouches, he removed the small device that Coryin had given him. It was rectangular and easily concealable in the palm of his hand. Uriah pulled on a small knob on the device's head and extended an antenna-like rod. He touched the antenna to the implant and waited a moment for it to confirm his suspicions. The implant beeped repeatedly. Voice was telling the truth. The implants were booby-trapped.

Uriah stuffed the implant and reading device into his pouch. He then ran to the wall adjacent to the double doors and peered through the small porthole windows. Two gangers were hiding in the next room, firing down the corridor at the Soulsplitters who'd taken reception. Several more Corsikan gangers were hiding in doorways and side-corridors to keep Slag's men at bay.

Inhaling deeply, Uriah counted three men that he could see between him and the window where he'd entered – two at the door and another using the stockroom. The good thing about firefights, however, was that they were chaotic. Breath held, Uriah raced out of the surgery bay and planted two shots into the two men firing from cover at the door. None of Corsikan's men saw them go down; the two men were behind everyone else.

As Uriah approached the open double-doors leading into the corridor, he fired again, this time hitting the ganger shooting from the stockroom. Uriah dashed into the room as gunshots erupted around him, and slammed the door shut. He ignored the blistering fire that pinged the metal door, instead grabbing the shelving units and pulling them down behind him. Uriah hit the window and scrambled out, driven forward by bullets and Las fire. He was out on the ledge and away from the window. He moved towards the building corner with the windowless expanse of plascrete wall.

Several panels of the stained glass window disintegrated and the echoes of a firefight drifted up to Uriah's ears. The fight was spreading, with more of the Shina Boys engaging the Soulsplitters. Uriah smiled briefly; he quickly noticed the floating skull probe hovering above the scene of carnage. It was looking straight at him.

'Kaden,' Uriah mumbled. 'Wonderful.'

Movement at the stockroom window caught his attention. One of Corsikan's gangers was trying to climb through it. Whether to escape or come after him, Uriah wasn't sure. All he knew was that he needed to climb down, and fast. The slightly pudgy ganger climbing through the window saw Uriah and fumbled for his pistol. Uriah knew he couldn't afford returning into the building where the fight raged. Instead, he fired at the man and hit the edge of the window; that frightened the Shina Boy back inside where he fell with an audible grunt.

Conserve ammunition, Uriah thought to himself. He scrambled over the side of the ledge and dropped down to the floor below, which was flush with the annexe's rooftop. The ferro-iron ribbed skylight arched half-a-storey higher still, but a rusted metal grated shelf ran its periphery between the skylight and the building's edge.

Uriah ran alongside the shelf, occasionally ducking as panels of stained glass in front of him or behind him exploded in a shower of shards.

The fight's really raging full pitch down there, Uriah thought. He chanced a quick glance through a hole in the skylight and saw the carnage. Corsikan's men were hidden throughout the area. They initially allowed the Soulsplitters to pass, but once the Shina Boys thought they'd been double crossed, they closed their fist around the Orlocks. Only the Orlocks weren't that helpless. Now the fight in the north-west building had spilled into the market annexe, with gangers hiding behind columns and half-walls.

What caught Uriah's attention were the farmers and market-goers caught inside when the gun battles began. Some were already dead. Some wounded. One couple on the second floor was trying to protect their small daughter, covering her with their bodies as they wedged themselves behind a half-column against a wall. Uriah hesitated. The ammunition being used in battle wouldn't stop for flesh or bone. It would travel through two or three people before lodging in the wall.

The daughter would die alongside her parents when the first bullet struck them. A couple of wild shots were already hammering the column they hid behind, gouging out fist-sized chunks.

Uriah wanted to move, to run, as instinct and training demanded. In minutes, the Enforcers would arrive in full force and execute any non-residents involved in the fracas.

Leave a voice told him. Nothing but the prize, Uriah heard Percal say.

Maybe, at one time, Uriah might have considered that sound advice. But that was before this entire sordid affair came along. That was before he understood Percal's game.

'Game,' Uriah muttered. To Percal it was a game – it eased the conscience. Uriah couldn't do that, however, not anymore. It was time to rectify past errors of judgement.

Uriah was about to crawl through the window to help the family, when a thought occurred to him. There was no reason not to plan this through; for that to work, Uriah needed a wildcard, something to throw the existing odds into chaos. When the outcome seemed certain, it was time to introduce new variables.

Uriah pulled the implant from his pouch and showed it to Kaden's floating skull-probe. 'Come and get it,' he said, 'before the Soulsplitters catch me and you fail once again.' With that, Uriah dropped through the hole and down to the second floor, where he hit the ground with a roll that absorbed most of his fall's impact. He ignored the jolt of pain to gain his bearings.

The gun battle was heated. From behind their cover, the gangers fired at one another – blind and wild – and all they managed to kill were civilians. Uriah scrambled to his feet and ran for the couple protecting their child. A gunman popped up from behind a half-wall to Uriah's right, but he fired once catching the man in the throat.

Uriah reached the couple and their screaming daughter. The mother was white and pretty in that 'untouched by poverty' way, while her ebony husband had some muscle to him. The daughter was a black-haired beauty caught in terror. Uriah felt strange doing this. He'd never played the hero before.

'When I say move, you move!' Uriah said. 'Run to that shop over there,' Uriah motioned with his head to the herbalist's shop.

The husband nodded, then hesitated. 'Wait, what if they come after us?'

'Head to the rear of the shop. They'll have an exit behind to throw trash.'

'Thank you,' the wife managed.

It was Uriah's turn to nod. He felt embarrassed.

The firefight continued, but the Soulsplitters were gaining the upper hand, eliminating the occasional Enforcer who arrived to help. It was now or never. Uriah gauged which gangers posed the greatest danger before shouting, 'Now!'

The family ran, hunched over with their daughter in the father's arms. Uriah put himself between the family and the shooters. As he feared, the movement of runners caught a couple of gangers' attentions, and they instinctively tried firing at the moving targets. Uriah fired back, forcing them to keep their heads down until the family reached the herbalist's.

Just before Uriah entered the shop, a hail of bullets mangled the balcony railing and wall near the herbalist's door. Uriah ducked, barely catching Slag firing at him with the behemoth Gordo at his side.

Uriah cursed and pushed the family further back into the unit as bullets and las-fire turned the storefront into a shower of steel and glass shards. Two dead bodies littered the floor.

'The exit,' Uriah shouted at the family. 'Go.'

'What about you?' the man asked, holding his daughter.

'Someone needs to hold them off. You don't want them following you, do you?'

'No,' the man replied.

The wife ran up to Uriah and kissed him on the cheek. 'Thank you,' she said. 'I don't know how we could ever repay you.'

'Survive this,' Uriah replied. 'Now run!'

With that, the family headed for the back of the store, past the racks of hanging spice jars and shelves filled with assorted goods. Uriah scrambled to the display window and fired a few shots outside to let Slag know he hadn't escaped. He wanted to give the family time to flee.

'There's no exit!'

Uriah turned to find the panicked father and mother back with their child.

'Damn it!' he said with a snarl. 'Hide in the back and keep your heads down no matter what. It's me they'll want. I'll draw them away from here. Stay here for hours if need be.'

'They'll kill you,' the man said.

'They'll try, but I promise you I'll get the better of them,' Uriah said. His eyes glittered with some wildness. 'I always do.'

'Good luck,' the woman said. They headed back into the shop.

Uriah sighed and steeled himself to the task. He removed a grenade from his pouch and threw it out of the window, over the balcony to the annexe floor below. Uriah counted to three before he ran out of the store.

His return into the line of fire was immediately followed by a brilliant flash of white and a booming bang from below. The windows shook and several gangers screamed in pain, their eyes burned from the phosphorus flash. Most were momentarily disoriented, allowing Uriah to run full pelt for ten metres alongside the second floor balcony before las-fire streamed past him. Uriah hit the ground a second before withering fire shredded a nearby wall.

Uriah realised he was running out of options. None of the commerce units had rear exits and the only ways out were over the railing to the ground floor, out through the skylight or into another building. Unfortunately, Slag was waiting for him on the ground floor, he couldn't reach the skylight, and the elevators – with their adjoining stairwell – to the nearest hab block were a good dozen metres away.

Uriah checked his ammunition and tried raising his head, but several shots ripped past him. He was pinned down, and it was only a matter of time before they came upstairs.

Uriah thought about crawling forward, but no sooner had he considered the idea than he heard Slag shout, 'Shoot the windows,' from below.

Windows collapsed under the immediate hail of bullets, showering the ground with giant splinters of glass. Bits rained down on Uriah, cutting his face and fingers with sharp nicks. Uriah cursed Slag for his forethought. Dragging himself across the ground would cut him open from his throat to his toes.

Time to return the favour, Uriah thought. He turned onto his back, aimed at the skylight and fired at the stained glass. Entire panels of glass, gravity propelled razors, rained down upon the first floor. It was a petty thing to do, but Uriah smiled at the panicked screams of the Soulsplitters as the guillotines of glass rained down upon their heads. He pushed off the ground, ignoring the cuts to his hand, and bolted for the stairwell to the other building.

Uriah was ten metres away from the elevators when the first shots rang out. Four metres later, an orchestra of shots rang out, and Uriah dived into the last commerce unit. He was six metres shy of the elevators and stairwell.

Uriah tried poking his head out from the store he was hidden in, but las-fire drove him back inside. The gangers were now on the second floor and had their gun sights trained on his hiding hole.

He was trapped. With Corsikan's men dead and the Enforcers yet to arrive in force, the Soulsplitters were coming up the stairs. Kaden's skull probe floated through the ruptured skylight and the broken display window, a couple of shots ringing out behind it.

'You're in a world of pain here,' Kaden's voice said through the speaker grille in the skull's mouth.

'So everything you said about not wanting me dead? Just wanting me humiliated? That was a lie?' Uriah spoke while searching the unit for additional cover. He moved behind a metal bin.

'That's not going to protect you much,' Kaden said.

'So you're here to watch the execution.'

The skull probe said nothing. Uriah took shot at a couple of Orlocks within sight of the store. They ducked behind cover.

'Listen,' Kaden said. 'I never wished you this kind of ill. How long do you think you can hold out for? Maybe I can get Percal to send help.'

'He won't. Or they won't arrive in time. Either way, Kaden, I'm dead unless you intercede.'

'Me? You must be some special kind of crazy.'

'Crazy? I must be to have believed Percal all these years.'

'What are you on about?'

Uriah ignored the question. 'Look, the fact is I have the last implant, the one you want. If I fall, the Orlocks get the implant. If you help me, House Delaque gets the implant. You have to decide when your dislike of me crosses that line of hurting the House, our House.' Uriah fired another shot at the Orlocks, but they were closing in on the commerce unit.

'Give me the implant,' Kaden said. 'This here skull's got itself a small compartment. I can fly it out, for the good of the House.'

'No. Help me,' Uriah said, 'as a brother of the House. This errand shouldn't be worth more than a brother's life no matter what Percal claims.'

Uriah did not receive his answer. The skull probe hovered in place for too long; a bullet slammed into the back of the skull and a shower of hot sparks spewed forth from its mouth. The probe fell to the ground and cracked open. Black smoke leaked from its eyes.

'Storm,' Slag called out from somewhere outside the shop. 'Your reckoning has arrived.'

While the air was troubled by the occasional shot as Orlocks kept the Enforcers at bay, most of the Soul-splitters were lined up on the balcony across from the unit. Uriah couldn't move without taking fire.

'Come out, Uriah,' Slag said. 'A quick bullet. I promise.'

'I have the implant,' Uriah said.

'You have my property. House Orlock paid for that. It's ours.'

'House Delaque also paid Slag.'

'Not my problem. I want the implant.'

'All right,' Uriah said. 'You get the implant and I walk.'

'You don't get it,' Slag said. 'I get the implant. And I get you. No way in hell are you walking away from this.'

'I fail to see my incentive in the matter,' Uriah said. 'Either I walk or I destroy the implant.'

'Incentive is in how you die,' Slag said.

Uriah realised the voice was closer now. He heard glass crunching under several heavy feet. Slag was inside the unit. Uriah glanced quickly and saw the broad frame of Gordo, standing just inside the doorway. Slag was hidden behind him.

'Hiding behind your men?' Uriah asked.

'Bet you my cover's better than yours,' Slag said. He fired a shot through the metal bin above Uriah's head. It punched clean through. Uriah might as well have been hiding behind paper.

'Fair enough,' Uriah said.

'Enough stalling. Your answer. And no explosives either. I'm ready for your tricks.'

Uriah rested his head against the cool metal. Every path he envisioned led to the same course – his death. This was the end; no exit, no escape. He was tired and the pain that Morgane had driven away was slowly seeping back inside him. He ached in truly ancient ways.

Still, if death was awaiting his response, he wasn't going to allow it an easy meal. Let it come. Let it wrest its morsel of food from his dying hands. Uriah unlatched the small knife hidden up his sleeve in his wrist sheath and tucked the pistol in his waistband.

Uriah stood from his hiding spot, arms raised. In one hand, he held the implant. In the other, an explosive device.

'I said no tricks!' Slag bellowed.

'Five… Four… Three…' Uriah began, counting down.

Slag's eyes widened when he realised the trigger was already in motion. He dived to the side, out of the store. The other gangers with him turned and ran.

'Two…' Uriah said, tossing the explosive to Gordo. Gordo caught the device with an ignorant smile and childlike guffaw.

'One…' Uriah concluded, running past Gordo and out of the store.

No explosion ensued, but that didn't stop Uriah from continuing the count in his head.

Three… no reason to tell Slag the real countdown, Uriah thought.

'I caught it,' Gordo exclaimed gleefully.

Two… Uriah was out the door and running for the stairwell.

One… The Orlocks across the way were only now reacting to events. They started taking aim.

'Shoot him!' Slag shouted, believing he'd been duped again.

Zero… Gordo caught the blast full in the face.

Uriah knew that tough or not, Gordo's upper body would have disintegrated in the explosion. Unfortunately, the yield was stronger than Uriah anticipated; the explosion threw Uriah to the floor, cutting his arm on the bed of broken glass.

The stairwell to the building was three metres away. Uriah tried rising to his knees; an Orlock boot slammed into his back and pushed him to the ground. More glass cut into him.

'Got 'em!' an unfamiliar voice said.

Before Uriah could react, he heard Slag roar; a large boot kicked him in his ribs. Two more kicks followed. Uriah almost blacked out from the sharp pain; several ribs cracked and for a moment he couldn't breathe.

Slag lifted Uriah to his feet and sent a meaty fist into his stomach. Uriah felt caught between trying to inhale and trying to vomit, opposite reactions that had him stutter-gasping for air. Two men grabbed Uriah by the arms and pulled the pistol from his waistband.

'Look at me,' Slag said, grabbing Uriah's jaw hard and lifting it up. 'Look at me! You devolved piece of excrement! You think you're better than me? Me! You're a fly! And I'm going to pull your wings off! Slowly!'

Uriah finally managed to catch his breath. He inhaled deeply.

'And when I'm done,' Slag said, 'I'm sticking your head on my flagstaff.'

Uriah laughed and asked with weakened breath: 'Did I upset you?'

Slag pummelled Uriah in the stomach and in the face with several fast blows. Another rib broke. Uriah dropped to the floor on his knees, his face bleeding, his lungs aching as though he'd swallowed glass. The two Orlocks pulled him back up.

Uriah felt something cold and metallic press into his forehead. Slag was holding a pistol. It was his pistol, the one stripped from him in Corval's building.

'Now you die!'

A shot rang out. Slag screamed as a sniper bullet tore through his gun shoulder; he dropped the pistol. More shots rang out, and the man holding Uriah's right arm fell away, the top of his head vanishing in a red smear. The other ganger let go of Uriah and scrambled for cover. A shot struck him in the back and he fell.

The other gangers fired blindly at the skylight, where a sniper had taken up position. It was Kaden.

Uriah reached for the pistol on the ground, but Slag was on top of him as quickly. Uriah grabbed the pistol, but a one-armed Slag grabbed his wrist. Both men rolled around on the broken glass, neither surrendering to the pain. Kaden continued firing, but he was now being pinned down by return fire.

Slag was strong, but Uriah had the use of both hands. And I'm smarter, he thought in the struggle.

Uriah let go of the pistol. Slag, with his one good hand reached over Uriah to grab it; with a triumphant smile, he clutched the pistol and was about to bring it to bear against Uriah's head. He stopped instead – shock registering across his face. He looked down to see the knife in his stomach.

'Surprise,' Uriah whispered and twisted the knife deeper into Slag's belly. It was the one he'd pulled from his wrist sheath. 'You broke my legs and you hurt my friend. Consider all debts repaid.'

Slag gurgled in response; Uriah pushed him off.

'And here's a secret,' Uriah said. He quickly whispered in Slag's ears and relished the look of surprise on the Orlock's face. 'That's right,' Uriah said. 'You died for *nothing*.'

Slag tried to say something, but it was lost in a blood-soaked gurgle. His eyes dimmed. Crimson briefly trickled from the Soulsplitter's mouth, but the trickle stopped at the same moment Slag did.

Uriah grabbed his old pistol from Slag as well as the one that the gangers had pulled from his waistband. He scrambled for the stairwell, grateful for Kaden's cover fire. He stumbled down the stairs and found an exit.

Uriah stumbled out into the night, the steady pops of gunfire growing in intensity. The Enforcers had arrived in greater numbers and were hopefully eliminating the last of Slag's minions. Uriah vanished into the shadows, his escape route a Delaque tunnel to be used only in emergencies.

CHAPTER: THIRTEEN

Last of all, never blink. The game is never won by the most skilled. It's won by the most daring.

– Delaque Operational Commandments
from the *Book of Lies*.

EVERYTHING WAS A BLUR, a smear that washed out the specifics into one jumbled mess of sight, sound and smell. Uriah stumbled upon moments of clarity, small islands of salvation in the stormy seas, when he needed them most. He was aware long enough to pull his two pistols on the young gangers about to rob him. When they ran, Uriah lost track of muddied time again.

Uriah found himself in a tunnel, moving down, deeper into the city's belly. When he regained his clarity for a moment, he was in a shuttle car, a vertical train barrelling down a shaft deep inside Hive Primus. He eyed his fellow passengers, a warning in his gaze to mind their own business. They complied. Time muddied again.

It continued like this for what felt like days; Uriah blacked out, coming to for just long enough to find himself closer to sanctuary. He was on the shuttle car, he was stumbling through the sewers, he was pulling out his green bike from its hiding hole, he was astride his bike, racing down at top speed and swerving to avoid crashing. It wasn't until he stumbled into Mother's den that he awoke for a final time. Mother loomed over him, checking his injuries.

'Hello Mother,' Uriah muttered.

'Sweet tears of oil,' Mother said, annoyed, 'can't you do anything in moderation?'

'I need you to call someone,' Uriah said, and told Mother how to reach Morgane. 'I love her,' he said.

'Well it's about time you found someone you selfish bastard,' Mother said.

Uriah smiled and felt as though he'd cracked his own face. The events and punishment of the past week came crashing down upon him. Everything went black under its weight.

EVERYONE STARED WHEN Uriah walked into Shadow-strohm. He'd been missing for a week following Kaden's report of the shootout in Shina District. Many had assumed he was dead, but Uriah was happy to disappoint.

Fact was, they weren't that far off. What could be seen of his body was covered in bandages and bruises. He looked like Hell's kickball, but there was an unexpected energy to his step, a macabre rejuvenation that belied his condition. He walked with purpose despite the slight limp. A week in Morgane's and Mother's care, being nursed back from death and exhaustion, worked its wonders. Uriah still ached and still needed plenty of rest, but he was finally strong enough to wrap up this matter.

Uriah walked straight for Derrik's office to pick up a file and give the dark-haired girl his regards. Before Derrik could barrage him with any questions, Uriah told him: 'Wait. I have one matter to finish first. I'll return. I promise.'

Then, Uriah made his way to Percal's office, where he knocked and waited. A moment later, gears shifted and whined, and the door opened.

'Where the hell have you been?' Percal roared as Uriah walked inside. Kaden was already seated.

'Ah, you received my message,' Uriah said to Kaden. 'Excellent.'

'Where… were… you?' Percal asked, emphasising each word as though ready to explode on any of them.

'Keep your nose on,' Uriah said, smiling.

Percal's face turned beet red; even Kaden looked shocked.

'I brought the implant,' Uriah said. He tossed the lung scrubber on the desk. Percal jumped.

'Have you gone mad?' Percal roared.

'Not at all,' Uriah said. 'I just needed some time to sort through some matters. But as promised I delivered you the implant.'

'I wanted all the implants,' Percal said. 'But all you and Kaden managed to acquire were three out of six. Two of the supposedly finest Handlers of House Delaque and you allow the Orlocks to steal away with three implants for study. Worse yet,' he said, pointing to Uriah, 'you only bring me one implant while Kaden procured the other two.'

Kaden smiled and shrugged at the off-handed compliment.

'In truth,' Uriah said. 'I recovered three implants. One, Kaden appropriated. The second one was destroyed in a bike crash.'

'You lost one of the implants? I'm disappointed in you, Uriah,' Percal said. 'I thought I was grooming a worthy successor.'

'Come now,' Uriah said. 'It's not all that bad and the truth is, you know that.' Uriah tossed the file folder on the desk.

'What's that?' Kaden asked. Percal, however, didn't budge. Instead, he kept a watchful eye on Uriah.

'A report of a massive explosion out of Stainstrip, an Orlock research facility. It occurred last week. I'm sure you know about the explosion?'

'And?' Kaden asked.

'You wish to answer that, or shall I?' Uriah asked Percal.

Percal said nothing. Instead, he leaned back in his chair, steepled his fingers and waited for Uriah to speak.

'Very well,' Uriah said. 'Stainstrip is where Slag sent the implant he recovered to be studied and tested.'

'Still not following you.'

'All right,' Uriah said. 'Let's take this back several steps. Soren was a Van Saar tech selling secrets to us.'

'I'm not that lost,' Kaden said.

'Well, Soren was also greedy. He was selling the same secrets to the Orlocks.'

'I'd already figured that out seeing as how the Soulsplitters were always around.'

'Soren was on his way to sell us the latest batch of implants when someone murdered him and scavenged his parts, selling them to the bio-surgeon Cantrall.'

'You haven't lost me yet.'

'Yes, well this part I bet you didn't know. The implants we recovered were of older technology. Hardly Van Saar's finest.'

'What? Somebody switched the tech on us?'

'Exactly. The technology given to Cantrall was not the technology promised to us. They weren't Soren's implants. Just sold as such with enough of Soren's flesh to give us a genetic match.'

'Damn it!' Kaden said. 'You mean we did this for nothing?'

'Depends on your definition of nothing,' Uriah said, smiling and maintaining his gaze on Percal.

'I don't get your meaning,' Kaden said. 'You know where the implants are?'

'Yes I do,' Uriah said. 'They're safe back at House Van Saar.'

'Come again?'

'The Van Saar orchestrated all this,' Uriah said. 'They discovered Soren's betrayal, so they hunted him down and killed him. Then they switched implants.'

'Then what's with the implants sold to Cantrall and all those gangers?' Kaden asked.

'The Van Saar idea of retribution. They wanted us scrambling to retrieve the implants. So they baited us by sending the implants to Cantrall and telling him they were top-of-the-line technology taken from Soren's body.'

'And we bought it,' Kaden said. 'But what's this got to do with the explosions at Stainstrip. I mean why even go through the effort of all this?'

'The Van Saar booby-trapped the implants. Each implant contained an explosive that was designed to detonate when someone tried tampering with its innards.'

Kaden's eyes shot to the lung device on the desk. 'Like that thing? It's got a bomb inside it?'

'Had,' Uriah replied. 'It had an explosive. And the reason they never activated when they were being attached or removed is because they'll only activate when taken apart and examined.'

Uriah allowed Kaden to absorb the information, though Percal was calm; this news had not been a surprise. Uriah thought back to Voice and how lucky she'd been to stumble across the explosive before it detonated. Something had worried her about the device, so her first detailed examination used what she called a microscopic fibre-opto to explore the heart accelerant's interior. That's when she found the bomb.

'Hey!' Kaden said, suddenly fitting two pieces together. 'Is that why Rot-Tongue couldn't sell his eye back to the Van Saar?'

'Correct,' Uriah said. 'The Van Saar weren't about to take back a booby-trapped item. Not when they were desperate for the Orlocks or us to have them.'

'What about the implants you sent to the lab?' Kaden asked Percal.

Uriah smiled. 'He already knew they were rigged with explosives.'

'I *suspected*,' Percal said. 'It's standard Van Saar procedure to booby-trap technology and leave it behind for the curious. I warned our techs of the danger and they discovered the explosives.'

'Then why didn't you tell us?' Kaden said, indignant.

'Because you weren't going to open the implants for examination. Not unless you knew how to speak with the Machine Spirit?' With that, he shot a look at Uriah.

Kaden caught the glance and looked at Uriah as well. Uriah however, was enjoying this moment.

'Kaden,' Uriah said. 'Mind if I have a word with Percal alone?'

'Sure,' Kaden said, standing. 'Just don't forget you owe me.'

'I do at that,' Uriah said with a smile. He waited for Kaden to leave before sitting.

'I don't remember inviting you to sit. I still consider your role in this a failure.'

'I don't need permission to sit from you. Not anymore,' Uriah said. His smile vanished, replaced by a feral gaze that no longer kowtowed to Percal.

'Is that so?' Percal said. 'Be careful when crossing words with me, boy. I've been at this game far longer than you.'

'Does it help?' Uriah asked. 'Does it ease your conscience to call it a game?'

'Leave,' Percal said. 'You've outstayed your welcome and my good graces.'

'No,' Uriah said. 'Not until you understand me perfectly.'

'Oh, I think I understand you already,' Percal said. His face was turning red.

'And I understand you,' Uriah replied; he felt calm.

'Oh really?' Percal said, laughing. 'Please. *Enlighten* me.'

'You betrayed Soren. You told the Van Saar about his dealings with us and with the Orlocks.'

'If I did,' Percal said, 'should I not be the hero for revealing a double-agent willing to court the Orlocks? If I did, that is.'

'Keep playing your game,' Uriah said. 'I want no part of it.'

'Are you so naïve as to think you can resign?' Percal asked, a bemused look on his face.

'Resign? No,' Uriah said. 'I'll still serve the House – as an independent with no affiliation to your operation. I've already made the request.'

'Through whom?' Percal asked, his eyes narrowing.

Uriah smiled. 'The only thing I want from you is the necklace Kaden stole from my hab.'

'Who says I–'

'I said no more games. The necklace, Percal. It's mine and it's not something you want to start a war over. Trust me.'

Percal considered the matter before removing the tearshaped, black diamond pendant necklace from somewhere inside his top drawer. 'Consider it a farewell present,' Percal said.

Uriah reached for it, but Percal pulled it away.

'I am curious, though,' he said. 'For old times sake, on whose neck does this belong?'

Uriah reached forward again. 'Her name is Bettyna,' Uriah said.

The smile on Percal's face evaporated. He shoved the pendant and chain into Uriah's hands. 'Leave,' Percal said. 'You are no longer welcome in my home.'

'Your home,' Uriah repeated as he stood and headed for the door. 'Big word for a man living alone.'

'You SAID THAT?' Derrik asked, in shock.

'I did at that,' Uriah said. 'But don't worry. I haven't told him that the Information Cullers and Requisitioners sponsored me with House Delaque as a freelance operative.'

'He'll find out soon enough, if he doesn't already know. At least your life is no longer bound on Percal's word.'

'True,' Uriah said. 'But he almost had me, you know?'

'How so?'

'Aside from the obvious traps?' Uriah said. 'He was grooming me to be another sacrificial lamb. Another Elias.'

Derrik shot Uriah an inquisitive look as he poured them both a drink from the bottle and shot cups in his desk drawer.

'Percal sent me deep undercover into House Van Saar on repeated occasions,' Uriah said. 'He knew I'd generate an affinity for the House, for its practices. You can't be an effective undercover agent without developing empathy for your targets. And like an idiot, I did.' Uriah decided not to mention the Machine Spirit or Morgane, but the other examples were suitable enough. 'I became familiar with their technology and I even befriended Soren.'

Derrik nodded. 'I see,' he said. 'So if there was ever a need to question your loyalties–'

'My own actions would condemn me,' Uriah said. 'I looked and acted like a Van Saar. I used their equipment on occasion. So much the easier to try me for treason and divert attention away from his action.'

Derrik nodded. 'You think that's what happened to Elias?'

'I know you do,' Uriah said. With that, he downed the shot of rat-bile and nodded his thanks to Derrik.

URIAH PULLED MORGANE tighter into his embrace and smelled her hair. He was enjoying this moment in bed with her though they'd discussed much of the day's events in detail.

'Taking a chance, aren't you?' she asked.

'Perhaps, but Percal's revealed far too many of his tricks over the years for me not to recognize his hand in matters. He's crooked.'

'How so?' Morgane asked.

'A long time ago, he was subtle enough to obfuscate the truth,' Uriah said. 'Not any more. I know he warned the Soulsplitters that I'd be going after Corval and Jaffa Hur. He knew I'd investigated them both previously. And he knew Corval was the easiest to reach and kill to set up the ambush.'

'You think he's working with the Orlocks?' Morgane asked.

'No, no, though at first, I couldn't figure out why he did it. I thought, perhaps he was trying to challenge me with greater obstacles, but that didn't ring true. He set Kaden and the Orlocks after me to keep me preoccupied and to prevent me from uncovering the truth.'

'And the truth is?'

'He's working for your House,' Uriah said.

'Are you certain?' Morgane asked, surprised.

'Certain enough to voice my suspicions,' Uriah said. 'That's why he was grooming me to seem like the Van Saar spy, in case his identity was ever in danger. That's why your House knew about Soren. As soon as Percal realised Soren was also dealing with the Orlocks, he decided to have him terminated.'

'But why allow Soren to continue betraying the Van Saar? Why encourage him?'

'I've been making new friends at Shadowstrohm,' Uriah said. 'Powerful friends. They told me that they've never heard of half the inventions that Soren told me he brought to House Delaque. Percal has been screening the technology we receive.'

'So why betray you to the Orlocks again?'

'Because Percal had no choice. He was told to investigate Soren's disappearance by his superiors, but he knew if I dug too deep, I might uncover his involvement.'

'Ah. So Kaden and the Soulsplitters were to distract you.'

'Or possibly even kill me.'

'That seems extreme,' Morgane said.

'Only if you don't understand Percal,' Uriah said. 'I'm not the Handler he wanted. I wasn't Elias.'

'Who's Elias?'

'Percal's former protégé. He was executed for betraying the House after Percal caught him selling secrets.'

'Sounds familiar,' Morgane said.

'Suspiciously so. It's likelier that Percal trained Elias as the sacrificial lamb to the point of unquestioning loyalty. Percal was the traitor and he'd indoctrinated Elias as well – I suspect he convinced Elias to take the fall for him when he could no longer hide.'

'You know Van Saar could use a man like you,' Morgane said.

'I know,' Uriah said. 'But that would put me back in Percal's court. Besides, if I'm to keep one step ahead of whatever retribution Percal has in mind I need to be inside House Delaque keeping an eye on him. I have allies now. They'll help me. Protect me.'

Morgane sighed and whispered, 'And I can't leave my position either.'

'I would never ask you to,' Uriah said, kissing Morgane. 'For now, we'll continue as we've done.'

'To do that, we need a new home. A hideaway for just you and me.'

'I know,' Uriah said, 'but we can't for the while.'

'Why?'

'Because,' Uriah said. 'In no uncertain terms, I just declared war against a very conniving and deadly foe. I don't have enough proof to lodge an official accusation, but he has more than enough cause to have me killed.'

'I'm not scared,' Morgane said.

'I know. We will find a place for ourselves, but not yet not when my life is about to come under heavy scrutiny. Nothing I find will be safe.'

'Then I'll find something. You concentrate on your battles and on eliminating Percal.'

Uriah nodded. 'And I know where to start,' he said.

PERCAL SAT IN his chair, in the darkness of his office, staring at the shadows. A grim expression sat squarely on his face, one made more macabre by the hollow of his nose. He reviewed the entire affair from beginning to end; there was nothing written down, nothing to implicate him in matters. Everything he possessed sat in the reservoir of his thoughts, to be called up with crystal clarity and often, verbatim whenever he needed it.

Uriah had proven far more cunning than he'd anticipated. Percal had seen the slow shift in Uriah's loyalties months ago. He was questioning more and pursuing matters without consulting his Overseer. He was acquiring help and equipment outside the regular channels, where Percal was once able to keep an eye on him.

Percal knew Uriah wasn't a House traitor, but it was a convenient lie he'd been trying to cultivate. Keep him isolated from everyone at Shadowstrohm to increase people's dislike of him, and send him on deep-cover assignments to where he'd start emulating Van Saar habits to survive, which he'd done. But Uriah's growing independent streak was troubling. Percal knew it was time to cut the strings that tied Uriah to House Delaque, but the entire Soren affair hadn't unfolded the way he'd intended. The Soulsplitters or Kaden should have eliminated Uriah and, in fact, had ample opportunity to do so. Instead, they'd failed.

I overestimated Slag's ability and underestimated Kaden's loyalties, Percal thought.

How Uriah had discovered the explosives, or the fact that the implants were fakes, or that Percal had orchestrated Soren's death was a mystery. Percal was using those events as his back-up plan to indict Uriah in betraying the House.

At the behest of his Van Saar handlers, Percal was ready to testify, Uriah Storm assassinated his friend Soren for betraying the Van Saar, and then knowingly brought booby-trapped implants into House Delaque. Had I not stopped him, his plan might have worked. I knew Uriah was the traitor when I saw him praying to the Machine Spirit and possessing Van Saar technology.

Now, however, Uriah had managed to protect himself from blame; he was under the aegis of the other gangs in Shadowstrohm; he'd revealed the presence of explosives in the implants himself, and he had exposed the Van Saar plot in the matter. Uriah was safe for the time being. Anything Percal did against him would heap suspicion back on himself.

With a sigh, Percal stood and headed over to the regicide board. Percal ignored his next move and instead pressed in sequence the tiles for D-3, F-8, C-6, H-5, F-2, and B-7. The pieces flickered. A moment later, a crackling voice emerged through hidden speakers.

'Did you receive my report?' Percal asked.

'We did,' the male voice said.

'My position here is in danger,' Percal said. 'You promised me a home should I need to leave this place.'

'And the promise stands,' the voice said. 'But you aren't in danger yet. Compromised, maybe, but I doubt they know enough to launch an investigation. If they did, we wouldn't be speaking. We still need you there.'

Percal sighed. 'I need to eliminate Uriah.'

'Yes,' the voice said. 'But not just yet. The timing must be right to remove you from suspicion. But you knew that already.'

'I did. And I need to start planning. I can't draw upon any Delaque resources to do it, either. I don't want any trails leading back to me. I need help from you. Technology and men, whatever you can spare.'

'Any way House Van Saar can help, consider it done,' the voice said.

With that, the voice cut out, leaving Percal standing over the board. A slow, unexpected smile crept across his face, and for the first time, Percal realised he was actually giddy.

It had been a long time since he'd entered the fray as a combatant. He was looking forward to playing the game once more.

VOICE AWOKE WITH a start and immediately groaned. The skin staples were still tight and her broken leg itched.

'Shh, shh, It's just me,' Uriah said, coming closer to her bed.

'Uriah. You scared me,' Voice said, admonishing the Handler.

'I'm sorry,' he said. 'How are you feeling?'

'Feeling? I hurt when I blink – that Mother is a tyrant.'

'I know,' Uriah said, smiling. 'I like her too.'

Voice chuckled. It was good to see her smile, despite the constant scowl she wore. Voice realised Uriah was studying her.

'What?' she asked.

'Nothing – well, truthfully, you're not at all how I imagined.'

'And how did you imagine me?' she asked.

'Taller. More hair, but black. I did expect the scowl, though.'

'Did you now? Uriah, what are you doing here?'

'I, uh, wanted to say I understand now.'

'Understand what?'

'Fleshworks,' he replied. 'For the want of tech, Soren sold his scruples and died in the exchange. I was betrayed and now a little more of me is artificial.' Uriah tapped his torso where two implants had replaced two shattered ribs. 'I'm less flesh then I was.'

'Told you. I'm always right. Anything else?' she asked with a smile.

'Actually, I was hoping you'd come work for me on a permanent basis.'

Voice laughed. 'Given our last enterprise?'

'I know,' Uriah said. 'But you're particularly gifted with machines. And to tell you the truth, I could use the help. I've made some powerful enemies and, I'd like to think, equally valuable friends.'

Voice shrugged.

'What say you?' Uriah asked.

'Offer the terms, but I'd likely say yes.'

'Excellent,' Uriah said slapping his knees. 'First thing we need to do when you're up and about is break into a certain person's regicide board. I'm sure he's using it to communicate with someone inside House Van Saar.'

'Very well,' Voice said, uncertain.

'Oh, and welcome to the shadowy world of House Delaque.'

'*What*? Hey! No! Wait!' Voice stammered. 'I never agreed–'

'Trust me, you'll love the experience,' Uriah said walking away.

'No, I don't like Houses. That's why I left–'

'The benefits are great,' Uriah said, walking for the door. 'They have to be with all the backbiting.'

'But I don't–'

'And you'll love Derrik. He can't wait to meet you. Has a thing for Escher women. Actually, women in general.'

'Jester,' Voice shouted after him. 'Get back here. *Jester!*'

'You said yes,' Uriah said, leaving the room. 'Can't back out now.'

'Uriah!' Voice shouted.

'Welcome to the Game, Voice! It's about to get interesting.'

ABOUT THE AUTHOR

Lucien Soulban has authored and co-written over 90 role-playing supplements for games including *Vampire: The Masquerade*, *Deadlands* and *Spycraft*. He also helped launch three roleplaying games including Guardians of Order's *Silver Age Sentinels* and White Wolf's award-winning *Orpheus*. Lucien wrote the script for Relic Entertainment's *Warhammer 40,000: Dawn of War* and *Winter Assault* video games, while February 2005 saw the release of his first novel, entitled: *Blood In, Blood Out*. He is now a scriptwriter for video-game giant Ubisoft Montreal.

READ TILL YOU BLEED

DO YOU HAVE THEM ALL?

WWW.BLACKLIBRARY.COM